1.00

RITES OF PASSAGE *is a journey of the soul. Set during the Napoleonic era, it is the story of the passengers aboard an ancient ship making its way from England to New Zealand, carrying seamen, soldiers, emigrants, cargo, and a few ladies and gentlemen. Among the latter is the observant Edmund Talbot, who records the ceremonies that mark a progress through life in the stratified society-in-miniature on board the ship. Death, birth, betrothal, betrayal, abortive court martial, disappearance at sea, funeral — each turn of events leads the reader on to the startling truth of the voyage.*

". . . beautifully poised between comedy and dread, and nearly all of it is splendidly, elegantly phrased."
KIRKUS REVIEWS

Also by William Golding

WILLIAM GOLDING

RITES OF PASSAGE

PLAYBOY
PAPERBACKS

RITES OF PASSAGE

Copyright © 1980 by William Golding

Cover illustration copyright © 1982 by PEI Books, Inc.

All rights reserved. No part of this book may be reproduced, stored in a retrieval system or transmitted in any form by an electronic, mechanical, photocopying, recording means or otherwise without prior written permission of the author.

Published simultaneously in the United States and Canada by Playboy Paperbacks, New York, New York. Printed in the United States of America. Library of Congress Catalog Card Number: 81-84143. Reprinted by arrangement with Farrar, Straus & Giroux.

Books are available at quantity discounts for promotional and industrial use. For further information, write to Premium Sales, Playboy Paperbacks, 1633 Broadway, New York, New York 10019.

ISBN: 0-867-21061-3

First Playboy Paperbacks printing May 1982.

(1)

Honoured godfather,

With those words I begin the journal I engaged myself to keep for you—no words could be more suitable!

Very well then. The place: on board the ship at last. The year: you know it. The date? Surely what matters is that it is the first day of my passage to the other side of the world; in token whereof I have this moment inscribed the number "one" at the top of this page. For what I am about to write must be a record of our *first day*. The month or day of the week can signify little since in our long passage from the south of Old England to the Antipodes we shall pass through the geometry of all four seasons!

This very morning before I left the hall I paid a visit to my young brothers, and they were such a trial to old Dobbie! Young Lionel performed what he conceived to be an Aborigine's war dance. Young Percy lay on his back and rubbed his belly, meanwhile venting horrid groans to convey the awful results of eating me! I cuffed them both into attitudes of decent dejection, then descended again to where my mother and father were waiting. My mother—contrived a tear or two? Oh no, it was the genuine article, for there was at that point a warmth in my own bosom which might not have been thought manly. Why, even my father— We have, I believe, paid more attention to sentimental Goldsmith and Richardson than lively old Fielding and Smollett! Your lordship would indeed have been convinced of my worth had you heard the invocations over me, as if I were a convict in irons rather than a young gentleman going to assist the governor in the administration of one of His Majesty's colonies! I felt much the better for my parents' evident feelings—and I felt the better for my own feelings too! Your godson is a good enough fellow at bottom. Recovery took him all the way down the drive, past the lodge and as far as the first turning by the mill!

Well then, to resume, I am aboard. I climbed the bulging and tarry side of what once, in her young days, may have been one of Britain's formidable *wooden walls*. I stepped through a kind of low doorway into the darkness of some deck or other and gagged at my first breath. Good God, it was quite nauseous! There was much bustling and hustling about in an artificial twilight. A fellow who announced himself as my servant conducted me to a kind of hutch against the vessel's side, which he assured me was my cabin. He is a limping old fellow with a sharp face and a bunch of white hair on either side of it. These bunches are connected over his pate by a shining baldness.

"My good man," said I, "what is this stink?"

He stuck his sharp nose up and peered round as if he might see the stink in the darkness rather than nose it. "Stink, sir? What stink, sir?"

"*The stink*," said I, my hand over my nose and mouth as I gagged, "the fetor, the stench, call it what you will!"

He is a sunny fellow, this Wheeler. He smiled at me then as if the deck, close over our heads, had opened and let in some light.

"Lord, sir!" said he. "You'll soon get used to that!"

"I do not wish to get used to it! Where is the captain of this vessel?"

Wheeler dowsed the light of his countenance and opened the door of my hutch for me.

"There's nothing Captain Anderson could do either, sir," said he. "It's sand and gravel you see. The new ships has iron ballast but she's older than that. If she was betwixt and between in age, as you might say, they'd have dug it out. But not her. She's too old you see. They wouldn't want to go stirring about down there, sir."

"It must be a graveyard then!"

Wheeler thought for a moment.

"As to that, I can't say, sir, not having been in her previous. Now you sit here for a bit and I'll bring a brandy."

With that, he was gone before I could bear to speak again and have to inhale more of the *'tween decks* air. So there I was and here I am.

Let me describe what will be my lodging until I can secure more fitting accommodation. The hutch contains a bunk like a trough laid along the ship's side with two drawers built under it. At one end of the hutch a flap lets down as a writing table and there is a canvas bowl with a bucket under it at the other. I must suppose the ship contains a more *commodious* area for the performance of our natural functions! There is room for a mirror above the bowl and two shelves for books at the foot of the bunk. A canvas chair is the movable furniture of this noble apartment. The door has a fairly big opening in it at eye-level through which some daylight filters, and the wall on either side of it is furnished with hooks. The floor, or deck as I must call it, is rutted deep enough to twist an ankle. I suppose these ruts were made by the iron wheels of her gun trolleys in the days when she was young and frisky enough to sport a full set of weapons! The hutch is new but the ceiling—the deckhead?—and the side of the ship beyond my bunk, old, worn and splintered and hugely patched. Imagine me, asked to live in such a coop, such a sty! However, I shall put up with it good-humouredly enough until I can see the captain. Already the act of breathing has moderated my awareness of our stench and the generous glass of brandy that Wheeler brought has gone near to reconciling me to it.

But what a noisy world this wooden one is! The south-west wind that keeps us at anchor booms and whistles in the rigging and thunders over her—over *our* (for I am determined to use this long voyage in becoming wholly master of the sea affair)—over our furled canvas. Flurries of rain beat a retreat of kettle-drums over every inch of her. If that were not enough, there comes from forward and on this very deck the baaing of sheep, lowing of cattle, shouts of men and yes, the shrieks of women! There is noise enough here too. My hutch, or sty, is only one on this side of the deck of a dozen such, faced by a like number on the other. A stark lobby separates the two rows and this lobby is interrupted only by the ascending and enormous cylinder of our *mizzen mast*. Aft of the lobby, Wheeler assures me, is the dining saloon for the passengers with the offices of necessity on either side of it. In the lobby dim figures pass or stand in clusters. They

—we—are the passengers I must suppose; and why an ancient ship of the line such as this one has been so transformed into a travelling store-ship and farm and passenger conveyance is only to be explained by the straits my lords of the Admiralty are in with more than six hundred warships in commission.

Wheeler has told me just this minute that we dine in an hour's time at four o'clock. On my remarking that I proposed to request more ample accommodation he paused for a moment's reflection, then replied it would be a matter of some difficulty and that he advised me to wait for a while. On my expressing some indignation that such a decrepit vessel should be used for such a voyage, he, standing in the door of my hutch with a napkin over his arm, lent me as much as he could of a seaman's philosophy—as: Lord sir she'll float till she sinks, and Lord sir she was built to be sunk; with such a lecture on lying in ordinary with no one aboard but the boatswain and the carpenter, so much about the easiness of lying to a hawser *in the good old way* rather than to a nasty iron chain that rattles like a corpse on a gibbet, he has sunk my heart clear down to her filthy ballast! He had such a dismissiveness of copper bottoms! I find we are no more than *pitched within and without* like the oldest vessel of all and suppose her first commander was none other than Captain Noah! Wheeler's parting comfort to me was that he was sure she is "safer in a blow than many a stiffer vessel". *Safer!* "For," said he, "if we get into a bit of a blow she'll render like an old boot." To tell the truth he left me with much of the brandy's good work undone. After all that, I found it was positively

required I should remove all articles that I should need
on the voyage from my chests before they were *struck
down below!* Such is the confusion aboard this vessel I
can find no one who has the authority to countermand
this singularly foolish order. I have resigned myself
therefore, used Wheeler for some of this unpacking,
set out my books myself, and seen my chests taken
away. I should be angry if the situation were not so
farcical. However, I had a certain delight in some of
the talk between the fellows who took them off, the
words were so perfectly nautical. I have laid Falconer's
Marine Dictionary by my pillow; for I am determined
to speak the tarry language as perfectly as any of these
rolling fellows!

LATER

We have dined by the light of an ample stern window
at two long tables in a great muddle. Nobody knew
anything. There were no officers, the servants were
harassed, the food poor, my fellow-passengers in a
temper, and their ladies approaching the hysterics. But
the sight of the other vessels at anchor outside the
stern window was undeniably exciting. Wheeler, my
staff and guide, says it is the remainder of the convoy.
He assures me that the confusion aboard will diminish
and that, as he phrases it, we shall *shake down*—presumably in the way the sand and gravel has shaken
down, until—if I may judge by some of the passengers
—we shall stink like the vessel. Your lordship may observe a certain pettishness in my words. Indeed, had it
not been for a tolerable wine I should be downright
angry. Our Noah, one Captain Anderson, has not

chosen to appear. I shall make myself known to him at the first opportunity but now it is dark. Tomorrow morning I propose to examine the topography of the vessel and form an acquaintance with the better sort of officer if there be any. We have ladies, some young, some middling, some old. We have some oldish gentlemen, a youngish army officer and a younger parson. This last poor fellow tried to ask a blessing on our meal and fell to eating as bashful as a bride. I have not been able to see Mr Prettiman but suppose he is aboard.

Wheeler tells me the wind will *veer* during the night and we shall get a-weigh, make sail, be off, start on our vast journey when the tide turns. I have told him I am a good sailor and have observed that same peculiar light, which is not quite a smile but rather an involuntary expansiveness, flit across his face. I made an immediate resolution to teach the man a lesson in manners at the first opportunity—but as I write these very words the pattern of our wooden world changes. There is a volleying and thundering up there from what must be the loosened canvas. There is the shrilling of pipes. Good God, can human throats emit such noises? But *that* and *that* must be signal guns! Outside my hutch a passenger has fallen with many oaths and the ladies are shrieking, the cattle are lowing and the sheep baaing. All is confusion. Perhaps then the cows are baaing, the sheep lowing and the ladies damning the ship and her timbers to all hell fire? The canvas bowl into which Wheeler poured water for me has shifted in its *gimbals* and now lies at a slight angle.

Our anchor has been plucked out of the sand and gravel of Old England. I shall have no connection with my native soil for three, or it may be four or five, years. I own that even with the prospect of interesting and advantageous employment before me it is a solemn thought.

How else, since we are being solemn, should I conclude the account of my first day at sea than with an expression of my profound gratitude? You have set my foot on the ladder and however high I climb—for I must warn your lordship that my ambition is boundless!—I shall never forget whose kindly hand first helped me upwards. That he may never be found unworthy of that hand, nor *do* anything unworthy of it—is the prayer—the *intention*—of your lordship's grateful godson

EDMUND TALBOT

II

RITES OF PASSAGE

(2)

I have placed the number "2" at the beginning of this entry though I do not know how much I shall set down today. Circumstances are all against careful composition. There has been so little strength in my limbs—the privehouse, the loo—I beg its pardon, I do not know what it should be called since in strict sea-language the *heads* are at the forward end of the vessel, the young gentlemen should have a *roundhouse* and the lieutenants should have—I do not know what the lieutenants should have. The constant movement of the vessel and the need constantly to adjust my body to it—

Your lordship was pleased to recommend that I should conceal nothing. Do you not remember conducting me from the library with a friendly arm across my shoulder, ejaculating in your jovial way, "Tell all, my boy! Hold nothing back! Let me live again through you!" The devil is in it, then, I have been most confoundedly seasick and kept my bunk. After all, Seneca off Naples was in my predicament was he not—but you will remember—and if even a stoic philosopher is reduced by a few miles of lumpy water, what will become of all us poor fellows on higher seas? I must own to have been reduced already to salt tears by exhaustion and to have been discovered in such a womanish state by Wheeler! However, he is a worthy fellow. I explained my tears by my exhaustion and he agreed cheerfully.

"You, sir," said he, "would hunt all day and dance

all night at the end of it. Now if you was to put me, or most seamen, on a horse, our kidneys would be shook clear down to our knees."

I groaned some sort of answer, and heard Wheeler extract the cork from a bottle.

"Consider, sir," said he, "it is but learning to ride a ship. You will do that soon enough."

The thought comforted me; but not as much as the most delectable odour which *came o'er my spirits like the warm south*. I opened my eyes and lo, what had Wheeler done but produce a huge dose of paregoric? The comfortable taste took me straight back to the nursery and *this* time with none of the melancholy attendant on memories of childhood and home! I sent Wheeler away, dozed for a while then slept. Truly, the poppy would have done more for old Seneca than his philosophy!

I woke from strange dreams and in such thick darkness that I knew not where I was but recollected all too soon and found our motion sensibly increased. I shouted at once for Wheeler. At the third shout—accompanied I admit with more oaths than I generally consider consistent with either common sense or gentlemanly conduct—he opened the door of my hutch.

"Help me out of here, Wheeler! I must get some air!"

"Now you lie still for a while, sir, and in a bit you'll be right as a trivet! I'll set out a bowl."

Is there, can there be, anything sillier, less comforting than the prospect of imitating a trivet? I saw them in my mind's eye as smug and self-righteous as a convocation of Methodists. I cursed the fellow to his face.

However, in the upshot he was being reasonable enough. He explained that we were having a *blow*. He thought my greatcoat with the triple capes too fine a garment to risk in flying salt spray. He added, mysteriously, that he did not wish me to look like a chaplain! He himself, however, had in his possession an unused suit of yellow oilskin. Ruefully enough, he said he had bought it for a gentleman who in the event had never embarked. It was just my size and I should have it for no more than he had given for it. Then at the end of the voyage I might sell it back to him at second hand if I chose. I closed there and then with this very advantageous offer, for the air was stifling me and I longed for the open. He eased and tied me into the suit, thrust India rubber boots on my feet and adjusted an oilskin hat on my head. I wish your lordship could have seen me for I must have looked a proper sailor, no matter how unsteady I felt! Wheeler assisted me into the lobby, which was running with water. He kept up his prattle as, for example, that we should learn to have one leg shorter than the other like mountain sheep. I told him testily that since I visited France during the late peace, I knew when a deck was atilt, since I had not walked across on the water. I got out into the waist and leaned against the bulwarks on the larboard, that is the downward, side of the deck. The main chains and the huge spread of the ratlines—oh Falconer, Falconer!—extended above my head, and above that a quantity of nameless ropes hummed and thrummed and whistled. There was an eye of light showing still, but spray flew over from the high, starboard side and clouds that raced past us seemed no higher than the masts. We had company, of course, the rest of the convoy being on our larboard hand and already showing lights, though spray and a smoky mist mixed with rain obscured them. I breathed with exquisite ease after the fetor of my hutch and could not but hope that this extreme, even violent, weather would blow some of the stench out of her. Somewhat restored I gazed about me, and found for the first time since the anchor was raised my intellect and interest reviving. Staring up and back, I could see two helmsmen at the wheel, black, tarpaulined figures, their faces lighted from below as they glanced alternately into the illuminated compass, then up at the set of the sails. We had few of these spread to the wind and I supposed it was due to the inclemency of the weather but learnt later from Wheeler—that walking Falconer —that it was so we should not run clear away from the rest of the convoy since we "have the legs" of all but a few. How he knows, if indeed he knows, is a mystery, but he declares we shall speak the squadron off Ushant, detach our other ship of the line to them, take over one of theirs, be convoyed by her to the latitude of Gibraltar after which we proceed alone, secured from capture by nothing but the few guns we have left and our intimidating appearance! Is this fair or just? Do their lordships not realize what a future Secretary of State they have cast so casually on the waters? Let us hope that like the Biblical bread they get me back again! However, the die is cast and I must take my chance. I stayed there, then, my back to the bulwark, and drank the wind and rain. I concluded that most of my extraordinary weakness had been due more to the fetor of the *hutch* than to the motion of the vessel.

There were now the veriest dregs of daylight but I was rewarded for my vigil by sight of the sickness I had escaped. There emerged from our lobby into the wind and rain of the waist, a parson! I supposed he was the same fellow who had tried to ask a blessing on our first dinner and been heard by no one but the Almighty. He wore knee-breeches, a long coat and bands that beat in the wind at his throat like a trapped bird at a window! He held his hat and wig crushed on with both hands and he staggered first one way, then the other, like a drunken crab. (Of *course* your lordship has seen a drunken crab!) This parson turned, like all people unaccustomed to a tilted deck, and tried to claw his way up it rather than down. He was, I saw, about to vomit, for his complexion was the mixed pallor and greenness of mouldy cheese. Before I could shout a warning he did indeed vomit, then slid down to the deck. He got on his knees—not, I think, for the purpose of devotion!—then stood at the very moment when a *heave* from the ship gave the movement an additional impetus. The result was he came, half-running, half-flying down the deck and might well have gone clean through the larboard ratlines had I not grabbed him by the collar! I had a glimpse of a wet, green face, then the servant who performs for the starboard passengers the offices that our Wheeler performs for the larboard ones rushed out of the lobby, seized the little man under the arms, begged my pardon and lugged him back out of sight. I was damning the parson for befouling my oilskins when a heave, shudder and convenient spout of mixed rain and sea water cleaned him off me. For some reason, though the water stung my face it put me in a good humour. Philosophy and religion—what are they when the wind blows and the water gets up in lumps? I stood there, holding on with one hand, and began positively to enjoy all this confusion, lit as it was by the last lees of light. Our huge old ship with her few and shortened sails from which the rain cascaded was beating into this sea and therefore shouldering the waves at an angle, like a bully forcing his way through a dense crowd. And as the bully might encounter here and there a like spirit, so she (our ship) was hindered now and then, or dropped or lifted or, it may be, struck a blow in the face that made all her forepart, then the waist and the afterdeck to foam and wash with white water. I began, as Wheeler had put it, to *ride a ship*. Her masts leaned a little. The shrouds to windward were taut, those to leeward slack, or very near it. The huge cable of her *mainbrace* swung out to leeward between the masts; and now here is a point which I would wish to make. Comprehension of this vast engine is not to be come at gradually nor by poring over diagrams in Marine Dictionaries! It comes, when it comes, at a bound. In that semi-darkness between one wave and the next I found the ship and the sea comprehensible not merely in terms of her mechanical ingenuity but as a—a what? As a steed, a conveyance, a means working to an end. This was a pleasure that I had not anticipated. It was, I thought with perhaps a touch of complacency, quite an addition to my understanding! A single sheet, a rope attached to the lower and leeward corner of a sail, was vibrating some yards above my head, wildly indeed, but understandably! As if to reinforce the comprehension, at the moment when I was examining the rope and its function there came a huge thud from forward, an explosion of water and spray, and the rope's vibration changed—was halved at the mid-point so that for a while its length traced out two narrow ellipses laid end to end—illustrated, in fact, the *first harmonic*, like that point on a violin string which if touched accurately enough will give the player the note an octave above the open one.

But this ship has more strings than a violin, more than a lute, more I think than a harp, and under the wind's tuition she makes a ferocious music. I will own that after a while I could have done with human company, but the Church has succumbed and the Army too. No lady can possibly be anywhere but in her bunk. As for the Navy—well, it is literally in its element. Its members stand here and there encased in tarpaulin, black with faces pale only by contrast. At a little distance they resemble nothing so much as rocks with the tide washing over them.

When the light had quite faded I felt my way back to my hutch and shouted for Wheeler, who came at once, got me out of my oilskins, hung the suit on the hook where it at once took up a drunken angle. I told him to bring me a lamp but he told me it was not possible. This put me in a temper but he explained the reason well enough. Lamps are dangerous to us all since once overset there is no controlling them. But I might have a candle if I cared to pay for it since a candle dowses itself when it falls, and in any case I must take a few safety measures in the management of it. Wheeler himself had a supply of candles. I replied that I had thought such articles were commonly obtained from the purser. After a short pause Wheeler agreed. He had not thought I would wish to deal directly with the purser who lived apart and was seldom seen. Gentlemen used not to have any traffic with him but employed their servants who ensured that the transaction was honest and above board. "For," said he, "you know what pursers are!" I agreed with an air of simplicity which in an instant—you observe, sir, that I was coming to myself—concealed a revised estimate of Mr Wheeler, his fatherly concern and his willingness to serve me! I made a mental note that I was determined always to see round and through him farther than he supposed that he saw round and through me. So by eleven o'clock at night—*six bells* according to the book —behold me seated at my table-flap with this journal open before me. But what pages of trivia! Here are none of the interesting events, acute observations and the, dare I say, sparks of wit with which it is my first ambition to entertain your lordship! However, our passage is but begun.

(3)

The third day has passed with even worse weather than the others. The state of our ship, or that portion of it which falls under my notice, is inexpressibly sordid. The deck, even in our lobby, streams with sea water, rain, and other fouler liquids, which find their way inexorably under the batten on which the bottom of the hutch door is supposed to close. Nothing, of course, fits. For if it did, what would happen in the next minute when this confounded vessel has changed her position from savaging the summit of a roller to plunging into the gulf on the other side of it? When this morning I had fought my way into the dining saloon—finding, by the way, nothing hot to drink there—I was unable for a while to fight my way out again. The door was jammed. I rattled the handle peevishly, tugged at it, then found myself hanging from it as she (the monstrous vessel has become "she" as a termagant mistress) she lurched. That in itself was not so bad but what followed might have killed me. For the door snapped open so that the handle flashed in a semicircle with a radius equal to the width of the opening! I saved myself from fatal or serious injury by the same instinct that drops a cat always on its feet. This alternate stiffness then too easy compliance with one's wishes by a door—one of those necessary objects in life on which I had never before bestowed much interest —seemed to me so animated a piece of impertinence on the part of a few planks of wood I could have believed the very genii, the dryads and hamadryads of the material from which our floating box is composed, had refused to leave their ancient dwelling and come to sea with us! But no—it was merely—"merely"—dear God what a world!—the good ship doing what Wheeler called "rendering like an old boot".

I was on all fours, the door having been caught neatly against the transverse or thwartships bulkhead (as Falconer would have it) by a metal springhook, when a figure came through the opening that set me laughing crazily. It was one of our lieutenants and he stumped along casually at such an angle to the deck— for the deck itself was my plane of reference—that he seemed to be (albeit unconsciously) clownish and he put me in a good humour at once for all my bruises. I climbed back to the smaller and possibly more exclusive of the two dining tables—that one I mean set directly under the great stern window—and sat once more. All is firmly fixed, of course. Shall I discourse to your lordship on "rigging screws"? I think not. Well then, observe me drinking ale at the table with this officer. He is one Mr Cumbershum, holding the King's Commission and therefore to be accounted a gentleman though he sucked in his ale with as nauseating an indifference to polite usage as you would find in a carter. He is forty, I suppose, with black hair cut short but growing nearly down to his eyebrows. He has been slashed over the head and is one of our heroes, however unformed his manners. Doubtless we shall hear *that* story before we have done! At least he was a source of information. He called the weather rough but not very. He thought those passengers who were staying in their bunks—this with a meaning glance at me—and taking light refreshment there, were wise, since we have no surgeon and a broken limb, as he phrased it, could be a nuisance to everyone! We have no surgeon, it appears, because even the most inept of young sawbones can do better for himself ashore. It is a mercenary consideration that gave me a new view of what I had always considered a profession with a degree of disinterestedness about it. I remarked that in that case we must expect an unusual incidence of mortality and it was fortunate we had a chaplain to perform all the other rites, from the first to the last. At this, Cumbershum choked, took his mouth away from the pot and addressed me in tones of profound astonishment.

"A chaplain, sir? We have no chaplain!"

"Believe me, I have seen him."

"No, sir."

"But law requires one aboard every ship of the line does it not?"

"Captain Anderson would wish to avoid it; and since parsons are in as short supply as surgeons it is as easy to avoid the one as it is difficult to procure the other."

"Come, come, Mr Cumbershum! Are not seamen notoriously superstitious? Do you not require the occasional invocation of Mumbo Jumbo?"

"Captain Anderson does not, sir. Nor did the great Captain Cook, I would have you know. He was a notable atheist and would as soon have taken the plague into his ship as a parson."

"Good God!"

"I assure you, sir."

"But how—my dear Mr Cumbershum! How is order to be maintained? You take away the keystone and the whole arch falls!"

Mr Cumbershum did not appear to take my point. I saw that my language must not be figurative with such a man and rephrased it.

"Your crew is not all officers! Forward there, is a crowd of individuals on whose obedience the order of the whole depends, the success of the voyage depends!"

"They are well enough."

"But sir—just as in a state the supreme argument for the continuance of a national church is the whip it holds in one hand and the—dare I say—illusory prize in the other, so here—"

But Mr Cumbershum was wiping his lips with the brown back of his fist and getting to his feet.

"I don't know about all that," he said. "Captain Anderson would not have a chaplain in the ship if he could avoid it—even if one was on offer. The fellow you saw was a passenger and, I believe, a very new-hatched parson."

I remembered how the poor devil had clawed up the wrong side of the deck and spewed right in the eye of the wind.

"You must be right, sir. He is certainly a very new-hatched seaman!"

I then informed Mr Cumbershum that at a convenient time I must make myself known to the captain. When he looked surprised I told him who I am, mentioned your lordship's name and that of His Excellency your brother and outlined the position I should hold in the governor's entourage—or as much as it is politic to outline, since you know what other business I am charged with. I did not add what I then thought. This was that since the governor is a naval officer, if Mr Cumbershum was an average example of the breed I should give the entourage some tone it would stand in need of!

My information rendered Mr Cumbershum more expansive. He sat down again. He owned he had never been in such a ship or on such a voyage. It was all strange to him and he thought to the other officers too. We were a ship of war, store ship, a packet boat or passenger vessel, we were all things, which amounted to—and here I believe I detected a rigidity of mind that is to be expected in an officer at once junior and elderly —amounted to being nothing. He supposed that at the end of this voyage she would moor for good, send down her top masts and be a sop to the governor's dignity, firing nothing but salutes as he went to and fro.

"Which," he added darkly, "is just as well, Mr Talbot sir, just as well!"

"Take me with you, sir."

Mr Cumbershum waited until the tilted servant had supplied us again. Then he glanced through the door at the empty and streaming lobby.

"God knows what would happen to her Mr Talbot if we was to fire the few great guns left in her."

"The devil is in it then!"

"I beg you will not repeat my opinion to the common sort of passenger. We must not alarm them. I have said more than I should."

"I was prepared with some philosophy to risk the

violence of the enemy; but that a spirited defence on our part should do no more than increase our danger is, is—"

"It is war, Mr Talbot; and peace or war, a ship is always in danger. The only other vessel of our rate to undertake this enormous voyage, a converted warship I mean, converted so to speak to general purposes—she was named the *Guardian*, I think—yes, the *Guardian*, did not complete the journey. But now I remember she ran on an iceberg in the Southern Ocean, so her rate and age was not material."

I got my breath again. I detected through the impassivity of the man's exterior a determination to roast me, precisely because I had made the importance of my position clear to him. I laughed good-humouredly and turned the thing off. I thought it a moment to try my prentice hand at the flattery which your lordship recommended to me as a possible *passe-partout*.

"With such devoted and skilful officers as we are provided with, sir, I am sure we need fear nothing."

Cumbershum stared at me as if he suspected my words of some hidden and perhaps sarcastic meaning.

"Devoted, sir? Devoted?"

It was time to "go about," as we nautical fellows say.

"Do you see this left hand of mine, sir? Yon door did it. See how scraped and bruised the palm is, you would call it my larboard hand I believe. I have a bruise on the larboard hand! Is that not perfectly nautical? But I shall follow your first advice. I shall take some food first with a glass of brandy, then turn in to keep my limbs entire. You will drink with me, sir?"

Cumbershum shook his head.

"I go on watch," he said. "But do you settle your stomach. However, there is one more thing. Have a care I beg you of Wheeler's paregoric. It is the very strongest stuff, and as the voyage goes on the price will increase out of all reason. Steward! A glass of brandy for Mr Talbot!"

He left me then with as courteous an inclination of the head as you would expect from a man leaning like the pitch of a roof. It was a sight to make one bosky out of hand. Indeed, the warming properties of strong drink give it a more seductive appeal at sea than it ever has ashore, I think. So I determined with that glass to regulate my use of it. I turned warily in my fastened seat and inspected the world of furious water that stretched and slanted beyond our stern window. I must own that it afforded me the scantiest consolation; the more so as I reflected that in the happiest outcome of our voyage there was not a single billow, wave, swell, *comber* that I shall cross in one direction without having, in a few years time, to cross it in the other! I sat for a great while eyeing my brandy, staring into its aromatic and tiny pool of liquid. I found little comfort in sight at that time except the evident fact that our other passengers were even more lethargic than I was. The thought at once determined me to eat. I got down some nearly fresh bread and a little mild cheese. On top of this I swallowed my brandy and gave my stomach a *dare* to misbehave; and so frightened it with the threat of an addiction to small ale, thence to brandy, then to Wheeler's paregoric and after that to the ultimate destructiveness of an habitual recourse, Lord help us, to laudanum that the poor, misused organ lay as quiet as a mouse that hears a kitchen-maid rattle the fire in the morning! I *turned in* and *got my head down* and *turned out* and ate; then toiled at these very pages by the light of my candle—giving your lordship, I doubt it not, a queasy piece of "living through" me for which I am as heartily sorry as yourself could be! I believe the whole ship, from the farm animals up or down to your humble servant, is nauseated to one degree or another—always excepting of course the leaning and streaming tarpaulins.

(4)

And how is your lordship today? In the best of health
and spirits, I trust, as I am! There is such a crowd of
events at the back of my mind, tongue, pen, what you
will, that my greatest difficulty is to know how to get
them on the paper! In brief, all things about our
wooden world have altered for the better. I do not
mean that I have got my *sea legs*; for even now that I
understand the physical laws of our motion they continue to exhaust me! But the motion itself is easier. It
was some time in the hours of darkness that I woke—
a shouted order perhaps—and feeling if anything even
more stretched on the rack of our lumbering, bullying
progress. For days, as I lay, there had come at irregular intervals a kind of impediment from our watery
shoulderings that I cannot describe except to say it was
as if our carriage wheels had caught for a moment on
the drag, then released themselves. It was a movement
that as I lay in my trough, my bunk, my feet to our
stern, my head to our bows—a movement that would
thrust my head more firmly into the pillow, which
being made of granite transmitted the impulsion
throughout the remainder of my person.

Even though I now understood the cause, the repe-
tition was unutterably wearisome. But as I awoke there
were loud movements on deck, the thundering of
many feet, then shouted orders prolonged into what
one might suppose to be the vociferations of the
damned. I had not known (even when crossing the
Channel) what an *aria* can be made of the simple in-

junction, "Ease the sheets!" then, "Let go and haul!" Precisely over my head, a voice—Cumbershum's perhaps—roared, "Light to!" and there was even more commotion. The groaning of the yards would have made me grind my teeth in sympathy had I had the strength; but then, oh then! In our passage to date there has been no circumstance of like enjoyment, bliss! The movement of my body, of the bunk, of the whole ship changed in a moment, in the twinkling of an eye as if—but I do not need to elaborate the allusion. I knew directly what had brought the miracle about. We had altered course more towards the south and in Tarpaulin language—which I confess I speak with increasing pleasure—we had brought the wind from *forrard of the starboard beam* to *large on the starboard quarter*! Our motion, ample as ever, was and is more yielding, more feminine and suitable to the sex of our conveyance. I fell healthfully asleep at once.

When I awoke there was no such folly as bounding out of my bunk or singing, but I did shout for Wheeler with a more cheerful noise than I had uttered, I believe, since the day when I was first acquainted with the splendid nature of my colonial employment—

But come! I cannot give, nor would you wish or expect, a moment by moment description of my journey! I begin to understand the limitations of such a journal as I have time to keep. I no longer credit Mistress *Pamela*'s pietistic accounts of every shift in her calculated resistance to the advances of her master! I will get myself up, relieved, shaved, breakfasted in a single sentence. Another shall see me on deck in my oilskin suit. Nor was I alone. For though the weather was in no way improved, we had it at our backs, or shoulders rather, and could stand comfortably in the shelter of our wall, that is, those *bulkheads* rising to the afterdeck and quarterdeck. I was reminded of convalescents at a spa, all up and about but wary in their new ability to walk or stagger.

Good God! Look at the time! If I am not more able to choose what I say I shall find myself describing the day before yesterday rather than writing about today for you tonight! For throughout the day I have walked, talked, eaten, drunk, explored—and here I am again, kept out of my bunk by the—I must confess—agreeable invitation of the page! I find that writing is like drinking. A man must learn to control it.

Well then. Early on, I found my oilskin suit too hot and returned to my cabin. There, since it would be in some sense an official visit, I dressed myself with care so as to make a proper impression on the captain. I was in greatcoat and beaver, though I took the precaution of securing this last on my head by means of a scarf passed over the crown and tied under my chin. I debated the propriety of sending Wheeler to announce me but thought this too formal in the circumstances. I pulled on my gloves, therefore, shook out my capes, glanced down at my boots and found them adequate. I went to climb the *ladders*—though of course they are staircases and broad at that—to the afterdeck and quarterdeck. I passed Mr Cumbershum with an underling and gave him good day. But he ignored my greeting in a way that would have offended me had I not known from the previous day's exchanges that his manners are uncouth and his temper uncertain. I approached the captain therefore, who was to be recognized by his elaborate if shabby uniform. He stood on the starboard side of the quarterdeck, the wind at his back where his hands were clasped, and he was staring at me, his face raised, as if my appearance was a shock.

Now I have to acquaint your lordship with an unpleasant discovery. However gallant and indeed invincible our Navy may be, however heroic her officers and devoted her people, a ship of war is an ignoble despotism! Captain Anderson's first remark—if such a growl may be so described—and uttered at the very moment when having touched my glove to the brim of my beaver I was about to announce my name, was an unbelievably discourteous one.

"Who the devil is this, Cumbershum? Have they not read my orders?"

This remark so astonished me that I did not attend to Cumbershum's reply, if indeed he made any. My first thought was that in the course of some quite incomprehensible misunderstanding Captain Anderson was about to strike me. At once, and in a loud voice, I made myself known. The man began to bluster and my anger would have got the better of me had I not been more and more aware of the absurdity of our position. For standing as we did, I, the captain, Cumbershum and his satellite, we all had one leg stiff as a post while the other flexed regularly as the deck moved under us. It made me laugh in what must have seemed an unmannerly fashion but the fellow deserved the rebuke even if it was accidental. It stopped his blusters and heightened his colour, but gave me the opportunity of producing your name and that of His Excellency your brother, much as one might prevent the nearer approach of a highwayman by quickly presenting a brace of pistols. Our captain squinted first—you will forgive the figure—down your lordship's muzzle, decided you were loaded, cast a fearful eye at the ambassador in my other hand and reined back with his yellow teeth showing! I have seldom seen a face at once so daunted and so atrabilious. He is a complete argument for the sovranty of the humours. This exchange and the following served to move me into the fringes of his local despotism so that I felt much like an envoy at the Grande Porte who may regard himself as reasonably safe, if uncomfortable, while all round him heads topple. I swear Captain Anderson would have shot, hanged, keel-hauled, marooned me if prudence had not in that instant got the better of his inclination. Nevertheless, if today when the French clock in the Arras room chimed ten and our ship's bell here was struck four times—at that time, I say, if your lordship experienced a sudden access of well-being and a warming satisfaction, I cannot swear that it may not have been some distant notion of what a silver-mounted and murdering piece of ordnance a noble name was proving to be among persons of a middle station!

I waited for a moment or two while Captain Anderson swallowed his bile. He had much regard for your lordship and would not be thought remiss in any attention to his, his—He hoped I was comfortable and had not at first known—The rule was that passengers came to the quarterdeck by invitation though of course in my case—He hoped (and this with a glare that would have frightened a wolf-hound), he hoped to see more of me. So we stood for a few more moments, one leg stiff, one leg flexing like reeds in the wind while the shadow of the *driver* (thank you, Falconer!) moved back and forth across us. Then, I was amused to see, he did not stand his ground, but put his hand to his hat, disguised this involuntary homage to your lordship as an attempt to adjust the set of it and turned away. He stumped off to the stern rail and stood there, his hands clasped behind his back, where they opened and shut as an unconscious betrayal of his irritation. Indeed, I was half sorry for the man, confounded as I saw him to be in the imagined security of his little kingdom. But I judged it no good time for gentling him. In politics do we not attempt to use only just sufficient force to achieve a desired end? I decided to allow the influence of this interview to work for a while and only when he has got the true state of affairs thoroughly grounded in his malevolent head shall I move towards some easiness with him. We have the whole long passage before us and it is no part of my business to make life intolerable for him, nor would I if I could. Today, as you may suppose, I am all good humour. Instead of time crawling past with a snail's gait—now *if* a crab may be said to be drunk a snail may be said to have a gait—instead of time crawling, it hurries, not to say dashes past me. I cannot get one tenth of the day down! It is late; and I must continue tomorrow.

(5)

That fourth day, then—though indeed the fifth—but to continue.

After the captain had turned to the stern rail I remained for some time endeavouring to engage Mr Cumbershum in conversation. He answered me in the fewest possible words and I began to understand that he was uneasy in the captain's presence. However, I did not wish to leave the quarterdeck as if retreating from it.

"Cumbershum," said I, "the motion is easier. Show me more of our ship. Or if you feel it inadvisable to interrupt the management of her, lend me this young fellow to be my conductor."

The young fellow in question, Cumbershum's satellite, was a midshipman—not one of your ancients, stuck in his inferior position like a goat in a bush, but an example of the breed that brings a tear to every maternal eye—in a sentence, a pustular lad of fourteen or fifteen, addressed, as I soon found in pious hope, as a "Young Gentleman." It was some time before Cumbershum answered me, the lad looking from the one to the other of us meanwhile. At last Mr Cumbershum said the lad, Mr Willis by name, might go with me. So my object was gained. I left the Sacred Precincts with dignity and indeed had despoiled it of a votary. As we descended the ladder there was a *hail* from Mr Cumbershum.

"Mr Willis, Mr Willis! Do not omit to invite Mr Talbot to glance at the captain's Standing Orders. You may transmit to me any suggestions he has for their improvement."

I laughed heartily at this sally though Willis did not seem to be amused by it. He is not merely pustular but pale, and he commonly lets his mouth hang open. He asked me what I would choose to see and I had no idea, having used him to get me off the quarterdeck suitably attended. I nodded towards the forward part of the vessel.

"Let us stroll thither," said I, "and see how the people live."

Willis followed me with some hesitation in the shadow of the boats on the boom, across the white line at the main mast, then between the pens where our beasts are kept. He passed me then and led the way up a ladder to the front or *fo'castle*, where was the capstan, some loungers and a woman plucking a chicken. I went towards the bowsprit and looked down. I became aware of the age of this old crone of a ship for she is positively *beaked* in the manner of the last century and flimsy, I should judge, about the bow withal. I looked over her monstrous figurehead, emblem of her name and which our people as is their custom have turned colloquially into an obscenity with which I will not trouble your lordship. But the sight of the men down there squatting in the heads at their business was distasteful and some of them looked up at me with what seemed like impertinence. I turned away and gazed along her vast length and to the vaster expanse of dark blue ocean that surrounded us.

"Well sir," said I to Willis, "we are certainly ἐπ' εὐρέα νῶτα θαλάσσης, are we not?"

Willis replied that he did not know French.

"What do you know then, lad?"

"The rigging sir, the parts of the ship, bends and hitches, the points of the compass, the marks of the leadline to take a bearing off a point of land or a mark and to shoot the sun."

"We are in good hands I see."

"There is more than that, sir," said he, "as for example the parts of a gun, the composition of powder to sweeten the bilge and the Articles of War."

"You must not sweeten the Articles of War," said I solemnly. "We must not be kinder to each other than the French are to us! It seems to me that your education is piled all on top of itself like my lady mother's sewing closet! But what is the composition of the powder that enables you to shoot the sun and should you not be careful lest you damage the source of light and put the day out?"

Willis laughed noisily.

"You are roasting me, sir," he said. "Even a landlubber I ask your pardon knows what shooting the sun is."

"I forgive you that 'even,' sir! When shall I see you do so?"

"Take an observation, sir? Why, at noon, in a few minutes. There will be Mr Smiles, the sailing master, Mr Davies and Mr Taylor, the other two midshipmen sir, though Mr Davies does not really know how to do it for all that he is so old and Mr Taylor my friend, I beg you will not mention it to the Captain, has a sextant that does not work owing to his having pawned the one that his father gave him. So we have agreed to take turn with mine and give altitudes that are two minutes different."

I put my hand to my forehead.

"And the safety of the whole hangs by such a spider's thread!"

"Sir?"

"Our position, my boy! Good God, we might as well be in the hands of my young brothers! Is our position to be decided by an antique midshipman and a sextant that does not work?"

"Lord, no, sir! In the first place Tommy Taylor and I believe we may persuade Mr Davies to swap his good one for Tommy's instrument. It would not really matter to Mr Davies you see. Besides, sir, Captain Anderson, Mr Smiles and some other officers are also engaged in the navigation."

"I see. You do not merely shoot the sun. You subject him to a British Broadside! I shall watch with interest and perhaps take a hand in shooting the sun too as we roll round him."

"You could not do that, sir," said Willis in what seemed a kindly way. "We wait here for the sun to climb up the sky and we measure the angle when it is greatest and take the time too."

"Now look, lad," said I. "You are taking us back into the Middle Ages! You will be quoting Ptolemy at me next!"

"I do not know of him, sir. But we must wait while the sun climbs up."

"That is no more than an apparent movement," said I patiently. "Do you not know of Galileo and his 'Eppur si muove?' The earth goes round the sun! The motion was described by Copernicus and confirmed by Kepler!"

The lad answered me with the purest simplicity, ignorance and dignity.

"Sir, I do not know how the sun may behave among those gentlemen ashore but I know that he climbs up the sky in the Royal Navy."

I laughed again and laid my hand on the boy's shoulder.

"And so he shall! Let him move as he chooses! To tell you the truth, Mr Willis, I am so glad to see him up there with the snowy clouds about him that he may dance a jig for all I care! Look—your companions are gathering. Be off with you and aim your instrument!"

He thanked me and dived away. I stood on the aftermost part of the fo'castle and looked back at the ceremony which, I own, pleased me. There was a number of officers on the quarterdeck. They waited on the sun, the brass triangles held to their faces. Now here was a curious and moving circumstance. All those of the ship's people who were on deck and some of the emigrants too, turned and watched this *rite* with silent attention. They could not be expected to understand the mathematics of the operation. That I have some notion of it myself is owing to education, an inveterate curiosity and a facility in learning. Even the passengers, or those of them on deck, stood at gaze. I should not have been surprised to see the gentlemen lift their hats! But the people, I mean the common sort, whose lives as much as ours depended on an accuracy of measurement beyond their comprehension and the application of formulae that would be as opaque to them as Chinese writing, these people, I say, accorded the whole operation a respect such as they might have paid to the solemnest moment of a religious service. You might be inclined to think as I did that the glittering instruments were their Mumbo Jumbo. Indeed, Mr Davies's ignorance and Mr Taylor's defective instrument were feet of clay; but I felt they might have a justifiable faith in some of the older officers! And then— their attitudes! The woman watched, the half-plucked hen in her lap. Two fellows who were carrying a sick girl up from below—why, even *they* stood and watched as if someone had said *hist*, while their burden lay helplessly between them. Then the girl, too, turned her head and watched where they watched. There was a moving and endearing pathos about their attention, as in a dog that watches a conversation it cannot possibly understand. I am not, as your lordship must be aware, a friend to those who approve the outrageous follies of democracy in this and the last century. But at the moment when I saw a number of our sailors in a posture of such intense regard I came as near as ever I have done to seeing such concepts as "duty", "privilege", and "authority" in a new light. They moved out of books, out of the schoolroom and university into the broader scenes of daily life. Indeed, until I saw these fellows like Milton's hungry sheep that "look up", I had not considered the nature of my own ambitions nor looked for the justification of them that was here presented to me. Forgive me for boring your lordship with my discovery of what you yourself must know so well.

How noble was the prospect! Our vessel was urged forward under the force of sufficient but not excessive wind, the billows sparkled, the white clouds were diversely mirrored in the deep—*et cetera*. The sun resisted without apparent effort our naval broadside! I went down the ladder and walked back towards where our navigators were breaking from their rank and descending from the quarterdeck. Mr Smiles, the sailing master, is old, but not as old as Mr Davies, our senior midshipman, who is nearly as old as the ship! He descended not merely the ladder to the level of the waist where I was but the next one down as well—going away with a slow and broken motion for all the world like a stage apparition returning to the tomb. After leave obtained, Mr Willis, my young acquaintance, brought his companion to me with some ceremony. Mr Tommy Taylor must be a clear two years younger than Mr Willis but has the spirit and well-knit frame that his elder lacks. Mr Taylor is from a naval family. He explained at once that Mr Willis was weak in his attic and needed retiling. I was to come to him, Mr Taylor, if I wished to find out about navigation, since Mr Willis would soon have me on the rocks. Only the day before, he had informed Mr Deverel that at the latitude of sixty degrees north, a degree of longitude would be reduced to half a nautical mile. On Mr Deverel asking him—evidently a wag, Mr Deverel—what it would be reduced to at sixty degrees south, Mr Willis had replied that he had not got as far as that in the book. The memory of these cataclysmic errors sent Mr Taylor into a long peal of laughter which Mr Willis did not appear to resent. He is devoted to his young friend evidently, admires him and shows him off to the best advantage. Behold me, then, pacing to and fro between the break of the afterdeck and the mainmast, a young acolyte on either side; the younger one on my *starboard hand*, full of excitement, information, opinion, gusto; the other, silent, but smiling with open mouth and nodding at his young friend's expressions of opinion on any subject under and, indeed, including the sun!

It was from these two young hopefuls that I learnt a little about our passengers—I mean of course those who have been accommodated aft. There is the Pike family, devoted to each other, all four. There is of *course*, one Mr Prettiman, known to us all. There is, I learn from precocious Mr Taylor, in the cabin between my own hutch and the dining saloon, a portrait-painter and his wife with their daughter—a young lady characterized by the aforesaid young gentleman as "a regular snorter"! I found this to be Mr Taylor's utmost in the description of female charm. Your lordship may imagine that this news of the presence on board of a fair *incognita* lent an added exhilaration to my animal spirits!

Mr Taylor might have conducted me through the whole list of passengers; but as we were returning from the mainmast for (it may be) the twentieth time, a— or rather, the—parson who had earlier spewed so copiously into his own face came out of the lobby of the passenger accommodation. He was turning to ascend the ladder to the afterdeck, but seeing me between my young friends, and perceiving me to be of some consequence I suppose, he paused and favoured me with a reverence. Observe I do not call it a bow or greeting. It was a sinuous deflection of the whole body, topped by a smile which was tempered by pallor and servility as his reverence was tempered by an uncertainty as to the movements of our vessel. As a gesture called forth by nothing more than the attire of a gentleman it could not but disgust. I acknowledged it by the briefest lifting of my hand towards the brim of my beaver and looked him through. He ascended the ladder. His calves were in thick, worsted stockings, his heavy shoes went up one after the other at an obtuse angle; so that I believe his knees, though his long, black coat covered them, must be by nature more than usually far apart. He wore a round wig and a shovel hat and seemed, I thought, a man who would not improve on acquaintance. He was hardly out of earshot when Mr Taylor gave it as his opinion that the *sky pilot* was on his way to interview Captain Anderson on the quarterdeck and that such an approach would result in his instant destruction.

"He has not read the captain's Standing Orders," said I, as one deeply versed in the ways of captains and their orders and warships. "He will be keel-hauled."

The thought of keel-hauling a parson overcame Mr Taylor completely. When Mr Willis had thumped him to a tear-stained and hiccupping recovery he declared it would be the best sport of all things and the thought set him off again. It was at this moment that a positive roar from the quarterdeck quenched him like a bucket of cold water. I believe—no, I am sure—the roar was directed at the parson but the two young gentlemen leapt as one, daunted, as it were, by no more than a ricochet or the splinters flying from where the captain's solid shot had landed. It appeared that Captain Anderson's ability to control his own officers, from Cumbershum down to these babes-in-arms, was not to be questioned. I must confess I did not desire more than the one engagement I had had with him as a ration *per diem*.

"Come lads," said I. "The transaction is private to Captain Anderson and the parson. Let us get out of earshot and under cover."

We went with a kind of casual haste into the lobby. I was about to dismiss the lads when there came the sound of stumbling footsteps on the deck above our heads, then a clatter from the ladder outside the lobby —which turned at once to a speedier rattle as of iron-shod heels that had slipped out and deposited their wearer at the bottom with a jarring thump! Whatever my distaste for the fellow's—shall I call it—*extreme unction*, in common humanity I turned to see if he required assistance. But I had taken no more than a step in that direction when the man himself staggered in. He had his shovel hat in one hand and his wig in the other. His parsonical bands were twisted to one side. But what was of all things the most striking was— no, not the expression—but the disorder of his face. My pen falters. Imagine if you can a pale and drawn countenance to which nature has afforded no gift beyond the casual assemblage of features; a countenance moreover to which she has given little in the way of flesh but been prodigal of bone. Then open the mouth wide, furnish the hollows under the meagre forehead with staring eyes from which tears were on the point of starting—do all that, I say, and you will still come short of the comic humiliation that for a fleeting moment met me eye to eye! Then the man was fumbling at the door of his hutch, got through it, pulled it to and was scrabbling at the bolt on the other side.

Young Mr Taylor started to laugh again. I took him by the ear and twisted it until his laugh turned into a yelp.

"Allow me to tell you, Mr Taylor," said I, but quietly as the occasion demanded, "that one gentleman does not rejoice at the misfortune of another in public. You may make your bows and be off, the two of you. We shall take a constitutional again some day, I don't doubt."

"Oh lord yes, sir," said young Tommy, who seemed to think that having his ear twisted half off was a gesture of affection. "Whenever you choose, sir."

"Yes, sir," said Willis with his beautiful simplicity. "We have missed a lesson in navigation."

They retreated down a ladder to what I am told is the Gun Room and suppose to be some sort of noisome pit. The last words I heard from them that day were spoken by Mr Taylor to Mr Willis in tones of high animation—

"Don't he hate a parson above anything?"

I returned to my cabin, called Wheeler and bade him get off my boots. He responds so readily to the demands I make on him I wonder the other passengers do not make an equal use of his services. Their loss is my gain. Another fellow—Phillips, I think—serves the other side of the lobby as Wheeler serves this one.

"Tell me, Wheeler", said I as he fitted himself

down in the narrow space, "why does Captain Anderson so dislike a parson?"

"A little higher if you please, sir. Thank you, sir. Now the other if you would be so good."

"Wheeler!"

"I'm sure I can't say, sir. Does he, sir? Did he say so, sir?"

"I know he does! I heard him as did the rest of the ship!"

"We do not commonly have parsons in the Navy, sir. There are not enough to go round. Or if there are, the reverend gentlemen do not choose the sea. I will give these a brush again, sir. Now the coat?"

"Not only did I hear him but one of the young gentlemen confirmed that Captain Anderson has a strong antipathy to the cloth, as did Lieutenant Cumbershum earlier, now I recollect it."

"Did he, sir? Thank you, sir."

"Is it not so?"

"I know nothing, Mr Talbot, sir. And now, sir, may I bring you another draught of the paregoric? I believe you found it very settling, sir."

"No thank you, Wheeler. As you see, I have eluded the demon."

"It *is* rather strong, sir, as Mr Cumbershum informed you. And of course as he has less left, the purser has to charge more for it. That's quite natural, sir. I believe there is a gentleman ashore as has wrote a book on it."

I bade him leave me and lay on my bunk for a while. I cast back in memory—could not remember what day of the voyage it was—took up this book, and it seemed

RITES OF PASSAGE

to be the sixth, so I have confused your lordship and myself. I cannot keep pace with the events and shall not try. I have, at a moderate estimate, already written ten thousand words and must limit myself if I am to get our voyage between the luxurious covers of your gift. Can it be that I have evaded the demon opium only to fall victim to the *furor scribendi?* But if your lordship do but leaf through the book—

A knock at the door. It is Bates, who serves in the passengers' saloon.

"Mr Summers's compliments to Mr Talbot and will Mr Talbot take a glass of wine with him in the saloon?"

"Mr Summers?"

"The first lieutenant, sir."

"He is second in command to the captain, is he not? Tell Mr Summers I shall be happy to wait on him in ten minutes' time."

It is not the captain, of course—but the next best thing. Come! We are beginning to move in society!

(X)

I *think* it is the seventh—or the fifth—or the eighth perhaps—let "X" do its algebraic duty and represent the unknown quantity. Time has the habit of standing still so that as I write in the evening or night when sleep is hard to come by, my candle shortens imperceptibly as stalactites and stalagmites form in a grotto. Then all at once, time, this indefinable commodity, is in short supply and a sheaf of hours has fled I know not whither!

Where was I? Ah yes! Well then—

I proceeded to the passenger saloon to keep my *rendez-vous* with the first lieutenant only to find that his invitation had been extended to every passenger in this part of the vessel and was no more than a kind of short preliminary to dinner! I have found out since, that they have heard such gatherings are customary in packets and company ships and indeed, wherever ladies and gentlemen take a sea voyage. The lieutenants have concluded to do the same in this vessel, to offset, I suspect, the peremptory and unmannerly prohibitions the captain has displayed in his "Orders regarding the Behaviour of the Ladies and Gentlemen who have been afforded"—*afforded*, mark you, not *taken*—"Passage."

Properly announced, then, as the door was held open, I stepped into a scene of animation that resembled more than anything else what you might find in the parlour or dining room of a coaching inn. All that distinguished the present gathering from such a *job lot* was the blue horizon a little tilted and visible above the crowded heads through the panes of the great stern window. The announcement of my name caused a silence for a moment or two and I peered at an array of pallid faces before me without being able to distinguish much between them. Then a well-built young man in uniform and two or three years my senior came forward. He introduced himself as Summers and declared I must meet Lieutenant Deverel. I did so, and thought him to be the most gentlemanlike officer I had yet found in the ship. He is slimmer than Summers, has chestnut hair and sidewhiskers but is cleanshaven about the chin and lips like all these fellows. We made an affable exchange of it and both determined, I don't doubt, to see more of each other. However, Summers said I must now meet the ladies and led me to the only one I could see. She was seated to the starboard side of the saloon on a sort of bench; and though surrounded or attended by some gentlemen was a severe-looking lady of uncertain years whose bonnet was designed as a covering for the head and as a genuine privacy for the face within it rather than as an ambush to excite the curiosity of the observer. I thought she had a Quakerish air about her, for her dress was grey. She sat, her hands folded in her lap, and talked directly up to the tall young army officer who smiled down at her. We waited on the conclusion of her present speech.

"—have always taught them such games. It is a harmless amusement for very young gentlemen and a knowledge of the various rules at least appropriate in the education of a young lady. A young lady with no gift for music may entertain her *parti* in that way as well as another might with the harp or other instrument."

The young officer beamed and drew his chin back to his collar.

"I am happy to hear you say so, ma'am. But I have seen cards played in some queer places, I can tell you!"

"As to that, sir, of course I have no knowledge. But surely games are not altered in themselves by the nature of the place in which they are played? I speak of it as I must, knowing no more of the games than as they are played in the houses of gentlefolk. But I would expect some knowledge of—let us say—whist, as necessary to a young lady, always provided—" and here I believe there must have been a change of expression on the invisible face, since a curiously ironic inflection entered the voice—"always provided she has the wit to lose prettily."

The tall young officer crowed in the way these fellows suppose to be *laughing* and Mr Summers took the opportunity of presenting me to the lady, Miss Granham. I declared I had overheard part of the conversation and felt inferior in not having a wide and deep knowledge of the games they spoke of. Miss Granham now turned her face on me and though I saw she could not be Mr Taylor's "regular snorter" her features were severely pleasant enough when lighted with the social smile. I praised the innocent hours of enjoyment afforded by cards and hoped that at some time in our long voyage I should have the benefit of Miss Granham's instruction.

Now there was the devil of it. The smile vanished. That word "instruction" had a *denotation* for me and a *connotation* for the lady!

"Yes, Mr Talbot," said she, and I saw a pink spot appear in either cheek. "As you have discovered, I am a governess."

Was this my fault? Had I been remiss? Her expectations in life must have been more exalted than their realization and this has rendered her tongue hair-triggered as a duelling pistol. I declare to your lordship that with such people there is nothing to be done and the only attitude to adopt with them is one of silent attention. That is how they are and one cannot detect their quality in advance any more than the poacher can see the gin. You take a step, and bang! goes the blunderbuss, or the teeth of the gin snap round your ankle. It is easy for those whose rank and position in society put them beyond the vexation of such trivial social distinctions. But we poor fellows who must work or, should I say operate, among these infinitesimal gradations find their detection in advance as difficult as what the papists call "the discernment of spirits".

But to return. No sooner had I heard the words "I am a governess", or perhaps even while I was hearing them, I saw that quite unintentionally I had ruffled the lady.

"Why, ma'am," said I soothingly as Wheeler's paregoric, "yours is indeed the most necessary and genteel profession open to a lady. I cannot tell you what a dear friend Miss Dobson, Old Dobbie as we call her, has been to me and my young brothers. I will swear you are as secure as she in the affectionate friendship of your young ladies and gentlemen!"

Was this not handsome? I lifted the glass that had been put in my hand as if to salute the whole useful race, though really I drank to my own dexterity in avoiding the lanyard of the blunderbuss or the footplate of the gin.

But it would not do.

"If," said Miss Granham severely, "I am secure in the affectionate friendship of my young ladies and gentlemen it is the only thing I am secure in. A lady who is daughter of a late canon of Exeter Cathedral and who is obliged by her circumstances to take up the offer of employment among a family in the Antipodes may well set the affectionate friendship of young ladies and gentlemen at a lower value than you do."

There was I, trapped and blunderbussed—unjustly, I think, when I remember what an effort I had made to smooth the lady's feathers. I bowed and was her servant, the army officer, Oldmeadow, drew his chin even further into his neck; and here was Bates with sherry. I gulped what I held and seized another glass in a way that it must have indicated my discomfiture, for Summers rescued me, saying he wished other people to have the pleasure of making my acquaintance. I declared I had not known there were so many of us. A large, florid and corpulent gentleman with a portwine voice declared he would wish to *turn* a group portrait since with the exception of his good lady and his gal we were all present. A sallow young man, a Mr Weekes, who goes I believe to set up school, declared that the *emigrants* would form an admirable background to the composition.

"No, no," said the large gentleman, "I must not be patronized other than by the nobility and gentry."

"The emigrants," said I, happy to have the subject changed. "Why, I would as soon be pictured for posterity arm in arm with a common sailor!"

"You must not have me in your picture, then," said Summers, laughing loudly. "I was once a 'common sailor' as you put it."

"You, sir? I cannot believe it!"

"Indeed I was."

"But how—"

Summers looked round with an air of great cheerfulness.

"I have performed the naval operation known as 'coming aft through the hawsehole.' I was promoted from the lower deck, or, as you would say, from among the common sailors."

Your lordship can have little idea of my astonishment at his words and my irritation at finding the whole of our small society waiting in silence for my reply. I fancy it was as dextrous as the occasion demanded, though perhaps spoken with a too magisterial aplomb.

"Well, Summers," I said, "Allow me to congratulate you on imitating to perfection the manners and speech of a somewhat higher station in life than the one you was born to."

Summers thanked me with a possibly excessive gratitude. Then he addressed the assembly.

RITES OF PASSAGE

"Ladies and gentlemen, pray let us be seated. There must be no ceremony. Let us sit where we choose. There will, I hope, be many such occasions in the long passage before us. Bates, bid them strike up out there."

At this there came the somewhat embarrassing squeak of a fiddle and other instruments from the lobby. I did what I could to ease what might well be called *constraint*.

"Come Summers," I said, "if we are not to be portrayed together, let us take the opportunity and pleasure of seating Miss Granham between us. Pray, ma'am, allow me."

Was that not to risk another set-down? But I handed Miss Granham to her seat under the great window with more ceremony than I would have shown a peeress of the realm, and there we were. When I exclaimed at the excellent quality of the meat Lieutenant Deverel, who had seated himself on my left hand, explained that one of our cows had broken a leg in the late blow so we were taking what we could while it was still there though we should soon be short of milk. Miss Granham was now in animated conversation with Mr Summers on her right so Mr Deverel and I conversed for some time on the topic of seamen and their sentimentality over a cow with a broken leg, their ingenuity in all manner of crafts both good and bad, their addiction to liquor, their immorality, their furious courage and their devotion, only half-joking, to the ship's figurehead. We agreed there were few problems in society that would not yield to firm but perceptive government. It was so, he said, in a ship. I replied that I had seen the firmness but was yet to be convinced of the perception. By now the, shall I say, animation of the whole party had risen to such a height that nothing could be heard of the music in the lobby. One topic leading to another, Deverel and I rapidly gained a degree of mutual understanding. He opened himself to me. He had wished for a proper ship of the line, not a superannuated third-rate with a crew small in number and swept up together in a day or two. What I had taken to be an established body of officers and men had known each other for at most a week or two since she came out of ordinary. It was a great shame and his father might have done better for him. This commission would do his own prospects no good at all let alone that the war was running down and would soon stop like an unwound clock. Deverel's speech and manner, indeed everything about him, is elegant. He is an ornament to the service.

The saloon was now as noisy as a public place can well be. Something was overset amidst shouts of laughter and some oaths. Already a mousey little pair, Mr and Mrs Pike with the small twin daughters, had scurried away and now at a particularly loud outburst, Miss Granham started to her feet, though pressed to stay both by me and Summers. He declared she must not mind the language of naval officers which became habitual and unconscious among the greater part of them. For my part I thought the ill-behaviour came more from the passengers than the ship's officers— Good God, said I to myself, if she is like this at the after end, what is she like at the other? Miss Granham had not yet moved from her seat when the door was opened for a lady of a quite different appearance. She appeared young yet richly and frivolously dressed. She came in with such a sweep and flutter that the bonnet fell to the back of her neck, revealing a quantity of golden curls. We rose—or most of us, at least—but with an admirable presence she seated us again at a gesture, went straight to the florid gentleman, leaned over his shoulder and murmured the following sentence in accents of exquisite, far, far too exquisite, beauty.

"Oh Mr Brocklebank, at last she has contrived to retain a mouthful of consom!"

Mr Brocklebank boomed us an explanation.

"My child, my little Zenobia!"

Miss Zenobia was at once offered a choice of places at the table. Miss Granham declared she was leaving so that her place at it was free if another cushion might be brought. But the young lady, as I must call her, replied with whimsical archness that she had relied on Miss Granham to protect her virtue among so many dangerous gentlemen.

"Stuff and nonsense, ma'am," said Miss Granham, even more severely than she had addressed your humble servant, "stuff and nonsense! Your virtue is as safe here as anywhere in the vessel!"

"Dear Miss Granham," cried the lady with a languishing air, "I am sure your virtue is safe anywhere!"

This was gross, was it not? Yet I am sorry to say that from at least one part of the saloon there came a shout of laughter, for we had reached that part of dinner where ladies are better out of the way and only such as the latest arrival was proving to be can keep in countenance. Deverel, I and Summers were on our feet in a trice but it was the army officer, Oldmeadow, who escorted Miss Granham from our midst. The voice of the port-wine gentleman boomed again. "Sit by me, Zenobia, child."

Miss Zenobia fluttered in the full afternoon sunlight that slanted across the great stern window. She held her pretty hands up to shield her face.

"It is too bright, Mr Brocklebank, pa!"

"Lord ma'am," said Deverel, "can you deprive us poor fellows in the shadows of the pleasure of looking at you?"

"I must," she said, "I positively must and will, take the seat vacated by Miss Granham."

She fluttered round the table like a butterfly, a painted lady perhaps. I fancy that Deverel would have been happy to have her by him but she sank into the seat between Summers and me. Her bonnet was still held loosely by a ribbon at the back of her neck so that a charming profusion of curls was visible by her cheek and ear. Yet it seemed to me even at the first sight that the very brightness of her eyes—or the one occasionally turned on me—owed a debt to the mysteries of her *toilette* and her lips were perhaps a trifle artificially coral. As for her perfume—

Does this appear tedious to your lordship? The many charmers whom I have seen to languish, perhaps in vain, near your lordship—devil take it, how am I to employ any flattery on my godfather when the simple truth—

To return. This bids fair to be a lengthy expatiation on the subject of a young woman's appearance. The danger here is to invent. I am, after all, no more than a young fellow! I might please myself with a rhapsody for she is the *only tolerable female object* in our company! There! Yet—and here I think the politician, the scurvy politician, as my favourite author would have it, is uppermost in my mind. I cannot get me glass eyes. I cannot rhapsodize. For Miss Zenobia is surely approaching her middle years and is defending indifferent charms before they disappear for ever by a continual animation which must surely exhaust her as much as they tire the beholder. A face that is never still cannot be subjected to detailed examination. May it not be that her parents are taking her to the Antipodes as a last resort? After all, among the convicts and Aborigines, among the emigrants and pensioned soldiers, the warders, the humbler clergy—but no. I do the lady an injustice for she is well enough. I do not doubt that the less continent of our people will find her an object of more than curiosity!

Let us have done with her for a moment. I will turn to her father and the gentleman opposite him, who became visible to me by leaping to his feet. Even in the resumed babble his voice was clearly to be heard.

"Mr Brocklebank, I would have you know that I am the inveterate foe of every superstition!"

This of course was Mr Prettiman. I have made a sad job of his introduction, have I not? You must blame Miss Zenobia. He is a short, thick, angry gentleman. You know of him. I know—it matters not how—that he takes a printing press with him to the Antipodes; and though it is a machine capable of little more than turning out handbills, yet the Lutheran Bible was produced from something not much bigger.

But Mr Brocklebank was booming back. He had not thought. It was a trifle. He would be the last person to offend the susceptibilities. Custom. Habit.

Mr Prettiman, still standing, vibrated with passion.

"I saw it distinctly, sir! You threw salt over your shoulder!"

"So I did, sir, I confess it. I will try not to spill the salt again."

This remark with its clear indication that Mr Brocklebank had no idea at all of what Mr Prettiman meant confounded the social philosopher. His mouth still open he sank slowly into his seat, thus almost passing from my sight. Miss Zenobia turned to me with a pretty seriousness round her wide eyes. She looked, as it were, under her eyebrows and up through lashes—but no. I will not believe that unassisted Nature—

"How angry Mr Prettiman is, Mr Talbot! I declare that when roused he is quite, quite terrifying!"

Anything less terrifying than the absurd philosopher would be difficult to imagine. However, I saw that we were about to embark on a familiar set of steps in an ancient dance. She was to become more and more the unprotected female in the presence of gigantic male creatures such as Mr Prettiman and your godson. We, for our part, were to advance with a threatening good humour so that in terror she would have to throw herself on our mercy, appeal to our generosity, appeal to our chivalry perhaps: and all the time the animal spirits, the, as Dr Johnson called them, "amorous propensities" of both sexes would be excited to that state, that *ambiance*, in which such creatures as she is or has been, have their being.

This was a distancing thought and brought me to
see something else. The size, the scale, was wrong. It
was too large. The lady has been at least an *habituée*
of the theatre if not a performer there! This was not a
normal encounter—for now she was describing her
terror in the late *blow*—but one, as it were, thrown outwards to where Summers at her side, Oldmeadow and
a Mr Bowles across the table and indeed anyone in
earshot could hear her. We were to perform. But before act one could be said to be well under weigh—and
I must confess that I dallied with the thought that she
might to some extent relieve the tedium of the voyage
—when louder exclamations from Mr Prettiman and
louder rumbles and even thunders from Mr Brocklebank turned her to seriousness again. She was accustomed to touch wood. I admitted to feeling more
cheerful if a black cat should cross the road before me.
Her lucky number was twenty-five. I said at once that
her twenty-fifth birthday would prove to be most fortunate for her—a piece of nonsense which went unnoticed, for Mr Bowles (who is connected with the law in
some very junior capacity and a thorough bore) explained that the custom of touching wood came from
a papistical habit of adoring the crucifix and kissing it.
I responded with my nurse's fear of crossed knives as
indication of a quarrel and horror at a loaf turned up-
side-down as presage of a disaster at sea—whereat she
shrieked and turned to Summers for protection. He
assured her she need fear nothing from the French,
who were quite beat down at this juncture; but the
mere mention of the French was enough to set her off
and we had another description of her trembling away

the hours of darkness in her cabin. We were a single ship. We were, as she said in thrilling accents,

> "—*alone, alone,*
> *All, all alone,*
> *Alone on a wide, wide sea!*"

Anything more crowded than the teeming confines of this ship is not to be found, I believe, outside a debtor's gaol or a prison hulk. But yes she had met Mr Coleridge. Mr Brocklebank—pa—had painted his portrait and there had been talk of an illustrated volume but it came to nothing.

At about this point, Mr Brocklebank, having presumably caught his daughter's recitation, could be heard booming on metrically. It was more of the poem. I suppose he knew it well if he had intended to illustrate it. Then he and the philosopher set to again. Suddenly the whole saloon was silent and listening to them.

"No, sir, I would not," boomed the painter. "Not in any circumstances!"

"Then refrain from eating chicken, sir, or any other fowl!"

"No sir!"

"Refrain from eating that portion of cow before you! There are ten millions of Brahmans in the East who would cut your throat for eating it!"

"There are no Brahmans in this ship."

"Integrity—"

"Once and for all, sir, I would not shoot an albatross. I am a peaceable person, Mr Prettiman, and I would shoot *you* with as much pleasure!"

"Have you a gun, sir? For I will shoot an albatross, sir, and the sailors shall see what befalls—"

"I have a gun, sir, though I have never fired it. Are you a marksman, sir?"

"I have never fired a shot in my life!"

"Permit me then, sir. I have the weapon. You may use it."

"You, sir?"

"I, sir!"

Mr Prettiman bounced up into full view again. His eyes had a kind of icy brilliance about them.

"Thank you, sir, I will, sir, and you shall see, sir! And the common sailors shall see, sir—"

He got himself over the bench on which he had been sitting, then fairly *rushed* out of the saloon. There was some laughter and conversation resumed but at a lower level. Miss Zenobia turned to me.

"Pa is determined we shall be protected in the Antipodes!"

"He does not propose going among the natives, surely!"

"He has some thought of introducing the art of portraiture among them. He thinks it will lead to complacency among them which he says is next door to civilization. He owns, though, that a black face will present a special kind of difficulty."

"It would be dangerous, I think. Nor would the governor allow it."

"But Mr Brocklebank—pa—believes he may persuade the governor to employ him."

"Good God! I am not the governor, but—dear lady, think of the danger!"

"If clergymen may go—"

"Oh yes, where is he?"

Deverel touched my arm.

"The parson keeps his cabin. We shall see little of him, I think, and thank God and the captain for that. I do not miss him, nor do you I imagine."

I had momentarily forgotten Deverel, let alone the parson. I now endeavoured to draw him into the conversation but he stood up and spoke with a certain meaning.

"I go on watch. But you and Miss Brocklebank, I have no doubt, will be able to entertain each other."

He bowed to the lady and went off. I turned to her again and found her to be thoughtful. Not I mean that she was solemn—no, indeed! But beyond the artificial animation of her countenance there was some expression with which I confess I was not familiar. It was—do you not remember advising me to *read* faces?—it was a directed stillness of the orbs and eyelids as if while the outer woman was employing the common wiles and archnesses of her sex, beyond them was a different and watchful person! Was it Deverel's remark about entertainment that had made the difference? What was—what is—she thinking? Does she meditate an *affaire*, as I am sure she would call it, *pour passer le temps*?

(12)

As your lordship can see by the number at the head of this section I have not been as attentive to the journal as I could wish—nor is the reason such as I could wish! We have had bad weather again and the motion of the vessel augmented a colic which I trace to the late and unlamented *Bessie*. However, the sea is now smoother. The weather and I have improved together and by dint of resting the book and inkstand on a tray I am able to write, though slowly. The one thing that consoles me for my indisposition is that during my long sufferings the ship has got on. We have been blown below the latitudes of the Mediterranean and our speed has been limited, according to Wheeler (that living *Falconer*), more by the ship's decrepitude than by the availability of wind. The people have been at the pumps. I had thought that pumps "clanked" and that I would hear the melancholy sound clearly but this was not so. In the worst of the weather I asked my visitor, Lieutenant Summers, fretfully enough why they did not pump, only to be assured the people were pumping all the time. He said it was a delusion caused by my sickness that made me feel the vessel to be low in the water. I believe I may be more than ordinarily susceptible to the movement of the vessel, that is the truth of it. Summers assures me that naval people accept the condition as nothing to be ashamed of and invariably adduce the example of Lord Nelson to bear them out. I cannot but think, though, that I have lost consequence. That Mr Brocklebank and La Belle Brocklebank were also reduced to the state in which the unfortunate Mrs Brocklebank has been ever since we left home is no kind of help. The condition of the two hutches in which that family lives must be one it is better not to contemplate.

There is something more to add. Just before the nauseating complaint struck me—I am nigh enough recovered, though weak—a *political* event convulsed our society. The captain, having through Mr Summers disappointed the parson's expectation that he would be allowed to conduct some services, has also forbidden him the quarterdeck for some infraction of the *Standing Orders*. What a little tyrant it is! Mr Prettiman, who parades the afterdeck (with a *blunderbuss!*), was our intelligencer. He, poor man, was caught between his detestation of any church at all and what he calls his *love of liberty!* The conflict between these attitudes and the emotions they roused in him was painful. He was soothed by, of all people, Miss Granham! When I heard this comical and extraordinary news I got out of my trough and shaved and dressed. I was aware that duty and inclination urged me forward together. The brooding captain should not dictate to me in this manner! What! Is *he* to tell *me* whether I should have a service to attend or not? I saw at once that the passenger saloon was suitable and no man unless his habit of command had become a mania could take it from our control.

The parson might easily hold a short evening service there for such of the passengers as chose to attend it. I walked as steadily as I could across the lobby and tapped on the door of the parson's hutch.

He opened the door to me and made his usual sinuous genuflection. My dislike of the man returned.

"Mr—ah—Mr—"

"James Colley, Mr Talbot, sir. The Reverend Robert James Colley at your service, sir."

"Service is the word, sir."

Now there was a mighty contortion! It was as if he accepted the word as a tribute to himself and the Almighty together.

"Mr Colley, when is the Sabbath?"

"Why today, sir, Mr Talbot, sir!"

The eyes that looked up at me were so full of eagerness, of such obsequious and devoted humility you would have thought I had a brace of livings in my coat pocket! He irritated me and I came near to abandoning my purpose.

"I have been indisposed, Mr Colley, otherwise I would have made the suggestion sooner. A few ladies and gentlemen would welcome it if you was to conduct a service, a short service in the passenger saloon at seven bells in the afternoon watch or, if you prefer to remain a landsman, at half-past three o'clock."

He grew in stature before my eyes! His own filled with tears.

"Mr Talbot, sir, this is—is—it is like you!"

My irritation increased. It was on the tip of my tongue to ask him how the devil he knew what I was like. I nodded and walked away, to hear behind my back some mumbled remark about *visiting the sick*. Good God, thought I—if he tries that, he will go off with a flea in his ear! However, I managed to get to the passenger saloon, for irritation is in part a cure for weakness in the limbs, and found Summers there. I told him what I had arranged and he greeted the information with silence. Only when I suggested that he should invite the captain to attend did he smile wryly and reply that he should have to inform the captain anyway. He would make bold to suggest a later hour. I told him the hour was a matter of indifference to me and returned to my hutch and canvas chair in which I sat and felt myself exhausted but recovered. Later in the morning, Summers came to me and said that he had altered my message somewhat and hoped I did not mind. He had made it a general request from the passengers! He hastened to add that this was more conformable to the customs of the sea service. Well. Someone who delights as I do in the strange but wholly expressive Tarpaulin language (I hope to produce some prize specimens for you) could not willingly allow the *customs of the sea service* to suffer. But when I heard that the little parson was to be allowed to address us I must own I began to regret my impulsive interference and understood how much I had enjoyed these few weeks of freedom from the whole paraphernalia of Established Religion!

However, in decency I could not back down now and I attended the service our little cleric was allowed to perform. I was disgusted by it. Just previous to the service I saw Miss Brocklebank and her face was fairly plastered with red and white! The Magdalene must have looked just so, it may be leaning against the outer wall of the temple precincts. Nor, I thought, was Colley one to bring her to a more decorous appearance. Yet later I found I had underestimated both her judge-

ment and her experience. For when it was time for the
service the candles of the saloon irradiated her face,
took from it the damaging years, while what had been
paint now appeared a magical youth and beauty! She
looked at me. Scarcely had I recovered from the shock
of having this battery play on me when I discovered
what further improvement Mr Summers had made on
my original proposal. He had allowed in, to share our
devotions with us, a number of the more respectable
emigrants—Grant, the farrier, Filton and Whitlock,
who are clerks I think, and old Mr Grainger with his
old wife. He is a scrivener. Of *course* any village
church will exhibit just such a mixture of the orders;
but here the society of the passenger saloon is so
pinchbeck—such a shoddy example to them! I was
recovering from this invasion when there entered to us
—we standing in respect—five feet nothing of parson
complete with surplice, cap of maintenance perched
on a round wig, long gown, boots with iron-shod heels
—together with a mingled air of diffidence, piety, triumph and complacency. Your lordship will protest at
once that some of these attributes cannot be got together under the same cap. I would agree that in the
normal face there is seldom room for them all and that
one in particular generally has the mastery. It is so in
most cases. When we smile, do we not do so with
mouth and cheeks and eyes, indeed, with the whole
face from chin to hairline! But this Colley has been
dealt with by Nature with the utmost economy. Nature has pitched—no, the verb is too active. Well then,
on some corner of Time's beach, or on the muddy rim
of one of her more insignificant rivulets, there have

been washed together casually and indifferently a number of features that Nature had tossed away as of no use to any of her creations. Some vital spark that might have gone to the animation of a sheep assumed the collection. The result is this fledgling of the church.

Your lordship may detect in the foregoing a tendency to *fine writing*: a not unsuccessful attempt, I flatter myself. Yet as I surveyed the scene the one thought uppermost in my mind was that Colley was a living proof of old Aristotle's dictum. There is after all an order to which the man belongs by nature though some mistaken quirk of patronage has elevated him beyond it. You will find that order displayed in crude medieval manuscripts where the colour has no shading and the drawing no perspective. Autumn will be illustrated by men, peasants, serfs, who are reaping in the fields and whose faces are limned with just such a skimped and jagged line under their hoods as Colley's is! His eyes were turned down in diffidence and possibly recollection. The corners of his mouth were turned up—and there was the triumph and complacency! Much bone was strewn about the rest of his countenance. Indeed, his schooling should have been the open fields, with stone-collecting and bird-scaring, his university the plough. *Then* all those features so irregularly scarred by the tropic sun might have been bronzed into a unity and one, modest expression animated the whole!

We are back with fine writing, are we not? But my restlessness and indignation are still hot within me. He knows of my consequence. At times it was difficult to

determine whether he was addressing Edmund Talbot
or the Almighty. He was theatrical as Miss Brocklebank. The habit of respect for the clerical office was
all that prevented me from breaking into indignant
laughter. Among the respectable emigrants that attended was the poor, pale girl, carried devotedly by
strong arms and placed in a seat behind us. I have
learned that she suffered a miscarriage in our first *blow*
and her awful pallor was in contrast with the manu-
factured allure of La Brocklebank. The decent and
respectful attention of her male companions was
mocked by these creatures that were ostensibly her
betters—the one in paint pretending devotion, the
other with his book surely pretending sanctity! When
the service began there also began the most ridiculous
of all the circumstances of that ridiculous evening. I
set aside the sound of pacing steps from above our
heads where Mr Prettiman demonstrated his anticleri-
calism as noisily on the afterdeck as possible. I omit
the trampings and shouts at the changing of the watch
—all done surely at the captain's behest or with his
encouragement or tacit consent with as much rowdi-
ness as can be procured among skylarking sailors. I
think only of the gently swaying saloon, the pale girl
and the farce that was played out before her! For no
sooner did Mr Colley catch sight of Miss Brocklebank
than he could not take his eyes off her. She for her
part—and "part" I am very sure it was—gave us such
a picture of devotion as you might find in the hedge
theatres of the country circuits. Her eyes never left his
face but when they were turned to heaven. Her lips
were always parted in breathless ecstasy except when

they opened and closed swiftly with a passionate
"Amen!" Indeed there was one moment when a sanc-
timonious remark in the course of his address from
Mr Colley, followed by an "Amen!" from Miss
Brocklebank was underlined, as it were (well, a *snail
has a gait!*) by a resounding fart from that wind-
machine Mr Brocklebank so as to set most of the congregation sniggering like schoolboys on their benches.

However much I attempted to detach myself from
the performance I was made deeply ashamed by it and
vexed at myself for my own feelings. Yet since that
time I have discovered a sufficient reason for my discomfort and think my feelings in this instance wiser
than my reason. For I repeat, we had a handful of the
common people with us. It is possible they had entered
the after part of the ship in much the same spirit as
those visitors who declare they wish to view your lordship's Canalettos but who are really there to see if they
can how the nobility live. But I think it more probable
that they had come in a simple spirit of devotion. Certainly that poor, pale girl could have no other object
than to find the comforts of religion. Who would deny
them to such a helpless sufferer, however illusory they
be? Indeed, the trashy show of the preacher and his
painted Magdalene may not have come between her
and the imagined object of her supplications, but what
of the honest fellows who attended her? They may
well have been stricken in the tenderest regions of loy-
alty and subordination.

Truly Captain Anderson detests the church! His attitude has been at work on the people. He had given
no orders, it is said, but would know how to esteem

those officers who did not agree with him in his obsession. Only Mr Summers and the gangling army officer, Mr Oldmeadow, were present. You know why *I* was there! I do not choose to submit to tyranny!

Most of the fellow's address was over before I made the major discovery in my, as it were, diagnosis of the situation. I had thought when I first saw how the painted face of the *actrice* engaged the eye of the reverend gentleman, that he experienced disgust mingled perhaps with the involuntary excitement, the first movement of warmth—no, lust—that an evident wanton will call from the male body rather than mind, by her very pronouncement of availability. But I soon saw that this would not do. Mr Colley has never been to a theatre! Where, too, would he progress, in what must surely be one of our remoter dioceses, from a theatre to a *maison d'occasion?* His book told him of painted women and how their feet go down to hell but did not include advice on how to recognize one by candlelight! He took her to be what her performance suggested to him! A chain of tawdry linked them. There came a moment in his address when having used the word of all others "gentlemen", he swung to her and with a swooning archness exclaimed, "Or ladies, madam, however beautiful," before going on with his theme. I heard a positive hiss from within Miss Granham's bonnet and Summers crossed then uncrossed his knees.

It ended at last, and I returned to my hutch, to write this entry, in, I am sorry to say, increasing discomfort though the motion of the ship is easy enough. I do not know what is the matter with me. I have written sourly and feel sour, that is the fact of the matter.

(17)

I think it is seventeen. What does it matter. I have suffered again—the colic. Oh Nelson, Nelson, how did you manage to live so long and die at last not from this noisome series of convulsions but by the less painful violence of the enemy?

(?)

I am up and about, pale, frail, convalescent. It seems that after all I may live to reach our destination!

I wrote that yesterday. My entries are becoming short as some of Mr Sterne's chapters! But there is one amusing circumstance that I must acquaint your lordship with. At the height of my misery and just before I succumbed to a large dose of Wheeler's paregoric there came a timid knock at my hutch door. I cried "Who is there?" To which a faint voice replied, "It is I, Mr Talbot, sir. Mr Colley, sir. You remember, the Reverend Mr Colley, at your service." By some stroke of luck rather than wit I hit on the only reply that would protect me from his *visitation*.

"Leave me I beg you, Mr Colley—" a dreadful convulsion of the guts interrupted me for a moment; then —"I am at prayer!"

Either a decent respect for my privacy or Wheeler approaching with the good draught in his hand rid me of him. The paregoric—it was a stiff and justifiable dose that *knocked me out*. Yet I do have some indistinct memory of opening my eyes in stupor and seeing that curious assemblage of features, that oddity of nature, Colley, hanging over me. God knows when that happened—if it happened! But now I am *up*, if not *about*, the man surely will not have the impertinence to thrust himself on me.

The dreams of paregoric must owe something surely to its constituent opium. Many faces, after all, floated through them so it is possible his was no more than a figment of my drugged delirium. The poor, pale girl haunted me—I hope indeed she may make a good recovery. There was under her cheekbone a right-angled hollow and I do not recollect ever having seen anything so painful to behold. The hollow and the affecting darkness that lived there, and moved did she but turn her head, touched me in a way I cannot describe. Indeed I was filled with a weak kind of rage when I returned in thought to the occasion of the service and remembered how her husband had exposed her to such a miserable farce! However, today I am more myself. I have recovered from such morbid thoughts. Our progress has been as excellent as my recovery. Though the air has become humid and hot I am no longer fevered by the pacing of Mr Prettiman overhead. He walks the afterdeck with a weapon provided of all things by the sot Brocklebank and will discharge a positive shower from his antique blunderbuss to destroy an albatross in despite of Mr Brocklebank and Mr Coleridge and Superstition together! He demonstrates to the thoughtful eye how really irrational a rationalist philosopher can be!

(23)

I think it is the twenty-third day. Summers is to explain the main parts of the rigging to me. I intend to surprise him with a landsman's knowledge—most collected out of books he has never heard of! I also intend to please your lordship with some choice bits of Tarpaulin language for I begin, haltingly it is true, to *speak Tarpaulin!* What a pity this noble vehicle of expression has so small a literature!

(27)

Can a man always be counting? In this heat and humidity—

It was Zenobia. Has your lordship ever remarked—but of course you have! What am I thinking of? There is a known, true, tried and tested link between the perception of female charms and the employment of strong drink! After three glasses I have seen twenty years vanish from a face like snow in summer! A sea voyage added to that stimulant—and one that has set us to move gently through the tropics of all places—has an effect on the male constitution that *may* be noted in the more recondite volumes of the profession—I mean the medical profession—but had not come my way in the course of an ordinary education. Perhaps somewhere in Martial—but I have not got him with me—or that Theocritus—you remember, midday and summer's heat τόν Πᾶνα δεδοίκαμες. Oh yes, we may well fear Pan here or his naval equivalent whoever it may be! But sea gods, sea nymphs were chill creatures. I have to admit that the woman is most damnably, most urgently attractive, *paint* and all! We have met and met again. How should we not? And again! It is all madness, tropical madness, a delirium, if not a transport! But now, standing by the bulwarks in the tropic night, stars caught among the sails and swaying very gently all together, I find that I deepen my voice so that her name vibrates and yet I know my own madness—she meanwhile, why she heaves her scarcely covered bosom with more motion than stirs the glossy deep. It is folly; but then, how to describe—

Noble godfather, if I do you wrong, rebuke me. Once ashore and I will be sane again, I will be that wise and impartial adviser, administrator, whose foot you have set on the first rung—but did you not say "Tell all"? You said, "Let me live again in you!"

I am but a young fellow after all.

Well then, the problem, devil take it, was a place of assignation. To meet the lady was easy enough and indeed unavoidable. But then so was meeting everyone else! Mr Prettiman paces the afterdeck. The *Famille* Pike, father, mother and little daughters, hurry up and down the afterdeck and the waist peering on this side and that lest they should be accosted, I suppose, and subjected to some indignity or impropriety. Colley comes by in the waist; and every time nowadays he not only favours me with his *reverence* but tops it off with a smile of such understanding and sanctity he is a kind of walking invitation to *mal de mer*. What could I do? I could scarcely hand the lady into the foretop! You will ask what is wrong with my hutch or her hutch. I answer "Everything!" Does Mr Colley but cry "Hem!" on the other side of the lobby he wakes Miss Granham in the hutch just aft of him. Does that windbag Mr Brocklebank but break wind—as he does every morning just after seven bells—our timbers shudder clear through my hutch and into Mr Prettiman's just forrard of me. I have had to prospect farther for a place suitable to the conduct of our *amours*. I had thought of finding and introducing myself to the purser—but to my surprise I found that all the officers shied away from mention of him as if the man were holy, or indecent, I cannot tell which, and he never appears on deck. It is a subject I propose to get clear in my mind—when I have a mind again and this, this surely temporary madness—

(30)

In sheer desperation I have got Mr Tommy Taylor to take me down to the gun room which, though it has only three midshipmen instead of the more usual complement, is nevertheless so roomy it is used for the warrant officers as well, because *their* mess—I cannot go into the politics of it all—is too far forrard and has been taken over for the better sort of emigrant. These elders, the gunner, the carpenter and the sailing master, sat in a row beyond a table and watched me in a silence that seemed more *knowing* than the regard of anyone else in the ship if we except the redoubtable Miss Granham. Yet I did not pay much attention to them at first because of the extraordinary object that Mr Willis revealed as he moved his bony length towards the ladder. It was, of all things, a plant, some kind of creeper, its roots buried in a pot and the stem roped to the bulkhead for a few feet. There was never a leaf; and wherever a tendril or branch was unsupported it hung straight down like a piece of seaweed—which indeed would have been more appropriate and useful. I exclaimed at the sight. Mr Taylor burst into his usual peal and pointed to Mr Willis as the not particularly proud owner. Mr Willis vanished up the ladder. I turned from the plant to Mr Taylor.

"What the devil is that for?"

"Ah," said the gunner. "Gentleman Jack."

"Always one for a joke, Mr Deverel," said the carpenter. "He put him up to it."

The sailing master smiled across at me with mysterious compassion.

"Mr Deverel told him it was the way to get on."

Tommy Taylor cried with laughter—literally cried, the tears falling from him. He choked and I beat his back more severely than he liked. But unalloyed high spirits are a nuisance anywhere. He stopped laughing.

"It's a creeper, you see!"

"Gentleman Jack," said the carpenter again. "I couldn't help laughing myself. God knows what sort of lark Mr Deverel will get up to in the badger bag."

"The what, sir?"

The gunner had reached below the table and brought up a bottle.

"You'll take an observation through a glass, Mr Talbot."

"In this heat—"

It was rum, fiery and sticky. It increased the heat in my blood and seemed to increase the oppressiveness of the air. I wished that I could shed my coat as the warrant officers had; but of course it would not do.

"This air is confoundedly close, gentlemen. I wonder you can endure it day after day."

"Ah," said the gunner. "It's a hard life Mr Talbot, sir. Here today and gone tomorrow."

"Here today and gone today," said the carpenter. "Do you mind that young fellow, Hawthorne I think, come aboard at the beginning of this commission? Boatswain gets him to tail on a rope with the others, only last man like and says, says he, 'Don't you go leaving go no matter what happens.' The boat begins to take charge on the yard and drops 'cause the rest jumps clear. Young Hawthorne, who don't know the crown of a block from its arse—he come off a farm, I shouldn't wonder—he holds on like he's been told."

The gunner nodded and drank.

"Obeys orders."

It seemed the story had come to an end.

"But what was wrong? What happened?"

"Why, see," said the carpenter, "the tail of the rope runs up to the block—swit!—just like that. Young Hawthorne he was on the end of it. He must have gone a mile."

"We never saw him again."

"Good God."

"Here today and gone today, like I said."

"I could tell you a story or two about guns if it comes to that," said the gunner. "Very nasty things, guns when they misbehave, which they can do so in ten thousand different ways. So if you take up to be a gunner, Mr Talbot, you need your head."

Mr Gibbs the carpenter nudged the sailing master.

"Why, even a gunner's mate needs a head, sir," he said. "Did you never hear the story of the gunner's mate who lost his head? It was off Alicante I believe—"

"Now then George!"

"This gunner, see, was walking up and down behind his battery with his pistol in his hand. They was swopping shot with a fort, a foolish thing to do in my view. A red hot shot come through a gun port and takes off the gunner's head clean as this gallantine the Frenchies make use of. Only see the shot was red hot and cauterizes the neck so the gunner goes on marching up and down and nobody notices nothing until they run out of orders. Laugh! They nigh on died until the first lieutenant wants to know why in the name of Christ the guns had fell silent in the after starboard maindeck battery, so they asks the gunner what to do but he had nothing with which to tell them."

"Really gentlemen! Oh come!"

"Another glass, Mr Talbot."

"It's getting so *stuffy* in here—"

The carpenter nodded and knocked on a timber with his knuckles.

"It's hard to tell whether the air sweats or her wood."

The gunner heaved once or twice with laughter inside him like a wave that does not break.

"We should open a winder," he said. "You remember the gals, Mr Gibbs? 'Couldn't we 'ave a winder open? I've come over queer like.'"

Mr Gibbs heaved like the gunner.

"Come over queer, have you? Along here, my little dear. It's the way for some nice fresh air."

"'Oh what was that, Mr Gibbs? Was it a rat? I can't abide rats! I'm sure it was a rat—'

"Just my little doggie, my dear. Here. Feel my little doggie."

I drank some of the fiery liquid.

"And commerce can be obtained even in such a vessel as this? Did no one see you?"

The sailing master smiled his beautiful smile.

"I saw them."

The gunner nudged him.

"Wake up, Shiner. You wasn't even in the ship. We hadn't hardly come out of ordinary."

"Ordinary," said Mr Gibbs. "That's the life that is. No nasty sea. Lying up a creek snug in a trot with your pick of the admirals' cabins and a woman on the books to do the galley work. That's the best berth there is in the Navy, Mr Talbot, sir. Seven years I was in her before they came aboard and tried to get her out of the mud. Then they didn't think they'd careen her what with one thing and another so they took what weed they could off her bottom with the drag rope. That's why she's so uncommon sluggish. It was sea water, you see. I hope this Sydney Cove or whatever they call it has berths in fresh water."

"If they took the weed off her," said the gunner, "they might take the bottom with it."

Clearly I was no nearer my original objective. I had but one possible resource left me.

"Does not the purser share this commodious apartment with you?"

Again there was that strange, uneasy silence. At last Mr Gibbs broke it.

"He has his own place up there on planks over the water casks among the cargo and dunnage."

"Which is?"

"Bales and boxes," said the gunner. "Shot, powder, slow match, fuse, grape and chain, and thirty twenty-four pounders, all of 'em tompioned, greased, plugged and bowsed down."

"Tubs," said the carpenter. "Tools, adzes and axes, hammers and chisels, saws and sledges, mauls, spikes, trenails and copper sheet, plugs, harness, gyves, wrought iron rails for the governor's new balcony, casks, barrels, tuns, firkins, pipkins, bottles and bins, seeds, samples, fodder, lamp oil, paper, linen."

"And a thousand other things," said the sailing master. "Ten thousand times ten thousand."

"Why don't you show the gentleman, Mr Taylor," said the carpenter. "Take the lantern. You can make believe as you're the captain going his rounds."

Mr Taylor obeyed and we went, or rather crept *forrard*. A voice called behind us.

"You may even glimpse the purser."

It was a strange and unpleasant journey where indeed rats scurried. Mr Taylor, being accustomed, I suppose, to this kind of journey, made short work of it. Until I ordered him back he got so far ahead of me that I was left in complete, and need I say, foetid, darkness. When he *did* return part way it was only to reveal with his lantern our narrow and irregular path between nameless bulks and shapes that seemed piled around us and indeed over us without order or any visible reason. Once I fell, and my boots trod that same noisome sand and gravel of her bilge that Wheeler had described to me on the *first day*: and it was while fumbling to extract myself from between two of her vast timbers that I had my one and only glimpse of our purser—or at least I suppose it was the purser. I glimpsed him up there through a kind of spyhole between, it may be, bales or whatnot; and since he of all people does not have to stint himself for light that hole, though it was far below deck, blazed like a sunny window. I saw a vast head with small spectacles bowed over a ledger—just that and nothing more. Yet *this* was the creature, mention of whom could produce a silence among these men so careless of life and death!

I scrambled out of the ballast and onto the planks over the *bowsed down* cannon and crawled after Mr Taylor till a quirk of our narrow passage hid the vision and we were alone with the lantern again. We reached the forepart of the ship. Mr Taylor led me up ladders, piping in his treble—"Gangway there!" You must not imagine he was ordering some mechanism to be lowered for my convenience. In Tarpaulin, a "gangway" is a space through which one may walk and he was acting as my usher, or lictor I suppose, and ensuring that the common people would not trouble me. So we rose from the depths, through decks crowded with people of all ages and sexes and smells and noises and smoke and emerged into the crowded fo'castle whence I positively fled out into the cool, sweet air of the waist! I thanked Mr Taylor for his convoy, then went to my hutch and had Wheeler take away my boots. I stripped and rubbed myself down with perhaps a pint of water and felt more or less clean. But clearly, however freely the warrant officers obtained the favours of young women in these shadowy depths, it was of no use for your humble servant. Sitting in my canvas chair and in a mood of near desperation I came close to confiding in Wheeler but retained just enough common sense to keep my wishes to myself.

I wonder what is meant by the expression "Badger Bag"? Falconer is silent.

(Y)

It has come to me in a flash! One's intelligence may march about and about a problem but the solution does not come gradually into view. One moment it is not. The next, and it is there. If you cannot alter the place all that is left to alter is the time! Therefore, when Summers announced that the people would provide us with an entertainment I brooded for a while, thinking nothing of it, then suddenly saw with a *political eye* that the ship was about to provide me not with a place but with an opportunity! I am happy to inform you—no, I do not think gaiety comes into it, rather a simple dignity; My lord, I have at sea emulated *one* of Lord Nelson's victories! Could the merely civil part of our country achieve more? Briefly, I let it be known that such trivial affairs as the seamen's entertainment held no attraction for me, that I had the headache and should pass the time in my cabin. I took care that Zenobia should hear me! I stood, therefore, gazing through the louvre as our passengers took their way to the afterdeck and quarterdeck, a clamorous crowd only too happy to find something out of the ordinary, and soon our lobby was empty and silent as—as it could well be. I waited, hearing the trampling of feet over my head; and soon, sure enough, Miss Zenobia came tripping down to find perhaps a shawl against the tropic night! I was out of my hutch, had her by the wrist and jerked her back in with me before she could even pretend a startled cry! But there was noise enough from other places and noise enough from the blood pounding in my ears so that I pressed my suit with positive ardour! We wrestled for a moment by the bunk, she with a nicely calculated exertion of strength that only just failed to resist me, I with mounting passion. My sword was in my hand and I boarded her! She retired in disorder to the end of the hutch where the canvas basin awaited her in its iron hoop. I attacked once more and the hoop collapsed. The bookshelf tilted. *Moll Flanders* lay open on the deck, *Gil Blas* fell on her and my aunt's parting gift to me, Hervey's *Meditations among the Tombs* (*MDCCLX*) *II vols London* covered them both. I struck them all aside and Zenobia's tops'ls too. I called on her to yield, yet she maintained a brave if useless resistance that fired me even more. I bent for the *main course*. We flamed against the ruins of the canvas basin and among the trampled pages of my little library. We flamed upright. Ah—she did yield at last to my conquering arms, was overcome, rendered up all the tender spoils of war!

However—if your lordship follows me—although it is our male privilege to *debellare* the *superbos*—the *superbas*, if you will—it is something of a duty I think to *parcere* the *subjectis!* In a sentence, having gained the favours of *Venus* I did not wish to inflict the pains of *Lucina!* Yet her abandonment was complete and passionate. I did not think female heat could increase —but as bad luck would have it, at that very critical moment there came from the deck above our heads the sound of a veritable explosion.

She clutched me frantically.

"Mr Talbot," she gasped, "Edmund! The French! Save me!"

Was there ever anything more mistimed and ridiculous? Like most handsome and passionate women she is a fool; and the explosion (which I at once identified) put her, if not me, in the peril from which it had been my generous intention to protect her. Well there it is. The fault was hers and she must bear the penalties of her follies as well as the pleasures. It was—and is all the same—confoundedly provoking. Moreover she is I believe too experienced a woman not to be aware of what she has done!

"Calm yourself, my dear," I muttered breathlessly, as my own too speedy paroxysm subsided—*confound* the woman—"It is Mr Prettiman who has at last seen an albatross. He has discharged your father's blunderbuss in its general direction. You will not be ravished by the French but by our common people if they find out what he is at."

(In fact I found that Mr Coleridge had been mistaken. Sailors are superstitious indeed, but careless of life in any direction. The only reason why they do not shoot seabirds is first because they are not allowed weapons and second because seabirds are not pleasant to eat.)

Above us, there was trampling on the deck and much noise about the ship in general. I could only suppose the entertainment was being rowdily successful, for such as like that sort of thing or have nothing better in view.

"Now my dear," said I, "we must get you back to the social scene. It will never do for us to appear together."

"Edmund!"

This with a great deal of heaving and—glowing, as it is called. Really, she was in a quite distasteful condition!

"Why—what is the matter?"

"You will not desert me?"

I paused and thought.

"Do you suppose I can step overboard into a ship of my own?"

"Cruel!"

We were now, as your lordship may observe, in about act three of an inferior drama. She was to be the deserted victim and I the heartless villain.

"Nonsense, my dear! Do not pretend that these are circumstances—even to our somewhat inelegant posture—that these are circumstances with which you are wholly unfamiliar!"

"What shall I do?"

"Fiddlesticks, woman! The danger is slight as you know very well. Or are you waiting for—"

I caught myself up. Even to pretend that there might be something about this commerce that was *commercial* seemed an unnecessary insult. To tell the truth I found there were a number of irritations combined with my natural sense of completion and victory and at the moment I wished nothing so much as that she would vanish like a soap bubble or anything evanescent.

"Waiting for what, Edmund?"

"For a reasonable moment to slip into your hutch—cabin I would say—and repair your, your toilette."

"Edmund!"

"We have very little time, Miss Brocklebank!"

"Yet if—*if* there should be—unhappy consequences—"

"Why, my dear, we must cross that bridge when you come to it! Now go, go! I will examine the lobby—yes the coast is clear!"

I favoured her with a light salute, then leapt back into my cabin. I restored the books to their shelves and did my best to wrench the iron support of the canvas basin back into shape. I lay at last in my bunk and felt, not the Aristotelian sadness but a continuance of my previous irritation. Really the woman is *such* a fool! The French! It was her sense of theatre that had betrayed her, I could not help thinking, at my expense. But the party was breaking up on deck. I thought that I would emerge later when the light in the lobby was a concealment rather than discovery. I would take the right moment to go to the passenger saloon and drink a glass with any gentleman who might be drinking late there. I did not care to light my candle but waited—and waited in vain! Nobody descended from the upper decks! I stole into the passenger saloon therefore and was disconcerted to find Deverel there already, seated at the table under the great stern window with a glass in one hand and of all things a carnival mask in the other! He was laughing to himself. He saw me at once and called out.

"Talbot my dear fellow! A glass for Mr Talbot, steward! What a sight it was!"

Deverel was elevated. His speech was not precise and there was a carelessness about his bearing. He drank to me with grace, however exaggerated. He laughed again.

"What famous sport!"

For a moment I thought he might refer to the passage between me and Miss Zenny. But his attitude was not exactly right for that. It was something else, then.

"Why yes," said I. "Famous, as you say, sir."

He returned nothing for a moment or two. Then—

"How he does hate a parson!"

I was, as we used to say in the nursery, getting warmer.

"You refer to our gallant captain."

"Old Rumble-guts."

"I must own, Mr Deverel, that I am no particular friend to the cloth myself; but the captain's dislike of it seems beyond anything. I have been told that he has forbidden Mr Colley the quarterdeck on account of some trivial oversight."

Deverel laughed again.

"The quarterdeck—which Colley supposes includes the afterdeck. So he is confined more or less to the waist."

"Such *passionate* detestation is mysterious. I myself found Colley to be a, a creature of—but I would not punish the man for his nature other than to ignore him."

Deverel rolled his empty glass on the table.

"Bates! Another brandy for Mr Deverel!"

"You are kindness itself, Talbot. I could tell you—"
He broke off, laughing.

"Tell me what, sir?"

The man, I saw too late, was deep in his cups. Only the habitual elegance of his behaviour and bearing had concealed the fact from me. He murmured.

"Our captain. Our damned captain."

His head fell forward on the saloon table, his glass dropped and broke. I tried to rouse him but could not. I called the steward who is accustomed enough to dealing with such situations. Now at last the audience were indeed returning from the upper decks, for I could hear feet on the ladder. I emerged from the saloon to be met by a crowd of them in the lobby. Miss Granham swept by me. Mr Prettiman hung at her shoulder and orated to what effect I know not. The Stocks were agreeing with Pike *père et mère* that the thing had gone too far. But here was Miss Zenobia, radiant among the officers as if she had made one of the audience from the beginning! She addressed me, laughing.

"Was it not diverting, Mr Talbot?"

I bowed, smiling.

"I have never been better entertained, Miss Brocklebank."

I returned to my cabin, where it seemed to me the woman's perfume yet lingered. To tell the truth, though irritation was still uppermost in my mind, as I sat down and began to make this entry—and as the entry has progressed—irritation has been subsumed into a kind of universal sadness—Good God! Is Aristotle right in this commerce of the sexes as he is in the orders of society? I must rouse myself from too dull a view of the farmyard transaction by which our wretched species is lugged into the daylight.

ZETA

It is the same night and I have recovered from what I now think a morbid view of practically everything! The truth is I am more concerned with what Wheeler may discover and pass on to his fellows than considerations of a kind of methodistical moralism! For one thing, I cannot get the iron ring back into precise shape and for another, that curst perfume lingers yet! Confound the fool of a woman! As I look back, it seems to me that what I shall ever remember is not the somewhat feverish and too brief pleasure of my *entertainment* but the occasional and astonishing recourse to the Stage which she employed whenever her feelings were more than usually roused—or perhaps when they were more than usually *definable!* Could an actress convey an emotion that is indefinable? And would she not therefore welcome with gratitude a situation where the emotion was direct and precise? And does this not account for *stagey* behaviour? In my very modest involvement with amateur theatricals at the university, those whom we had hired to be our professional advisers named for us some of the technicalities of the art, craft or *trade*. Thus, I should have said that after my remark "Why, my dear, we must cross that bridge when you come to it!" she did not reply in words; but being half-turned away she turned wholly away and started forward away from me—would have gone much further had the hutch allowed of it—would have performed the movement we were told constituted *a break down stage right!* I laughed to remember it and was somewhat more myself again. Good God, as the captain would agree, one parson in a ship is one too many, and the stage serves as an agreeable alternative to moralism! Why, was there not a performance given us by the reverend gentleman and Miss Brocklebank in the course of the one service we have had to suffer? I am this very moment possessed by a positively and literally Shakespearean concept. *He* had found her attractive and *she* had shown herself, as women will, anxious to kneel before a male officiant—they made a pair! Should we not do them good—or, as an imp whispered to me, do us all three good? Should not this unlikely Beatrice and Benedict be brought into a mountain of affection for each other? "I will do any modest office to help my cousin to a good husband." I laughed aloud as I wrote that—and can only hope that the other passengers, lying in their bunks at *three bells of the middle watch* think that like Beatrice I laughed in my sleep! I shall for the future single out Mr Colley for the most, shall I say, distinguished attentions on my part—or at least until Miss Brocklebank proves to be no longer in danger from *the French!*

RITES OF PASSAGE

(Z)

Zed, you see, zed, I do not know what the day is—but here was a to-do! What a thing!

I rose at the accustomed hour with a faint stricture about the brows, caused I think by my somewhat liberal potations with Mr Deverel of a rather inferior brandy. I dressed and went on deck to blow it away—when who should emerge from our lobby but the reverend gentleman for whom I planned to procure—the word is unfortunate—such a pleasant future. Mindful of my determination I raised my beaver to him and gave him good day. He bowed and smiled and raised his tricorn but with more dignity than I had thought he had in him. Come, thought I to myself, does Van Diemen's Land require a bishop? I watched him in some surprise as he walked steadily up the ladder to the afterdeck. I followed him to where Mr Prettiman still stood and cradled his ridiculous weapon. I saluted him; for if I have a personal need, now, of Mr Colley, as you know, Mr Prettiman must always be an object of interest to me.

"You hit the albatross, sir?"

Mr Prettiman bounced with indignation.

"I did not, sir! The whole episode—the weapon was snatched from my hands—the whole episode was grotesque and lamentable! Such a display of ignorance, of monstrous and savage superstition!"

"No doubt, no doubt," said I soothingly. "Such a thing could never happen in France."

I moved on towards the quarterdeck; climbed the ladder; and what was my astonishment to find Mr Colley there! In round wig, tricorn and black coat he stood before Captain Anderson on the very planks sacred to the tyrant! As I came to the top of the ladder Captain Anderson turned abruptly away, went to the rail and spat over the side. He was red in the face and grim as a gargoyle. Mr Colley lifted his hat gravely, then came towards the ladder. He saw Lieutenant Summers and went across to him. They saluted each other with equal gravity.

"Mr Summers, I believe it was you who discharged Mr Prettiman's weapon?"

"It was, sir."

"I trust you injured no one?"

"I fired over the side."

"I must thank you for it."

"It was nothing, sir. Mr Colley—"

"Well, sir?"

"I beg of you, be advised by me."

"In what way, sir?"

"Do not go immediately. We have not known our people long enough, sir. After yesterday—I am aware that you are no friend to intoxicants of any sort—I beg you to wait until the people have been issued with their rum. After that there will ensue a period when they will, even if they are no more than now open to reason, be at least calmer and more amiable—"

"I have armour, sir."

"Believe me, I know of what I speak! I was once of their condition—"

RITES OF PASSAGE

"I bear the shield of the Lord."

"Sir! Mr Colley! As a personal favour to me, since you declare yourself indebted—I beg of you, wait for one hour!"

There was a silence. Mr Colley saw me and bowed gravely. He turned back to Mr Summers.

"Very well, sir. I accept your advice."

The gentlemen bowed once again, Mr Colley came towards me so *we* bowed to each other! Versailles could have done no better! Then the gentleman descended the ladder. It was too much! A new curiosity mingled with my *Shakespearean* purposes for him. Good God, thought I, the whole southern hemisphere has got itself an archbishop! I hurried after him and caught him as he was about to enter our lobby.

"Mr Colley!"

"Sir?"

"I have long wished to be better acquainted with you but owing to an unfortunate indisposition the occasion has not presented itself—"

His *mug* split with a grin. He swept off his hat, clasped it to his stomach and bowed, or sinuously reverenced over it. The archbishop diminished to a country curate—no, to a hedge priest. My contempt returned and quenched my curiosity. But I remembered how much Zenobia might stand in need of his services and that I should keep him *in reserve*—or as the Navy would say—*in ordinary!*

"Mr Colley. We have been too long unacquainted. Will you not take a turn with me on deck?"

It was extraordinary. His face, burned and blistered

as it was by exposure to the tropic sun, reddened even more, then as suddenly paled. I swear that tears stood in his eyes! His Adam's apple positively *danced* up and down beneath and above his bands!

"Mr Talbot, sir—words cannot—I have long desired—but at such a moment—this is worthy of you and your noble patron—this is generous—this is Christian charity in its truest meaning—God bless you, Mr Talbot!"

Once more he performed his sinuous and ducking bow, retired a yard or two backwards, ducked again as if leaving the presence, then disappeared into his hutch.

I heard a contemptuous exclamation above me, glanced up and saw Mr Prettiman gazing down at us over the forrard rail of the afterdeck. He bounced away again out of sight. But for the moment I spared him no attention. I was still confounded by the remarkable effect of my words on Colley. My appearance is that of a gentleman and I am suitably dressed. I have some height and perhaps—I say no more than perhaps—consciousness of my future employment may have added more dignity to my bearing than is customary in one of my years! In which case, sir, you are obliquely to be blamed for—but I wrote earlier did I not that I would not continue to trouble you with my gratitude? To resume then, there was nothing about me to warrant this foolish fellow treating me as a Royal! I paced between the break of the afterdeck and the mainmast for half an hour, perhaps to rid myself of that same stricture of the brows, and pondered this ridiculous circumstance. Something had happened and I did not know what it was—something, I saw, during the ship's entertainment while I was so closely engaged with the Delicious Enemy! What it was, I could not tell, nor why it should make my recognition of Mr Colley more than ordinarily delightful to him. And Lieutenant Summers had discharged Mr Prettiman's blunderbuss without injuring anyone! That seemed like an extraordinary failure on the part of a *fighting seaman!* It was a great mystery and puzzle; yet the man's evident gratitude for my attentions—it was annoying that I could not demand a solution to the mystery from the gentlemen or officers, for it would not be politic to reveal an ignorance based on a pleasant preoccupation with a member of the Sex. I could not at once think how to go on. I returned to our lobby, proposing to go into the saloon and discover if I could by attending to casual conversations the source of Mr Colley's extreme gratitude and dignity. But as I entered the lobby Miss Brocklebank hurried out of her hutch and detained me with a hand on my arm.

"Mr Talbot—Edmund!"

"How may I serve you, ma'am?"

Then throatily, contralto but pianissimo—

"A letter— Oh God! What shall I do?"

"Zenobia! Tell me all!"

Does your lordship detect a theatricality in my response? It was so indeed. We were at once borne along on a tide of melodrama.

"Oh heavens—it, it is a *billet*—lost, lost!"

"But my dear," said I, leaving the stage at once, "I have written you nothing."

Her magnificent but foolish bosom heaved.

"It was from Another!"

"Well," I murmured to her, "I refuse to be responsible for every gentleman in the ship! You should employ his offices, not mine. And so—"

I turned to leave but she held me by the arm.

"The note is wholly innocent but may be—might be misconstrued—I may have dropped it—oh Edmund, you well know where!"

"I assure you," said I, "that while I rearranged my hutch where it had been disturbed by a certain exquisite occasion I should have noticed—"

"Please! Oh please!"

She gazed into my eyes with that look of absolute trust mingled with anguish which so improves a pair of orbs however lustrous. (But who am I to instruct your lordship, still surrounded as you are by adorers who gaze on what they would have but cannot obtain—by the way, is my flattery too gross? Remember you declared it most effective when seasoned with truth!)

Zenobia came close and murmured up at me.

"It must be in your cabin. Oh should Wheeler find it I am lost!"

The devil, thought I. If Wheeler finds it, *I* am lost or near enough—is she trying to implicate me?

"Say no more, Miss Brocklebank. I will go at once."

I exited right—or should it be left? I have never been certain, where the theatre is concerned. Say then that I moved towards my spacious apartment on the larboard side of the vessel, opened the door, went in, shut it and began to search. I do not know anything more irritating than to be forced to search for an object in a confined space. All at once I was aware that there were two feet by mine. I glanced up.

"Go away, Wheeler! Go *away!*"

He went. After that I found the paper but only when I had given up looking for it. I was about to pour water into my canvas basin when what should I see in the centre of it but a sheet of paper, folded. I seized it at once and was about to return it to Zenobia's hutch when I was stopped by a thought. In the first place I had performed my ablutions earlier in the morning. The canvas basin had been emptied and the bunk re-made.

Wheeler!

At once, I unfolded the note, then breathed again. The hand was uneducated.

DEAREST MOST ADORABLE WOMAN I CAN WATE NO
LONGER! I HAVE AT LAST DISCOVERED A PLACE AND
NO ONE IS IN THE NO! MY HART THUNDERS IN
MY BOSSOM AS IT NEVER DID IN MY FREQUENT
HOURS OF PERIL! ONLY ACQUAINT ME WITH THE
TIME AND I WILL CONDUCT YOU TO OUR HEVEN!
YOUR SAILOR HERO

Good God, thought I, this is Lord Nelson raised to a higher power of the ridiculous! She is having an attack of the *Emmas* and has infected this Unknown Sailor Hero with her own style of it! I fell into a state of complete confusion. Mr Colley, all dignity—now this note —Summers with Prettiman's blunderbuss that was really Brocklebank's—I began to laugh, then shouted for Wheeler.

"Wheeler, you have been busy in my cabin. What should I do without you?"

He bowed but said nothing.

"I am pleased with your attentiveness. Here is a half-guinea for you. You are sometimes forgetful though, are you not?"

The man's eyes did not flicker towards the canvas bowl.

"Thank you, Mr Talbot, sir. You may rely on me in every way sir."

He withdrew. I examined the note again. It was not Deverel's, obviously, for the illiteracy was not that of a gentleman. I wondered what I should do.

Then—really, at some later date I must amuse myself by seeing how the thing would fit into a farce—I saw how the theatre would provide a means whereby I might rid myself of Zenobia and the parson together —I had but to drop the note in his cabin, pretend to discover it—Is not this note addressed to Miss Brocklebank sir? And you a minister of religion! Confess, you dog, and let us congratulate you on your success with your inamorata!

It was at this point that I caught myself up in astonishment and irritation. Here was I, who considered myself an honourable and responsible man, contemplating an action which was not merely criminal but despicable! How did that come about? You see I hide nothing. Sitting on the edge of my bunk I examined the train that had led me to such gross thoughts and found its original in the dramatic nature of Zenobia's appeal—straight back to farce and melodrama—in a word, to the theatre! Be it proclaimed in all the schools—

Plato was right!

I rose, went to the next hutch, knocked. She opened, I handed her the note and came away.

(Ω)

Omega, omega, omega. The last scene surely! Nothing more can happen—unless it be fire, shipwreck, the violence of the enemy or a miracle! Even in this last case, I am sure the Almighty would appear theatrically as a *Deus ex Machina!* Even if I refuse to disgrace myself by it, I cannot, it seems, prevent the whole ship from indulging in theatricals! I myself should come before you now, wearing the cloak of a messenger in a play— why not your Racine—forgive me the "Your" but I cannot think of him as otherwise—

Or may I stay with the Greeks? It is a play. Is it a farce or a tragedy? Does not a tragedy depend on the dignity of the protagonist? Must he not be great to fall greatly? A farce, then, for the man appears now a sort of Punchinello. His fall is in social terms. Death does not come into it. He will not put out his eyes or be pursued by the Furies—he has committed no crime, broken no law—unless our egregious tyrant has a few in reserve for the unwary.

After I had rid myself of the *billet* I went to the afterdeck for air, then to the quarterdeck. Captain Anderson was not there, but Deverel had the watch together with our ancient midshipman Mr Davies, who in bright sunlight looks more decayed than ever. I saluted Deverel and returned to the afterdeck, meaning to have some kind of exchange with Mr Prettiman who still patrols in all his madness. (I am becoming more and more convinced that the man cannot conceivably be any danger to the state. No one would heed him. Nevertheless, I thought it my duty to keep an acquaintance with him.) He paid no attention to my approach. He was staring down into the waist. My gaze followed his.

What was my astonishment to see the back view of Mr Colley appear from beneath the afterdeck and proceed towards the people's part of the vessel! This in itself was astonishing enough, for he crossed the white line at the mainmast which delimits their approach to us unless by invitation or for duty. But what was even more astonishing was that Colley was dressed in a positive delirium of ecclesiastical finery! That surplice, gown, hood, wig, cap looked quite simply silly under our vertical sun! He moved forward at a solemn pace as he might in a cathedral. The people who were lounging in the sun stood at once and, I thought, with a somewhat sheepish air. Mr Colley disappeared from my sight under the break of the fo'castle. This, then, was what he had spoken of with Summers. The people must have had their rum—and indeed now I recollected that I had heard the pipe and the cry of "Up Spirits!" earlier on without paying any attention to a sound that by now had become so familiar. The movement of the vessel was easy, the air hot. The people themselves were indulged with a holiday or what Summers calls a "Make and Mend". I stood on the afterdeck for a while, hardly attending to Mr Prettiman's diatribe on what he called this survival of barbaric finery, for I was waiting with some curiosity to see the parson come out again! I could not think that he proposed to conduct a full service! But the sight of a parson not so much walking into such a place as proc-

essing into it—for there had been about him that movement, that air, which would suppose a choir, a handful
of canons and a dean at least—this sight I say at once
amused and impressed me. I understood his mistake.
He lacked the natural authority of a gentleman and
had absurdly overdone the dignity of his calling. He
was now advancing on the lower orders in all the majesty of the Church Triumphant—or should it be the
Church Militant? I was moved at this picture in little
of one of the elements that have brought English—
and dare I say British—Society to the state of perfection it now enjoys. Here before me was the Church;
there, *aft* of me and seated in his cabin was the State
in the person of Captain Anderson. Which whip I
wondered would prove to be the more effective? The
cat-o'-nine-tails, only too material in its red serge bag
and at the disposal of the captain, though I have not
known him order its use; or the notional, the *Platonic
Idea* of a whip, the threat of hell fire? For I had no
doubt (from the dignified and outraged appearance
of the man before the captain) that the people had
subjected Mr Colley to some slight, real or imagined.
I should not have been too surprised had I heard the
fo'castle to resound with wails of repentance or
screams of terror. For a time—I do not know how
long—I waited to see what would happen and concluded that nothing would happen at all! I returned to
my cabin, where I continued with the *warm* paragraphs which I trust you will have enjoyed. I broke off
from that employment at a noise.

Can your lordship guess what the noise was? No sir,

not even you! (I hope to come by practice to subtler forms of flattery.)

The first sound I heard from the fo'castle was applause! It was not the sort of applause that will follow an *aria* and perhaps interrupt the business of an opera for whole minutes together. This was not hysteria, the audience was not beside itself. Nor were the people throwing roses—or guineas, as I once saw some young bloods try to into the bosom of the Fantalini! They were, my *social* ears told me, doing what was proper, the done thing. They applauded much as I for my part have applauded in the Sheldonian among my fellows when some respectable foreigner has been awarded an honorary degree by the university. I went out on deck quickly, but there was now silence after that first round of applause. I thought I could just hear the reverend gentleman speaking. I had half a mind to advance on the scene, conceal myself by the break of the fo'castle and listen. But then I reflected on the number of sermons I had heard in my life and the likely number to come. Our voyage, so wretched in many ways, has nevertheless been an almost complete holiday from them! I decided to wait, therefore, until our newly triumphant Colley should have persuaded our captain that our ancient vessel needed a sermon or, worse, a formal series of them. There even floated before my thoughtful eyes the image of, say, *Colley's Sermons* or even *Colley on Life's Voyage*, and I decided in advance not to be a subscriber.

I was about to return from where I stood in the gently moving shadow of some sail or other when I heard, incredulously, a burst of applause, warmer this time and spontaneous. I do not have to point out to your lordship the rarity of the occasions on which a parson is applauded in full fig or as what young Mr Taylor describes as "Dressed over all". Groans and tears, exclamations of remorse and pious ejaculations he may look for if his sermon be touched with any kind of *enthusiasm:* silence and covert yawns will be his reward if he is content to be a dull, respectable fellow! But the applause I was hearing from the fo'-castle was more proper for an entertainment! It was as if Colley were an acrobat or juggler. This second round of applause sounded as if (having earned the first one by keeping six dinner plates in the air at once) he now had added a billiard cue stood on his forehead with a chamber pot revolving on the top of it!

Now my curiosity was really roused and I was about to go forrard when Deverel descended from his watch and at once, with what I can only call deliberate meaning, began to discuss La Brocklebank! I felt myself detected and was at once a little flattered as any young fellow might be and a little apprehensive, when I imagined the possible consequences of my connection with her. She herself I saw standing on the starboard side of the afterdeck and being lectured by Mr Prettiman. I drew Deverel with me into the lobby, where we fenced a little. We spoke of the lady with some freedom and it crossed my mind that during my indisposition Deverel might have had more success than he cared to admit, though he hinted at it. We may both be in the same basket. Heavens above! But though a naval officer he is a gentleman, and however things turn out we shall not give each other away. We drank a *tot* in the passenger saloon, he had gone about his business and I was returning to my hutch when I was stopped in my tracks by a great noise from the fo'castle and the most unexpected noise of all—a positive crash of laughter! I was quite overcome by the thought of Mr Colley as a wit and concluded at once that he had left them to themselves and they were, like schoolboys, amusing themselves with a mocking pantomime of the master, who has rebuked then left them. I went up to the afterdeck for a better view, then to the quarterdeck, but could see no one on the fo'castle except the man stationed there as a lookout. They were all inside, all gathered. Colley had said something, I thought, and is now in his hutch, changing out of his *barbaric finery*. But word had flown round the ship. The afterdeck was filling below me with ladies and gentlemen and officers. Those who dared had stationed themselves by me at the forrard rail of the quarterdeck. The theatrical image that had haunted my mind and coloured my speculations in the earlier events now seemed to embrace the whole vessel. For one dizzy moment I wondered if our officers were out in the expectation of mutiny! But Deverel would have known, and he had said nothing. Yet everyone was looking forward to the great, unknown part of the ship where the people were indulging in whatever sport was afoot. We were spectators and there, interruptedly seen beyond the boats on the boom and the huge cylinder of the mainmast, was the stage. The break of the fo'castle rose like the side of the house, yet furnished with two ladders and two entrances, one on either side, that were provokingly like a stage—provoking, since a performance could not be guaranteed and our strange expectations were likely to be disappointed. I was never made so aware of the distance between the disorder of real life in its multifarious action, partial exhibition, irritating concealments and the stage simulacra that I had once taken as a fair representation of it! I did not care to ask what was going on and could not think how to find out unless I was willing to show an unbecoming degree of curiosity. Of course your lordship's favourite would have brought forward the heroine and her confidante—mine would have added the stage instruction *Enter two sailors.* Yet all I could hear was amusement growing in the fo'castle and something the same among our passengers, not to say officers. I waited on the event, and unexpectedly it came! Two ship's boys—not Young Gentlemen—shot out of the larboard doorway of the fo'castle, crossed out of sight behind the mainmast, then shot as suddenly into the starboard entrance! I was reflecting on the abject nature of the sermon that could be the occasion of such general and prolonged hilarity when I became aware of Captain Anderson, who also stood by the forward rail of the quarterdeck and stared forward inscrutably. Mr Summers, the first lieutenant, came racing up the ladder, his every movement conveying anxiety and haste. He went straight to Captain Anderson.

"Well, Mr Summers?"

"I beg you will allow me to take charge, sir."

"We must not interfere with the church, Mr Summers."

"Sir—the men, sir!"

III

RITES OF PASSAGE

"Well, sir?"

"They are in drink, sir!"

"Then see they are punished for it, Mr Summers."

Captain Anderson turned away from Mr Summers and for the first time appeared to notice me. He called out across the deck.

"Good day, Mr Talbot! I trust you are enjoying our progress?"

I replied that I was, couching my rejoinder in words I have forgotten, for I was preoccupied by the extraordinary change in the captain. The face with which he is accustomed to await the approach of his fellow men may be said to be welcoming as the door of a gaol. He has, too, a way of projecting his under-jaw and lowering the sullen mass of his face on it, all the while staring up from under his brows, that I conceive to be positively terrifying to his inferiors. But today there was in his face and indeed in his speech a kind of gaiety!

But Lieutenant Summers had spoken again.

"At least allow me—look at that, sir!"

He was pointing. I turned.

Has your lordship ever reflected on the quaintness of the tradition that signalizes our attainment of learning by hanging a medieval hood round our necks and clapping a plasterer's board on our heads? (Should not the chancellor have a silver gilt hod carried before him? But I digress.) Two figures had appeared at the larboard entry. They were now *processing* across the deck to the starboard one. Perhaps the striking of the ship's bell and the surely sarcastic cry of "All's well!" persuaded me that these figures were those in some fantastic clock. The foremost of the figures wore a black hood edged with fur, and wore it not hung down his back but up and over his head as we see in illuminated manuscripts from the age of Chaucer. It was up and round his face and held by one hand close under the chin in the fashion that I believe ladies would describe as a tippet. The other hand was on the hip with elbow akimbo. The creature crossed the deck with an exaggeratedly mincing parody of the female gait. The second figure wore—apart from the loose garments of canvas which are the people's common wear—a mortarboard of decidedly battered appearance. It followed the first figure in shambling pursuit. As the two of them disappeared into the fo'castle there was another crash of laughter, then a cheer.

Dare I say what from its subtlety your lordship may well consider to be retrospective wisdom? This playacting was not directed only inwards towards the fo'castle. It was aimed *aft* at us! Have you not seen an actor consciously throw a soliloquy outwards and upwards to the gallery and even into one corner of it? These two figures that had paraded before us had cast their portrayal of human weakness and folly directly *aft* to where their betters were assembled! If your lordship has any concept of the speed with which scandal spreads in a ship you will the more readily credit the immediacy—no, the instantaneity—with which news of the business in the fo'castle, whatever it was, now flashed through the ship. The people, the men, the crew—they had purposes of their own! They were astir! We were united, I believe, in our awareness of the threat to social stability that might at any moment arise among the common sailors and emigrants! It was horseplay and insolence at liberty in the fo'castle. Mr Colley and Captain Anderson were at fault—the one for being the occasion of such insolence, the other for allowing it. During a whole generation (granted the glory attendant on our successful arms) the civilized world has had cause to lament the results of indiscipline among the Gallic Race. They will hardly recover, I believe. I began to descend from the quarterdeck in disgust with a bare acknowledgement of salutations on every side. Mr Prettiman now stood with Miss Granham on the afterdeck. He might well, I thought bitterly enough, have an ocular demonstration of the results of the liberty he advocated! Captain Anderson had left the quarterdeck to Summers, who still stared forward with a tense face as if he expected the appearance of the enemy or Leviathan or the sea serpent. I was about to descend to the waist when Mr Cumbershum appeared from our lobby. I paused, wondering whether to interrogate him; but while I did so, young Tommy Taylor positively burst out of the fo'castle of all places and came racing aft. Cumbershum grabbed him.

"More decorum about the deck, young fellow!"

"Sir—I must see the first lieutenant, sir—it's true as God's my judge!"

"Swearing are you again, you little sod?"

"It's the parson, sir, I told you it was!"

"Mr Colley to you, sir, and damn your impudence for a squeaking little bugger!"

"It's true, sir, it's true! Mr Colley's there in the fo'castle as drunk as the butcher's boots!"

"Get below, sir, or I'll masthead you!"

Mr Taylor disappeared. My own astonishment was complete at finding the parson had been present in the fo'castle during all the various noises that had resounded thence—had been there while yet there was play-acting and the clock-figures mountebanking for our instruction. I no longer thought of retiring to my hutch. For now not merely the afterdeck and quarterdeck were crowded. Those persons who were sufficiently active had climbed into the lower parts of the mizzen shrouds while below me, the waist—the pit, I suppose in theatrical terms—had yet more spectators. What was curious was that round me on the afterdeck, the ladies no less than the gentlemen were in, or exhibited a condition of, shocked cheerfulness. They would, it seemed, have been glad to be assured the news was not true—would rather be assured—were desperately sorry if it *was* true—would not for the wide world have had such a thing happen—and if, against all probability, no, possibility, it *was* true, why never, never, never— Only Miss Granham descended with a set face from the afterdeck, turned and vanished into the lobby. Mr Prettiman with his gun stared from her to the fo'castle and back again. Then he hastened after her. But other than this severe pair the afterdeck was full of whispering and nodding animation fitted more for the retiring room at an assembly than the deck of a man-of-war. Below me Mr Brocklebank leaned heavily on his stick with the women nodding their bonnets at him on either side. Cumbershum stood by them, silent. It was at some point in this period of expectancy that the silence became general so that the gentle noises of the ship—sea noises against her planks, the soft touch of the wind fingering her rigging—became audible. In the silence, and as if produced by it, my ears—*our* ears—detected the distant sound of a man's voice. It sang. We knew at once it must be Mr Colley. He sang and his voice was meagre as his appearance. The tune and the words were well enough known. It might be heard in an alehouse or a drawing room. I cannot tell where Mr Colley learnt it.

"*Where have you been all the day, Billy Boy?*"

Then there followed a short silence, after which he broke into a different song that I did not know. The words must have been warm, I think, country matters perhaps, for there was laughter to back them. A peasant, born to stone-gathering and bird-scaring, might have picked them up under the hedge where the workers pause at noon.

When I go over the scene in my mind I am at a loss to account for our feeling that Colley's misdemeanour would be rounded out to the fullness of the event. I had been vexed earlier to see how little the stage of the fo'castle was to be relied on for conveying to us the shape and dimensions of this drama! Yet now I too waited. Your lordship might demand with reason, "Have you never heard of a drunken parson before?" I can only reply that I had indeed heard of one but had not yet seen one. Moreover, there are times and places.

The singing stopped. There began to be laughter again, applause, then a clamour of shouts and jeers. It seemed after a while that we were indeed to be cheated of the event—which was hardly to be borne, seeing how

much in sickness, danger and boredom we had paid for
our seats. However, it was at this critical juncture that
Captain Anderson ascended from his cabin to the
quarterdeck, took his place at the forrard rail of it and
surveyed the theatre and audience. His face was as
severe as Miss Granham's. He spoke sharply to Mr
Deverel, who now had the watch, informing him (in a
voice which seemed to make the fact directly attributa-
ble to some negligence on Mr Deverel's part) that *the
parson was still there*. He then took a turn or two
round his side of the quarterdeck, came back to the
rail, stopped by it, and spoke to Mr Deverel more
cheerfully.

"Mr Deverel. Be good enough to have the parson
informed he must now return to his cabin."

I believe not another muscle stirred in the ship as
Mr Deverel repeated the order to Mr Willis, who
saluted and went forward with all eyes on his back.
Our astonished ears heard Mr Colley address him
with a string of endearments that would have—and
perhaps *did*—make La Brocklebank blush like a pae-
ony. The young gentleman came stumbling out of the
fo'castle and ran back sniggering. But in truth none
among us paid him much attention. For now, like
some pigmy Polyphemus, like whatever is at once
strange and disgusting, the parson appeared in the
lefthand doorway of the fo'castle. His ecclesiastical
garment had gone and the marks of his degree. His
wig had gone—his very breeches, stockings and shoes
had been taken from him. Some charitable soul had in
pity, I supposed, supplied him with one of the loose

canvas garments that the common people wear about
the ship; and this because of his diminutive stature was
sufficient to cover his loins. He was not alone. A young
stalwart had him in charge. This fellow was supporting
Mr Colley, whose head lay back on the man's breast.
As the curious pair came uncertainly past the mainmast, Mr Colley pushed back so that they stopped. It
was evident that his mind had become only lightly
linked to his understanding. He appeared to be in a
state of extreme and sunny enjoyment. His eyes moved
indifferently, as if taking no print of what they saw.
Surely his frame was not one that could afford him any
pleasure! His skull now the wig no longer covered it
was seen to be small and narrow. His legs had no
calves; but dame Nature in a frivolous mood had furnished him with great feet and knots of knees that
betrayed their peasant origin. He was muttering some
nonsense of *fol de rol* or the like. Then, as if seeing his
audience for the first time, he heaved himself away
from his assistant, stood on splayed feet and flung out
his arms as if to embrace us all.

"Joy! Joy! Joy!"

Then his face became thoughtful. He turned to his
right, walked slowly and carefully to the bulwark and
pissed against it. What a shrieking and covering of
faces there was from the ladies, what growls from us!
Mr Colley turned back to us and opened his mouth.
Not even the captain could have caused a more immediate silence.

Mr Colley raised his right hand and spoke, though
slurredly.

"The blessing of God the Father Almighty, God the Son and God the Holy Ghost be with you and remain with you always."

Then there was a commotion I can tell you! If the man's uncommonly public micturation had shocked the ladies, to be blessed by a drunk man in a canvas shirt caused screams, hasty retreats and, I am told, one *évanouissement!* It was no more than seconds after this that the servant, Phillips, and Mr Summers, the first lieutenant, lugged the poor fool out of sight while the seaman who had helped him aft stood and stared after them. When Colley was out of sight the man looked up at the quarterdeck, touched his forelock and went back to the fo'castle.

On the whole I think the audience was well enough satisfied. Next to the ladies Captain Anderson seemed to be the principal beneficiary of Colley's performance. He became positively sociable with the ladies, voluntarily breaking away from his sacred side of the quarterdeck and bidding them welcome. Though he firmly but courteously declined to discuss *l'affaire Colley*, there was a lightness about his step and indeed a light in his eye that I had supposed occasioned in a naval officer only by the imminence of battle! What animation had possessed the other officers passed away quickly enough. They must have seen enough drunkenness and been part of enough to see this as no more than an event in a long history. And what was the sight of Colley's urine to naval gentlemen who had perhaps seen decks smeared with the viscera and streaming with the blood of their late companions? I returned to my hutch, determined to give you as full and vivid an account of the episode as was in my power. Yet even while I was busy leading up to the events, the further events of his fall raced past me. While I was yet describing the strange noises from the fo'castle, I heard the sound of a door opened clumsily on the other side of the lobby. I jumped up and stared (by means of my *louvre* or spyhole) across it. Lo, Colley came out of his cabin! He held a sheet of paper in his hand and he still smiled that smile of aery contentment and joy. He went in this joyous distraction in the direction of the necessary offices on that side of the ship. Evidently he still dwelt in a land of faery which would vanish presently and leave him—

Well. Where will it leave him? He is quite unpractised in the management of spiritous liquors. I imagined his distress on coming to himself and I started to laugh—then changed my mind. The closeness of my cabin became a positive fetor.

(51)

This is the fifty-first day of our voyage, I think; and then again perhaps it is not. I have lost interest in the calendar and almost lost it in the voyage too. We have our shipboard calendar of events which are trivial enough. Nothing has happened since Colley entertained us. He is much condemned. Captain Anderson continues benign. Colley himself has not been out of his hutch in the four days which have passed since his drunkenness. No one but the servant has seen him if you except me on the occasion when he took his own paper to the loo! Enough of him.

What might amuse you more is the kind of *country dance* we young fellows have been performing round La Brocklebank. I have not yet identified her *Sailor Hero* but am sure that Deverel has had to do with her. I taxed him with it and drew an admission from him. We agreed that a man might well suffer shipwreck on *that* coast and have decided to stand shoulder to shoulder in mutual defence. A mixed metaphor, my lord, so you can see how dull I find myself. To resume. We both think that at the moment she is inclined to Cumbershum. I owned that this was a relief to me and Deverel agreed. We had feared, both of us, to be in the same difficulty over our common *inamorata*. You will remember that I had some hare-brained scheme, since Colley was so clearly *épris* with her, of having a MUCH ADO ABOUT NOTHING and bringing this Beatrice and Benedict into a mountain of affection for each other! I told Deverel this, at which he was silent for a

RITES OF PASSAGE

while, then burst out laughing. I was about to inform him plainly that I took exception to his conduct when he asked my pardon in the most graceful way. But, said he, the coincidence was past the wit of man to invent and he would share the jest with me if I would give him my word to say nothing of what he told me. We were interrupted at this point and I do not know what the jest is, but you shall have it when I do.

ALPHA

I have been remiss and let a few days go by without attention to the journal. I have felt a lethargy. There has been little to do but walk the deck, drink with any-one who will, walk the deck again, perhaps speaking to this passenger or that. I believe I did not tell you that when "Mrs Brocklebank" issued from the cabin she proved to be if anything younger than her daughter! I have avoided both her and the fair Zenobia, who *glows* in this heat so as almost to turn a man's stomach! Cumbershum is not so delicate. The boredom of the voyage in these hot and next to windless latitudes has increased the consumption of strong spirits among us. I had thought to give you a full list of our passengers but have given up. They would not interest you. Let them remain κωφὰ πρόσωπα. What is of some interest however is the behaviour—or the lack of it—of Colley. The fact is that since the fellow's fall he has not left his cabin. Phillips the servant goes in occasionally and I believe that Mr Summers has visited him, I suppose thinking it part of a first lieutenant's duty. A lustreless fellow like Colley might well feel some diffidence at coming again among ladies and gentlemen. The ladies are particularly strict on him. For my own part, the fact that Captain Anderson *rode the man hard*, in Dever-el's phrase, is sufficient to temper any inclination I might have absolutely to reject Colley as a human being!

Deverel and I agree that Brocklebank is or has been the keeper of both the doxies. I had known that the world of art is not to be judged by the accepted standards of morality but would prefer him to set up his brothel in another place. However, they have two hutches, one for the "parents" and one for the "daughter," so he does at least make a tiny gesture towards preserving appearances. Appearances are preserved and everyone is happy, even Miss Granham. As for Mr Prettiman, I suppose he notices nothing. Long live illusion, say I. Let us export it to our colonies with all the other benefits of civilization!

(60)

I have just come from the passenger saloon, where I have sat for a long time with Summers. The conversation is worth recording, though I have an uneasy feeling that it tells against me. I am bound to say that Summers is the person of all in this ship who does His Majesty's Service the most credit. Deverel is naturally more the gentleman but not assiduous in his duties. As for the others—they may be dismissed *en masse*. The difference had been in my mind and I did, in a way I now fear he may have found offensive, discuss the desirability of men being elevated above their first station in life. It was thoughtless of me and Summers replied with some bitterness.

"Mr Talbot, sir, I do not know how to say this or indeed whether I should—but you yourself made it plain in a way that put the matter beyond misunderstanding, that a man's original is branded on his forehead, never to be removed."

"Come, Mr Summers—I did not so!"

"Do you not remember?"

"Remember what?"

He was silent for a while. Then—

"I understand. It is plain when I see it from your point of view. Why should you remember?"

"Remember *what*, sir?"

Again he was silent. Then he looked away and seemed to be reading the words of the following sentence off the bulkhead.

" 'Well, Summers, allow me to congratulate you on

imitating to perfection the manners and speech of a somewhat higher station in life than the one you was born to.' "

Now it was my turn to be silent. What he said was true. Your lordship may, if you choose, turn back in this very journal and find the words there. I have done so myself, and re-read the account of that first meeting. I believe Summers does not give me credit for the state of bewilderment and embarrassment in which I had then found myself, but the words, the very words, are there!

"I ask your pardon, Mr Summers. It was—insufferable."

"But true, sir," said Summers, bitterly. "In our country for all her greatness there is one thing she cannot do and that is translate a person wholly out of one class into another. Perfect translation from one language into another is impossible. Class is the British language."

"Come, sir," said I, "will you not believe me? Perfect translation from one language to another is possible and I could give you an example of it. So is perfect translation from class to class."

"*Imitating* to perfection—"

"Perfect in this, that you are a gentleman."

Summers flushed red and his face only slowly resumed its wonted bronze. It was high time we moved our ground.

"Yet you see, my dear fellow, we have at least one example among us where the translation is not a success!"

"I must suppose you to refer to Mr Colley. It was my purpose to raise that subject."

"The man has stepped out of his station without any merit to support the elevation."

"I do not see how his conduct can be traced to his original for we do not know what it was."

"Come. It appears in his physique, his speech and above all in what I can only call his habit of subordination. I swear he has got out of the peasantry by a kind of greasy obsequiousness. Now for example—Bates, the brandy, please!—I can myself drink brandy as long as you please and I issue a guarantee that no man and particularly no lady will see in me the kind of behaviour by which Mr Colley has amused us and affronted them. Colley, plied, as we must suppose, with spirits there in the fo'castle, had neither the strength to refuse it nor the breeding which would have enabled him to resist its more destructive effects."

"This wisdom should be put in a book."

"Laugh if you will, sir. Today I must not be offended with you."

"But there is another matter and I had intended to raise it. We have no physician and the man is mortally sick."

"How can that be? He is young and suffering from no more than over-indulgence in liquor."

"Still? I have talked with the servant. I have entered the cabin and seen for myself. In many years of service neither Phillips nor I have seen anything like it. The bed is filthy, yet the man, though he breathes every now and then, does not stir in it. His face is pressed down and hidden. He lies on his stomach, one hand above his head and clutched into the bolster, the other clutching an old ringbolt left in the timber."

"I marvel you can eat after it."

"Oh that! I tried to turn him over."

"Tried? You must have succeeded. You have three times his strength."

"Not in these circumstances."

"I own, Mr Summers, that I have not observed much intemperance in Colley's line of life. But the story goes that the Senior Tutor at my own college, having dined too well before a service, rose from his seat, staggered to the lectern, slumped, holding on to the brass eagle and was heard to mutter, 'I should have been down had it not been for this bleeding Dodo.' But I daresay you never heard the story."

Mr Summers shook his head.

"I have been much abroad," he replied gravely. "The event made little noise in that part of the Service where I then was."

"A hit, a palpable hit! But depend on it, young Colley will lift up his head."

Summers stared into his untouched glass.

"He has a strange power. It is almost as if the New-tonian Force is affected. The hand that holds the ring-bolt might be made of steel. He lies, dinted into his bunk, drawn down into it as if made of lead."

"There he must stay then."

"Is that all, Mr Talbot? Are you as indifferent to the man's fate as others are?"

"I am not an officer in this ship!"

"The more able to help, sir."

"How?"

"I may speak to you freely, may I not? Well then—how has the man been treated?"

"He was at first an object of one man's specific dislike, then an object of general indifference that was leading to contempt even before his latest—escapade."

Summers turned and stared out of the great stern window for a while. Then he looked back at me.

"What I say now could well ruin me if I have misjudged your character."

"Character? *My* character? You have examined my character? You set yourself up—"

"Forgive me—nothing is further from my mind than offending you and if I did not believe the case desperate—"

"What case, for God's sake?"

"We know your birth, your prospective position—why—men—and women—will flatter you in the hope or expectation of gaining the governor's ear—"

"Good God—Mr Summers!"

"Wait, wait! Understand me, Mr Talbot—I do not complain!"

"You sound uncommonly like a man complaining, sir!"

I had half-risen from my seat; but Summers stretched out his hand in a gesture of such simple—"supplication" I suppose I must call it—that I sat down again.

"Proceed then, if you must!"

"I do not speak in my own behalf."

For a while we were both silent. Then Summers swallowed, deeply as if there had been a real drink in his mouth and that no small one.

"Sir, you have used your birth and your prospective position to get for yourself an unusual degree of attention and comfort—I do not complain—dare not! Who am I to question the customs of our society or indeed, the laws of nature? In a sentence, you have exercised the privileges of your position. I am asking you to shoulder its responsibilities."

During—it may be—half a minute; for what is time in a ship, or to revert to that strange metaphor of existence that came to me so strongly during Mr Colley's exhibition, what is time in a theatre? During that time, however long or short, I passed through numberless emotions—rage I think, confusion, irritation, amusement and an embarrassment for which I was most annoyed, seeing that I had only now discovered the seriousness of Mr Colley's condition.

"That was a notable impertinence, Mr Summers!"

As my vision cleared I saw that the man had a positive pallor under his brown skin.

"Let me think, man! Steward! Another brandy here!"

Bates brought it at the run for I must have ordered it in a more than usually peremptory voice. I did not drink at once but sat and stared into my glass.

The trouble was that in everything the man had said, he was right!

After a while, he spoke again.

"A visit from you, sir, to such a man—"

"I? Go in that stinking hole?"

"There is a phrase that suits your situation, sir. It is *Noblesse oblige*."

"Oh be damned to your French, Summers! But I

tell you this and make what you choose of it! I believe in fair play!"

"That I am prepared to accept."

"You? That is profoundly generous of you, sir!"

Then we were silent again. It must have been in a harsh enough voice that I spoke at last.

"Well, Mr Summers, you were right, were you not? I have been remiss. But those who administer correction out of school must not expect to be thanked for it."

"I fear not."

This was too much.

"Fear nothing, man! How mean, how vindictive, how small do you think I am? Your precious career is safe enough from me. I do not care to be lumped in with the enemy!"

At this moment, Deverel came in with Brocklebank and some others so that the conversation perforce became general. As soon as possible I took my brandy back to my hutch and sat there, thinking what to do. I called Wheeler and told him to send Phillips to me. He had the insolence to ask me what I wanted the man for and I sent him about his business in no uncertain terms. Phillips came soon enough.

"Phillips, I shall pay a call on Mr Colley. I do not wish to be offended by the sights and smells of a sick-room. Be good enough to clean up the place and, as far as you can, the bunk. Let me know when it is done."

I thought for a moment he would demur but he changed his mind and withdrew. Wheeler stuck his head in again but I had plenty of rage left over and told him if he was so idle he might as well go across and lend Phillips a hand. This removed him at once. It must have been a full hour before Phillips tapped on my door and said he had done *what he could*. I rewarded him, then fearing the worst went across the lobby attended by Phillips but with Wheeler hovering as if expecting a half-guinea for allowing Phillips the use of me. These fellows are as bad as parsons over fees for christenings, weddings and funerals! They were disposed to mount guard at the door of Mr Colley's cabin but I told them to be off and watched till they disappeared. I then went in.

Colley's hutch was a mirror image of mine. Phillips, if he had not rid it completely of stench, had done the next best thing by covering it with some pungent but not unpleasantly aromatic odour. Colley lay as Summers had said. One hand still clutched what both Falconer and Summers agreed was a ringbolt in the side of the ship. His scrubby head was pressed into the bolster, the face turned away. I stood by the bunk and was at a loss. I had little experience of visiting the sick.

"Mr Colley!"

There was no reply. I tried again.

"Mr Colley, sir. Some days ago I desired further acquaintance with you. But you have not appeared. This was too bad, sir. May I not expect your company on deck today?"

That was handsome enough, I thought in all conscience. I was so certain of success in raising the man's spirits that a fleeting awareness of the boredom I should experience in his company passed through my mind and took some edge off my determination to rouse him. I backed away.

"Well sir, if not today, then when you are ready! I will await you. Pray call on me!"

Was that not a foolish thing to say? It was an open invitation to the man to pester me as much as he would. I backed to the door and turned in time to see Wheeler and Phillips vanish. I looked round the cabin. It contained even less than mine. The shelf held a Bible, a prayer book, and a dirty, dog-eared volume, purchased I imagine at third hand and clumsily rebound in brown paper, which proved to be *Classes Plantarum*. The others were works of devotion—Baxter's *Saints Everlasting Rest*, and the like. There was a pile of manuscript on the flap of the table. I closed the door and went back to my hutch again.

Scarce had I got my own door open when I found Summers following me close. He had, it appeared, watched my movements. I motioned him inside.

"Well Mr Talbot?"

"I got no response from him. However, I visited him as you saw and I did what I could. I have, I believe, discharged those responsibilities you were so kind as to bring to my notice. I can do no more."

To my astonishment he raised a glass of brandy to his lips. He had carried it concealed or at least unnoticed—for who would look for such a thing in the hands of so temperate a man?

"Summers—my dear Summers! You have taken to drink!"

That he had not indeed was seen only too clearly

when he choked and coughed at the first taste of the liquid.

"You need more practice, man! Join Deverel and me some time!"

He drank again, then breathed deeply.

"Mr Talbot, you said that today you could not be angry with me. You jested but it was the word of a gentleman. Now I am to come at you again."

"I am weary of the whole subject."

"I assure you, Mr Talbot, this is my last."

I turned my canvas chair round and sank into it.

"Say what you have to say, then."

"Who is responsible for the man's state?"

"Colley? Devil take it! Himself! Let us not mince round the truth like a pair of church spinsters! You are going to spread the responsibility, are you not? You will include the captain and I agree—who else?—Cumbershum? Deverel? Yourself? The starboard watch? The world?"

"I will be plain, sir. The best medicine for Mr Colley would be a gentle visit from the captain of whom he stands in such awe. The only man among us with sufficient influence to bring the captain to such an action, is yourself."

"Then devil take it again, for I shall not!"

"You said I would 'Spread the responsibility'. Let me do so now. *You* are the man most responsible—"

"Christ in his heaven, Summers, you are the—"

"Wait! Wait!"

"Are you drunk?"

"I said I would be plain. I will stand shot, sir, though my career is now in far more danger from you than it ever was from the French! They, after all, could do no more than kill or maim me—but you—"

"You *are* drunk—you must be!"

"Had you not in a bold and thoughtless way out-faced our captain on his own quarterdeck—had you not made use of your rank and prospects and connections to strike a blow at the very foundations of his authority, all this might not have happened. He is brusque and he detests the clergy, he makes no secret of it. But had you not acted as you did at that time, he would never in the very next few minutes have crushed Colley with his anger and continued to humiliate *him* because he could not humiliate *you*."

"If Colley had had the sense to read Anderson's Standing Orders—"

"You are a passenger as he is. Did you read them?"

Through my anger I thought back. It was true to some extent—no, wholly true. On my first day Wheeler had murmured something about them—they were to be found outside my cabin and at a suitable opportunity I should—

"*Did* you read them, Mr Talbot?"

"No."

Has your lordship ever come across the odd fact that to be seated rather than erect induces or at least tends towards a state of calm? I cannot say that my anger was sinking away but it was stayed. As if he, too, wished us both to be calm, Summers sat on the edge of my bunk, thus looking slightly down at me. Our relative positions seemed to make the *didactic* inevitable.

"The captain's Standing Orders would seem to you as brusque as he is, sir. But the fact is they are wholly necessary. Those applying to passengers lie under the same necessity, the same urgency, as the rest."

"Very well, very well!"

"You have not seen a ship at a moment of crisis, sir. A ship may be taken flat aback and sunk all in a few moments. Ignorant passengers, stumbling in the way, delaying a necessary order or making it inaudible—"

"You have said enough."

"I hope so."

"You are certain I am responsible for nothing else that has gone awry? Perhaps Mrs East's miscarriage?"

"If our captain could be induced to befriend a sick man—"

"Tell me, Summers—why are you so curious about Colley?"

He finished his drink and stood up.

"Fair play, *noblesse oblige*. My education is not like yours, sir, it has been strictly practical. But I know a term under which both phrases might be—what is the word?—subsumed. I hope you will find it."

With that, he went quickly out of my hutch and away somewhere, leaving me in a fine mixture of emotions! Anger, yes, embarrassment, yes—but also a kind of rueful amusement at having been taught two lessons in one day by the same schoolmaster! I damned him for a busybody, then half undamned him again, for he is a likeable fellow, common or not. What the devil had he to do with *my* duty?

Was that the word? An odd fellow indeed! Truly as good a translation as yours, my lord! All those countless leagues from one end of a British ship to the other! To hear him give orders about the deck—and then to meet him over a glass—he can pass between one sentence and the next from all the jargoning of the Tarpaulin language to the plain exchanges which take place between gentlemen. Now the heat was out of my blood I could see how he had thought himself professionally at risk in speaking so to me and I laughed a little ruefully again. We may characterize him in our theatrical terms as—enter a Good Man!

Well, thought I to myself, there is this in common between Good Men and children—we must never disappoint them! Only half of the confounded business had been attended to. I had visited the sick—now I must try my influence in adjusting matters between Colley and our gloomy captain. I own the prospect daunted me a little. I returned to the passenger saloon and brandy and in the evening, to tell the truth, found myself in no condition to exercise judgement. I think this was deliberate and an endeavour to postpone what I knew must be a difficult interview. At last I went with what must have been a stately gait to my bunk and have some recollection of Wheeler assisting me into it. I was bosky indeed and fell into a profound sleep to wake later with the headache and some queasiness. When I tried my repeater I found it was yet early in the morning. Mr Brocklebank was snoring. There were noises coming from the hutch next to mine from which I inferred that the fair Zenobia was busy with yet another lover or, it may be, client. Had *she*, I wondered, also wanted to reach the governor's ear? Should I one day find myself approached by her to get an official portrait of the governor executed by Mr Brocklebank? It was a sour consideration for the early hours that stemmed straight from Summers's frankness. I damned him all over again. The air in my hutch was thick, so I threw on my greatcoat, scuffed my feet into slippers and felt my way out on deck. Here there was light enough to make out the difference between the ship, the sea, and the sky but no more. I remembered my resolution to speak with the captain on Colley's behalf with positive revulsion. What had seemed a boring duty when I was elevated with drink now presented itself as downright unpleasant. I called to mind that the captain was said to take a constitutional on the quarterdeck at dawn, but such a time and place was too early for our interview.

Nevertheless, the early morning air, unhealthy as it may have been, seemed in a curious way to alleviate the headache, the queasiness and even my slight uneasiness at the prospect of the interview. I therefore set myself to marching to and fro between the break of the afterdeck and the mainmast. While I did so, I tried to see all round the situation. We had yet more months of sea travel before us in the captain's company. I neither liked nor esteemed Captain Anderson nor was able to think of him as anything but a petty tyrant. Endeavour—it could be no more—to assist the wretched Colley could not but exacerbate the dislike that lay just beyond the bounds of the unacknowledged truce between us. The captain accepted my position as your lordship's godson, *et cetera*. I accepted his as a captain of one of His Majesty's ships. The limit of his powers in respect of passengers was obscure; and so was the limit of my possible influence with his superiors! Like dogs cautious of each other's strength we stepped high and round each other. And now I was to try to influence his behaviour towards a contemptible member of the profession he hated! I was thus, unless I was very careful, in danger of putting myself under an obligation to him. The thought was not to be borne. At one time and another in my long contemplation I believe I uttered a deal of oaths! Indeed, I had half a mind to abandon the whole project.

However, the damp but soft air of these latitudes, no matter what the subsequent effect on one's health, is certainly to be recommended as an antidote to an aching head and sour stomach! As I came more and more to myself I found it more and more in my power to exercise judgement and contemplate action. Those ambitious of attaining to statecraft or whose birth renders the exercise of it inevitable would do well to face the trials of a voyage such as ours! It was, I remember, very clearly in my mind how your lordship's benevolence had got for me not only some years of employment in a new and unformed society but had also ensured that the preliminary voyage should give me time for reflection and the exercise of my not inconsiderable powers of thought. I decided I must proceed on the principle of the use of *least force*. What would move Captain Anderson to do as I wished? Would there be anything more powerful with him than self-interest? That wretched little man, Mr Colley! But there was no doubt about it. Whether it was, as Summers said, *my* fault in part or not, there was no doubt he had been persecuted. That he was a fool and had made a cake of himself was neither here nor there.

Deverel, little Tommy Taylor, Summers himself—they all implied that Captain Anderson for no matter what reason had deliberately made the man's life intolerable to him. The devil was in it if I could find any word to sum up both Summers's phrase of "*Noblesse Oblige*" and mine of "Fair Play" other than "Justice". There's a large and schoolbook word to run directly on like a rock in mid-ocean! There was a kind of terror in it too since it had moved out of school and the university onto the planks of a warship—which is to say the planks of a tyranny in little! What about *my* career?

Yet I was warmed by Summers's belief in my ability and more by his confident appeal to my sense of justice. What creatures we are! Here was I, who only a few weeks before had thought highly of myself because my mother wept to see me go, now warming my hands at the small fire of a lieutenant's approval!

However, at last I saw how to go on.

(61)

Well! I returned to my hutch, washed, shaved and dressed with care. I took my morning draught in the saloon and then drew myself up as before *a regular stitcher*. I did not enjoy the prospect of the interview, I can tell you! For if I had established my position in the ship, it was even more evident that the captain had established his! He was indeed our moghool. To remove my foreboding I went very briskly to the quarterdeck, positively bounding up the ladders. Captain Anderson, the wind now being on the starboard quarter, was standing there and facing into it. This is his privilege; and is said by seamen to rise from the arcane suggestion that "Danger lies to windward" though in the next breath they will assure you that the most dangerous thing in the world is "a lee shore". The first, I suppose, refers to a possible enemy ship, the second to reefs and suchlike natural hazards. Yet I have, I believe, a more penetrating suggestion to make as to the origin of the captain's privilege. Whatever sector of the ship is to windward is almost free from the stench she carries everywhere with her. I do not mean the stink of urine and ordure but that pervasive stench from the carcass of the ship herself and her rotten bilge of gravel and sand. Perhaps more modern ships with their iron ballast may smell more sweetly; but captains, I dare say, in this Noah's service will continue to walk the windward side even if ships should run clean out of wind and take to rowing. The tyrant must live as free of stink as possible.

RITES OF PASSAGE

I find that without conscious intention I have delayed this description as I had dallied over my draught. I live again those moments when I drew myself together for the jump!

Well then, I stationed myself on the opposite side of the quarterdeck, affecting to take no notice of the man other than to salute him casually with a lifted finger. My hope was that his recent gaiety and elevation of spirits would lead him to address me first. My judgement was correct. His new air of satisfaction was indeed apparent, for when he saw me he came across, his yellow teeth showing.

"A fine day for you, Mr Talbot!"

"Indeed it is, sir. Do we make as much progress as is common in these latitudes?"

"I doubt that we shall achieve more than an average of a knot over the next day or two."

"Twenty-four sea miles a day."

"Just so, sir. Warships are generally slower in their advance than most people suppose."

"Well sir, I must confess to finding these latitudes more agreeable than any I have experienced. Could we but tow the British Isles to this part of the world, how many of our social problems would be solved! The mango would fall in our mouths."

"You have a quaint fancy there, sir. Do you mean to include Ireland?"

"No sir. I would offer her to the United States of America, sir."

"Let them have the first refusal, eh, Mr Talbot?"

"Hibernia would lie snugly enough alongside New England. We should see what we should see!"

"It would remove half a watch of my crew at a blow."

"Well worth the loss, sir. What a noble prospect the ocean is under a low sun! Only when the sun is high does the sea seem to lack that indefinable air of Painted Art which we are able to observe at sunrise and sunset."

"I am so accustomed to the sight that I do not see it. Indeed, I am grateful—if the phrase is not meaningless in the circumstances—to the oceans for another quality."

"And that is?"

"Their power of isolating a man from his fellows."

"Of isolating a captain, sir. The rest of humanity at sea must live only too much herded. The effect on them is not of the best. Circe's task must not have been hindered, to say the least, by the profession of her victims!"

Directly I had said this I realized how cutting it might sound. But I saw by the blankness of the captain's face, then its frown, that he was trying to remember what had happened to any ship of that name.

"Herded?"

"Packed together, I ought to have said. But how balmy the air is! I declare it seems almost insupportable that I must descend again and busy myself with my journal."

Captain Anderson checked at the word "journal" as if he had trodden on a stone. I affected not to notice but continued cheerfully.

"It is partly an amusement, captain, and partly a duty. It is, I suppose, what you would call a 'log'."

"You must find little to record in such a situation as this."

"Indeed, sir, you are mistaken. I have not time nor paper sufficient to record all the interesting events and personages of the voyage together with my own observations on them. Look—there is Mr Prettiman! A personage for you! His opinions are notorious, are they not?"

But Captain Anderson was still staring at me.

"Personages?"

"You must know," said I laughing, "that had I not his lordship's direct instructions to me I should still have been scribbling. It is my ambition to out-Gibbon Mr Gibbon and this gift to a godfather falls conveniently."

Our tyrant was pleased to smile, but quiveringly, like a man who knows that to have a tooth pulled is less painful than to have the exquisite torturer left in.

"We may all be famous, then," said he. "I had not looked for it."

"That is for the future. You must know, sir, that to the unhappiness of us all, his lordship has found himself temporarily vexed by the gout. It is my hope that in such a disagreeable situation, a frank, though private account of my travels and of the society in which I find myself may afford him some diversion."

Captain Anderson took an abrupt turn up and down the deck, then stood directly before me.

"The officers of the ship in which you travel must bulk large in such an account."

"They are objects of a landsman's interest and curiosity."

"The captain particularly so?"

"You sir? I had not considered that. But you are, after all, the king or emperor of our floating society with prerogatives of justice and mercy. Yes. I suppose you do bulk large in my journal and will continue to do so."

Captain Anderson turned on his heel and marched away. He kept his back to me and stared up wind. I saw that his head was sunk again, his hands clasped behind his back. I supposed that his jaw must be projecting once more as a foundation on which to sink the sullenness of his face. There was no doubt at all of the effect of my words, either on him or on *me!* For I found myself quivering as the first lieutenant had quivered when he dared to beard Mr Edmund Talbot! I spoke, I know not what, to Cumbershum, who had the watch. He was discomforted, for it was clean against the tyrant's Standing Orders and I saw, out of the corner of my eye, how the captain's hands tightened on each other behind his back. It was not a situation that should be prolonged. I bade the lieutenant good day and descended from the quarterdeck. I was glad enough to get back into my hutch, where I found of all things that my hands still had a tendency to tremble! I sat, therefore, getting my breath back and allowing my pulse to slow.

At length I began to consider the captain once more and try to predict his possible course of action. Does not the operation of a *statist* lie wholly in his power to affect the future of other people; and is not that power founded directly on his ability to predict their behaviour? Here, thought I, was the chance to observe the success or failure of my prentice hand! How would the man respond to the hint I had given him? It was not a subtle one; but then, I thought, from the directness of his questions that he was a simple creature at bottom. It was possible that he had not noticed the suggestiveness of my mentioning Mr Prettiman and his extreme beliefs! Yet I felt certain that mention of my journal would force him to look back over the whole length of the voyage and consider what sort of figure he might cut in an account of it. Sooner or later he would stub his toe over the Colley affair and remember how he had treated the man. He must see that however I myself had provoked him, nevertheless, by indulging his animosity against Colley, he had been cruel and unjust.

How would he behave then? How had I behaved when Summers had revealed to me my portion of responsibility in the affair? I tried out a scene or two for our floating theatre. I pictured Anderson descending from the quarterdeck and walking in the lobby casually, so as not to seem interested in the man. He might well stand consulting his own fading Orders, written out in a fair and clerkly hand. Then at a convenient moment, no one being by—oh no! he would have to let it be seen so that I should record it in my journal! —he would march into the hutch where Colley lay, shut the door, sit by the bunk and chat till they were a couple of bosoms. Why, Anderson might well stand in for an archbishop or even His Majesty! How could Colley not be roused by such amiable condescension? The captain would confess that he himself had committed just such a folly a year or two before—

I could not imagine it, that is the plain truth. The conceit remained artificial. Such behaviour was beyond Anderson. He might, he might just come down and gentle Colley somewhat, admitting his own brusqueness but saying it was habitual in a captain of a ship. More likely he would come down but only to assure himself that Colley was lying in his bunk, prone and still and not to be roused by a jesting exordium. But then, he might not even come down. Who was I to dip into the nature of the man, cast the very waters of his soul and by that chirurgeonly experiment declare how his injustice would run its course? I sat before this journal, upbraiding myself for my folly in my attempt to play the politician and manipulator of his fellow men! I had to own that my knowledge of the springs of human action was still in the egg. Nor does a powerful intellect do more than assist in the matter. Something more there must be, some distillation of experience, before a man can judge the outcome in circumstances of such quantity, proliferation and confusion.

And then, *then* can your lordship guess? I have saved the sweet to the last! He did come down. Before my very eyes he came down as if my prediction had drawn him down like some fabulous spell! I am a wizard, am I not? Admit me to be a prentice-wizard at least! I had said he would come down and come down he did! Through my louvre I saw him come down, abrupt and grim, to take his stand in the centre of the lobby. He stared at one hutch after another, turning on his heel, and I was only just in time to pull my face away from the spyhole before his louring gaze swept over it with an effect I could almost swear like the heat from a burning coal! When I risked peeping again—for somehow it seemed positively dangerous that the man should know I had seen him—he had his back to me. He stepped to the door of Colley's hutch and for a long minute stared through it. I saw how one fist beat into the palm of the other hand behind his back. Then he swung impatiently to his left with a movement that seemed to cry out—*I'll be damned if I will!* He stumped to the ladder and disappeared. A few seconds later I heard his firm step pass along the deck above my head.

This was a modified triumph, was it not? I had said he would come down and he had come down. But where I had pictured him endeavouring to comfort poor Colley he had shown himself either too heartless or too little politic to bring himself to do so. The nearer he had come to dissimulating his bile the higher it had risen in his throat. Yet now I had some grounds for confidence. His knowledge of the existence of this very journal would not let him be. It will be like a splinter under the nail. He would come down again—

BETA

Wrong again, Talbot! Learn another lesson, my boy! You fell at that fence! Never again must you lose yourself in the complacent contemplation of a first success! Captain Anderson did not come down. He sent a messenger. I was just writing the sentence about the splinter when there came a knock at the door and who should appear but Mr Summers! I bade him enter, sanded my page—imperfectly as you can see—closed and locked my journal, stood up and indicated my chair. He declined it, perched himself on the edge of my bunk, laid his cocked hat on it and looked thoughtfully at my journal.

"Locked, too!"

I said nothing but looked him in the eye, smiling slightly. He nodded as if he understood—which indeed I think he did.

"Mr Talbot, it cannot be allowed to continue."

"My journal, you mean?"

He brushed the jest aside.

"I have looked in on the man by the captain's orders."

"Colley? I looked in on him myself. I agreed to, you remember."

"The man's reason is at stake."

"All for a little drink. Is there still no change?"

"Phillips swears he has not moved for three days."

I made a perhaps unnecessarily blasphemous rejoinder. Summers took no notice of it.

"I repeat, the man is losing his wits."

"It does indeed seem so."

RITES OF PASSAGE

"I am to do what I can, by the captain's orders, and you are to assist me."

"I?"

"Well. You are not ordered to assist me but I am ordered to invite your assistance and profit by your advice."

"Upon my soul, the man is flattering me! Do you know, Summers, I was advised myself to practice the art? I little thought to find myself the object of such an exercise!"

"Captain Anderson feels that you have a social experience and awareness that may make your advice of value."

I laughed heartily and Summers joined in.

"Come Summers! Captain Anderson never said that!"

"No, sir. Not precisely."

"Not precisely indeed! I tell you what, Summers—"

I stopped myself in time. There were many things I felt like saying. I could have told him that Captain Anderson's sudden concern for Mr Colley began not at any moment of appeal by me but at the moment when he heard that I kept a journal intended for influential eyes. I could have given my opinion that the captain cared nothing for Colley's wits but sought cunningly enough to involve me in the events and so obscure the issue or at the very least soften what might well be your lordship's acerbity and contempt. But I am learning, am I not? Before the words reached my tongue I understood how dangerous they might be to Summers—and even to me.

"Well, Mr Summers, I will do what I can."

"I was sure you would agree. You are co-opted among us ignorant tars as the civil power. What is to be done?"

"Here we have a parson who—but come, should we not have co-opted Miss Granham? She is the daughter of a canon and might be presumed to know best how to handle the clergy!"

"Be serious, sir and leave her to Mr Prettiman."

"No! It cannot be! Minerva herself?"

"Mr Colley must claim all our attention."

"Well then. Here we have a clergyman who—made too much of a beast of himself and refines desperately upon it."

Summers regarded me closely, and I may say curiously.

"You know what a beast he made of himself?"

"Man! I saw him! We all saw him, including the ladies! Indeed, I tell you, Summers, I saw something more than the rest!"

"You interest me deeply."

"It is of little enough moment. But some few hours after his exhibition I saw him wander through the lobby towards the *bog*, a sheet of paper in his hand and for what it is worth a most extraordinary smile on that ugly mug of his."

"What did the smile suggest to you?"

"He was silly drunk."

Summers nodded towards the forward part of the vessel.

"And there? In the fo'castle?"

"How can we tell?"

"We might ask."

"Is that wise, Summers? Was not the play-acting of the common people—forgive me!—directed not to themselves but to those in authority over them? Should you not avoid reminding them of it?"

"It is the man's wits, sir. Something must be risked. Who set him on? Beside the common people there are the emigrants, decent as far as I have met them. *They* have no wish to mock at authority. Yet they must know as much as anyone."

Suddenly I remembered the poor girl and her emaciated face where a shadow lived and was, as it were, feeding where it inhabited. She must have had Colley's beastliness exhibited before her at a time when she had a right to expect a far different appearance from a clergyman!

"But this is terrible, Summers! The man should be—"

"What is past cannot be helped, sir. But I say again it is the man's wits that stand in danger. For God's sake, make one more effort to rouse him from his, his— lethargy!"

"Very well. For the second time, then. Come."

I went briskly and, followed by Summers across the lobby, opened the door of the hutch and stood inside. It was true enough. The man lay as he had lain before; and indeed seemed if anything even stiller. The hand that had clutched the ringbolt had relaxed and lay with the fingers hooked through it but without any evidence of muscular tension.

Behind me, Summers spoke gently.

"Here is Mr Talbot, Mr Colley, come to see you."

I must own to a mixture of confusion and strong distaste for the whole business which rendered me even more than usually incapable of finding the right kind of encouragement for the wretched man. His situation and the odour, the stench, emanating I suppose from his unwashed person was nauseous. It must have been, you will agree, pretty *strong* to contend with and overcome the general stench of the ship to which I was still not entirely habituated! However, Summers evidently credited me with an ability which I did not possess for he stood away from me, nodding at the same time as if to indicate that the affair was now in my hands.

I cleared my throat.

"Well Mr Colley, this is an unfortunate business but believe me, sir, you are refining too much on it. Uncontrolled drunkenness and its consequences is an experience every man ought to have at least once in his life or how is he to understand the experience of others? As for your relieving nature on the deck—do but consider what those decks have seen! And in the peaceful counties of our own far-off land—Mr Colley I have been brought to see, by the good offices of Mr Summers, that I am in however distant a way partly responsible for your predicament. Had I not enraged our captain—but there! I shall confess, sir, that a number of young fellows, ranged at upper-storey windows, did once, at a given signal, make water on an unpopular and bosky tutor who was passing below! Now what was the upshot of that shocking affair? Why nothing, sir! The man held out his hand, stared frowning into the evening sky, then opened his umbrella! I swear to

you, sir, that some of those same young fellows will
one day be bishops! In a day or two we shall all laugh
at your comical interlude together! You are bound for
Sydney Cove I believe and thence to Van Diemen's
Land. Good Lord, Mr Colley, from what I have heard
they are more likely to greet you drunk than sober.
What you need now is a dram, then as much ale as
your stomach can hold. Depend upon it, you will soon
see things differently."

There was no response. I glanced enquiringly at
Summers but he was looking down at the blanket, his
lips pressed together. I spread my hands in a gesture of
defeat and left the cabin. Summers followed me.

"Well, Summers?"

"Mr Colley is willing himself to death."

"Come!"

"I have known it happen among savage peoples.
They are able to lie down and die."

I gestured him into my hutch and we sat side by
side on the bunk. A thought occurred to me.

"Was he perhaps an enthusiast? It may be that he
is taking his religion too much to heart—come now,
Mr Summers! There is nothing to laugh at in the matter! Or are you so disobliging as to find my remark
itself a subject for your hilarity?"

Summers dropped his hands from his face, smiling.

"God forbid, sir! It is pain enough to have been shot
at by an enemy without the additional hazard of presenting oneself as a mark to—dare I say—one's friends.
Believe me properly sensible of my privilege in being
admitted to a degree of intimacy with your noble god-

father's genteel godson. But you are right in one thing. As far as poor Colley is concerned there is nothing to laugh at. Either his wits are gone or he knows nothing of his own religion."

"He is a parson!"

"The uniform does not make the man, sir. He is in despair I believe. Sir, I take it upon myself as a Christian—as a humble follower at however great a distance —to aver that a Christian *cannot* despair!"

"My words were trivial then."

"They were what you could say. But of course they never reached him."

"You felt that?"

"Did not you?"

I toyed with the thought that perhaps someone of Colley's own class, a man from among the ship's people but unspoilt by education or such modest preferment as had come his way, might well find a means to approach him. But after the words that Summers and I had exchanged on a previous occasion I felt a new delicacy in broaching such a subject with him. He broke the silence.

"We have neither priest nor doctor."

"Brocklebank owned to having been a medical student for the best part of a year."

"Did he so? Should we call him in?"

"God forbid—he does so prose! He described his turning from doctoring to painting as 'deserting Aesculapius for the Muse'."

"I shall enquire among our people forrard."

"For a doctor?"

"For some information as to what happened."

"Man, we *saw* what happened!"

"I mean in the fo'castle or below it, rather than on deck."

"He was made beastly drunk."

I found that Summers was peering at me closely.

"And that was all?"

"All?"

"I see. Well, sir, I shall report back to the captain."

"Tell him I shall continue to consider how we may devise some method of bringing the wretched fellow to his senses."

"I will do so; and must thank you for your assistance."

Summers left and I was alone with my thoughts and this journal. It was so strange to think that a young fellow not much above my years or Deverel's and certainly not as old as Cumbershum should have so strong an instinct for self-destruction! Why, Aristotle or no, half an hour of La Brocklebank—even Prettiman and Miss Granham—and *there*, thought I, is a situation I must get acquainted with for a number of reasons, the least of them entertainment: and then—

What do you suppose was the thought that came into my mind? It was of the pile of manuscript that had lain on the flap of Colley's table! I had not noticed the flap or the papers when Summers and I entered the cabin; but now, by the incomprehensible faculties of the human mind I, as it were, entered the cabin *again* and surveying the scene I had just left, I saw in my mind that the writing-flap was empty! There is a subject for a savant's investigation! How can a man's mind go back and see what he saw not? But so it was.

Well. Captain Anderson had co-opted me. He should find out, I thought, what sort of overseer he had brought into the business!

I went quickly to Colley's cabin. He lay as before. Only when I was inside the hutch did I return to a *kind* at least of apprehension. I intended the man nothing but good and I was acting on the captain's behalf; yet there was in my mind an unease. I felt it as the effect of the captain's rule. A tyrant turns the slightest departure from his will into a crime; and I was at the least contemplating bringing him to book for his mistreatment of Mr Colley. I looked quickly round the cabin. The ink and pens and sander were still there, as were the shelves with their books of devotion at the foot of the bed. It seemed there was a limit to their efficacy! I leaned over the man himself.

It was then that I perceived without seeing—I knew, but had no real means of knowing—

There had been a time when he had awakened in physical anguish which had quickly passed into a mental one. He lay like that in deepening pain, deepening consciousness, widening memory, his whole being turning more and more from the world till he could desire nothing but death. Phillips could not rouse him nor even Summers. Only I—my words after all had touched something. When I left him after that first visit, glad enough to be gone, he had leapt from his bunk in some *new* agony! Then, in a passion of self-disgust he had swept his papers from the table. Like a child he had seized the whole and had jammed them into a convenient crack as if it would stay unsearched till doom's day! Of course. There was, between the bunk and the side of the vessel a space, just as in my own hutch, into which a man might thrust his hand as I then did in Colley's. They encountered paper and I drew out a crumpled mass of sheets all written, some cross-written, and all, I was certain, material evidence against our tyrant in the case of Colley versus Anderson! I put the papers quickly into the bosom of my coat, came out—unseen I pray God!—and hurried to my cabin. There I thrust the mass of papers into my own writing-case and locked it as if I were concealing the spoils of a burglary! After that I sat and began to write all this in my journal as if seeking, in a familiar action, some legal security! Is that not comic?

Wheeler came to my cabin.

"Sir, I have a message, sir. The captain requests that you give him the pleasure of your company at dinner in an hour's time."

"My compliments to the captain and I accept with pleasure."

GAMMA

What a day this has been. I commenced it with some
cheerfulness and I end it with—but you will wish to
know all! It seems so long ago that the affair was misty
and my own endeavours to pierce the mist so complacent, so self-satisfied—

Well. As Summers said, I am partly to blame. So are
we all in one degree or another; but none of us, I think,
in the same measure as our tyrant! Let me take you
with me, my lord, step by step. I promise you—no, not
entertainment but at the very least a kind of generous
indignation and the exercise not of my, but *your* judgement.

I changed and dismissed Wheeler only to find his
place taken by Summers, who looked positively elegant.

"Good God, Summers, are you also bidden to the
feast?"

"I am to share that pleasure."

"It is an innovation, for sure."

"Oldmeadow makes a fourth."

I took out my repeater.

"It still wants more than ten minutes. What is eti-
quette for such a visit on shipboard?"

"Where the captain is concerned, on the last stroke
of the bell."

"In that case I shall disappoint his expectations and
arrive early. He anticipates, I believe, knowing me,
that I shall arrive late."

My entry into Captain Anderson's stateroom was as

ceremonious as an admiral could wish. The cabin, or
room, rather, though not as large as the passengers'
saloon or even the saloon where the lieutenants
messed, was yet of palatial dimensions when compared with our meagre individual quarters. Some of
the ship's full width was pared off on either side for the
captain's own sleeping quarters, his closet, his personal
galley, and another small cabin where I suppose an
admiral would have conducted the business of a fleet.
As in the lieutenants' wardroom and the passenger
saloon, the rear wall, or in Tarpaulin language *the
after bulkhead*, was one vast, leaded window by means
of which something like a third of the horizon might
be seen. Yet part of this window was obscured in a
way that at first I could scarcely credit. Part of the
obscuration was the captain, who called out as soon as
I appeared in what I can only call a holiday voice.

"Come in, Mr Talbot, come in! I must apologize
for not greeting you at the threshold! You have caught
me in my garden."

It was so indeed. The obscuration to the great window was a row of climbing plants, each twisting itself
round a bamboo that rose from the darkness near the
deck where I divined the flower pots were. Standing a
little to one side I could see that Captain Anderson
was serving each plant into its flower pot with water
from a small watering can with a long spout. The can
was the sort of flimsy trifle you might find a lady using
in the orangery—not indeed, to serve the trees in their
enormous vats, but some quaintness of Dame Nature's
own ingenuity. The morose captain might be thought

to befit such a picture ill; but as he turned I saw to my astonishment that he was looking positively amiable, as if I were a lady come to visit him.

"I did not know that you had a private paradise, captain."

The captain smiled! Yes, positively, he smiled!

"Do but think, Mr Talbot, this flowering plant that I am tending, still innocent and unfallen, may have been one with which Eve garlanded herself on the first day of her creation."

"Would that not presuppose a loss of innocence, captain, precursor to the fig leaves?"

"It might be so. How acute you are, Mr Talbot."

"We were being fanciful, were we not?"

"I was speaking my mind. The plant is called the Garland Plant. The ancients, I am told, crowned themselves with it. The flower, when it appears, is agreeably perfumed and waxen white."

"We might be Grecians then and crown ourselves for the feast."

"I do not think the custom suited to the English. But do you see I have three of the plants? Two of them I actually raised from seed!"

"Is that a task as difficult as your triumphant tone would imply?"

Captain Anderson laughed happily. His chin was up, his cheeks creased, twin sparks in his little eyes.

"Sir Joseph Banks said it was impossible! 'Anderson,' he said, 'take cuttings, man! You might as well throw the seeds overboard!' But I have persevered and in the end I had a box of them—seedlings, I mean—

enough to supply a Lord Mayor's banquet, if—to follow your fancy—they should ever require their aldermen to be garlanded. But there! It is not to be imagined. Garlands would be as out of place as in the painted hall at Greenwich. Serve Mr Talbot. What will you drink, sir? There is much to hand, though I take no more than an occasional glass myself."

"Wine for me, sir."

"Hawkins, the claret if you please! This geranium you see, Mr Talbot, has some disease of the leaf. I have dusted it with flowers of sulphur but to no effect. I shall lose it no doubt. But then, sir, he who gardens at sea must accustom himself to loss. On my first voyage in command I lost my whole collection."

"Through the violence of the enemy?"

"No sir, through the uncommon nature of the weather which held us for whole weeks without either wind or rain. I could not have served water to my plants. There would have been mutiny. I see the loss of this one plant as no great matter."

"Besides, you may exchange it for another at Sydney Cove."

"Why must you—"

He turned away and stowed the waterpot in a box down by the plants. When he turned back I saw the creases in his cheeks again and the sparks in his eyes.

"We are a long way and a long time from our destination, Mr Talbot."

"You speak as though you do not anticipate our arrival there with pleasure."

The sparks and creases vanished.

"You are young, sir. You cannot understand the pleasures of, no, the necessity of solitude to some natures. I would not care if the voyage lasted for ever!"

"But surely a man is connected to the land, to society, to a family—"

"Family? Family?" said the captain with a kind of violence. "Why should a man not do without a family? What is there about a family, pray?"

"A man is not a, a garland plant, Captain, to fertilize his own seed!"

There was a long pause in which Hawkins, the captain's servant, brought us the claret. Captain Anderson made a token gesture towards his face with half a glass of wine.

"At least I may remind myself how remarkable the flora will be at the Antipodes!"

"So you may replenish your stock."

His face was gay again.

"Many of Nature's inventions in that region have never been brought back to Europe."

I saw now there was a way, if not to Captain Anderson's heart, at least to his approval. I had a sudden thought, one worthy of a *romancier*, that perhaps the stormy or sullen face with which he was wont to leave his paradise was that of the expelled Adam. While I was considering this and my glass of claret, Summers and Oldmeadow entered the stateroom together.

"Come in, gentlemen," cried the captain. "What will you take, Mr Oldmeadow? As you see, Mr Talbot is content with wine—the same for you, sir?"

Oldmeadow cawed into his collar and declared he would be agreeable to a little dry sherry. Hawkins brought a broad-bottomed decanter and poured first for Summers, as knowing already what he would drink, then for Oldmeadow.

"Summers," said the captain, "I had meant to ask you. How does your patient?"

"Still the same, sir. Mr Talbot was good enough to comply with your request. But his words had no more effect than mine."

"It is a sad business," said the captain. He stared directly at me. "I shall enter in the ship's log that the patient—for such I believe we must consider him—has been visited by you, Mr Summers, and by you, Mr Talbot."

It was now that I began to understand Captain Anderson's purpose in getting us into his cabin and his clumsy way about the business of Colley. Instead of waiting till the wine and talk had worked on us he had introduced the subject at once and far too abruptly. It was time I thought of myself!

"You must remember, sir," said I, "that if the wretched man is to be considered a patient, my opinion is valueless. I have no medical knowledge whatsoever. Why, you would do better to consult Mr Brocklebank!"

"Brocklebank? Who is Brocklebank?"

"The artistic gentleman with the port-wine face and female entourage. But I jested. He told me he had begun to study medicine but had given it up."

"He has some medical experience, then?"

"No, no! I jested. The man is—what is the man, Summers? I doubt he could take a pulse!"

"Nevertheless—Brocklebank you said? Hawkins,

find Mr Brocklebank and ask him to be good enough to come and see me at once."

I saw it all—saw the entry in the log—*visited by a gentleman of some medical experience!* He was crude but cunning, was the captain! He was, as Deverel would say, "keeping his yardarm free." Observe how he is forcing me to report to your lordship in my journal that he has taken every care of the man, had him visited by his officers, by me, and by a gentleman *of some medical experience!*

No one said anything for a while. We three guests stared into our glasses as if rendered solemn by a reminder of the sick. But it could not have been more than two minutes before Hawkins returned to say that Mr Brocklebank would be happy to wait on the captain.

"We will sit down, then," said the captain. "Mr Talbot on my right—Mr Oldmeadow here, sir! Summers, will you take the bottom of the table? Why, this is delightfully domestic! Have you room enough, gentlemen? Summers has plenty of course. But we must allow him free passage to the door in case one of ten thousand affairs takes him from us about the ship's business."

Oldmeadow remarked that the soup was excellent. Summers, who was eating his with the dexterity acquired in a dozen fo'castles, remarked that much nonsense was talked about Navy food.

"You may depend upon it," he said, "where food has to be ordered, gathered, stored and served out by the thousands of ton there will be cause of complaint

here and there. But in the main, British seamen eat
better at sea than they do ashore."

"Bravo!" I cried. "Summers, you should be on the
government benches!"

"A glass of wine with you, Mr Summers," said the
captain. "What is the phrase? 'No heel taps'? A glass
with all you gentlemen! But to return—Summers, what
do you say to the story of the cheese clapped on the
main as a mastcapping? What of the snuff-boxes
carved out of beef?"

I saw out of the corner of my eye how the captain
did no more than sniff the bouquet of his wine, then
set the glass down. I determined to humour him if
only to see round his schemes.

"Summers, I must hear you answer the captain.
What of the snuff-boxes and mastcheeses—"

"Mastcappings—"

"What of the bones we hear are served to our gallant tars with no more than a dried shred of meat
adhering?"

Summers smiled.

"I fancy you will sample the cheese, sir; and I believe the captain is about to surprise you with bones."

"Indeed I am," said the captain. "Hawkins, have
them brought in."

"Good God," I cried, "marrow bones!"

"Bessie, I suppose," said Oldmeadow. "A very prof-
itable beast."

I bowed to the captain.

"We are overwhelmed, sir. Lucullus could do no
better."

"I am endeavouring to supply you with material for your journal, Mr Talbot."

"I give you my word, sir, the *menu* shall be preserved for the remotest posterity together with a memorial of the captain's hospitality!"

Hawkins bent to the captain.

"The gentleman is at the door, sir."

"Brocklebank? I will take him for a moment into the office if you will excuse me, gentlemen."

Now there occurred a scene of farce. Brocklebank had not remained at the door but was inside it and advancing. Either he had mistaken the captain's message for such an invitation as had been issued to me, or he was tipsy, or both. Summers had pushed back his chair and stood up. As if the first lieutenant had been a footman, Brocklebank sank into it.

"Thankee, thankee. Marrow bones! How the devil did you know, sir? I don't doubt one of my gals told you. Confusion to the French!"

He drained Summers's glass at a draught. He had a voice like some fruit which combines the qualities—if there be such a fruit—of peach and plum. He stuck his little finger in his ear, bored for a moment, inspected the result on the end of it while no one said anything. The servant was at a loss. Brocklebank caught a clearer sight of Summers and beamed at him.

"You too, Summers? Sit down, man!"

Captain Anderson, with what for him was rare tact, broke in.

"Yes, Summers, pull up that chair over there and dine with us."

Summers sat at a corner of the table. He was breathing quickly as if he had run a race. I wondered whether he was thinking what Deverel thought and had confided to me in his, or perhaps I ought to say *our*, cups—No, *Talbot, this is not a happy ship.*

Oldmeadow turned to me.

"There was mention of a journal, Talbot. There is a devil of a lot of writing among you government people."

"You have advanced me, sir. But it is true. The offices are paved with paper."

The captain pretended to drink, then set the glass down.

"You might well think a ship is ballasted with paper. We record almost everything somewhere or another, from the midshipmen's logs right up to the ship's log kept by myself."

"In my case I find there is hardly time to record the events of a day before the next two or three are upon me."

"How do you select?"

"Salient facts, of course—such trifles as may amuse the leisure of my godfather."

"I hope," said the captain heavily, "that you will record our sense of obligation to his lordship for affording us your company."

"I shall do so."

Hawkins filled Brocklebank's glass. It was for the third time.

"Mr, er, Brocklebank," said the captain, "may we profit from your medical experience?"

"My what, sir?"

"Talbot—Mr Talbot here," said the captain in a vexed voice, "Mr Talbot—"

"What the devil is wrong with him? Good God! I assure you that Zenobia, dear, warm-hearted gal—"

"I myself," said I swiftly, "have nothing to do with the present matter. Our captain refers to Colley."

"The parson is it? Good God! I assure you it doesn't matter to me at my time of life. Let them enjoy themselves I said—on board I said it—or did I?"

Mr Brocklebank hiccupped. A thin streak of wine ran down his chin. His eyes wandered.

"We need your medical experience," said the captain, his growls only just below the surface, but in what for him was a conciliatory tone. "We have none ourselves and look to you—"

"I have none either," said Mr Brocklebank. "Garçon, another glass!"

"Mr Talbot said—"

"I looked round you see but I said, Wilmot, I said, this anatomy is not for you. No indeed, you have not the stomach for it. In fact as I said at the time, I abandoned Aesculapius for the Muse. Have I not said so to you, Mr Talbot?"

"You have so, sir. On at least two occasions. I have no doubt the captain will accept your excuses."

"No, no," said the captain irritably. "However little the gentleman's experience, we must profit by it."

"Profit," said Mr Brocklebank. "There is more profit in the Muse than in the other thing. I should be a rich man now had not the warmth of my constitution, an attachment more than usually firm to the Sex and the opportunities for excess forced on my nature by the shocking corruption of English Society—"

"I could not abide doctoring," said Oldmeadow. "All those corpses, good God!"

"Just so, sir. I prefer to keep reminders of mortality at arm's length. Did you know I was first in the field after the death of Lord Nelson with a lithograph portraying the happy occasion?"

"You were not present!"

"Arm's length, sir. Neither was any other artist. I must admit to you freely that I believed at the time that Lord Nelson had expired on deck."

"Brocklebank," cried I, "I have seen it! There is a copy on the wall in the tap of the Dog and Gun! How the devil did that whole crowd of young officers contrive to be kneeling round Lord Nelson in attitudes of sorrow and devotion at the hottest moment of the action?"

Another thin trickle of wine ran down the man's chin.

"You are confusing art with actuality, sir."

"It looked plain silly to me, sir."

"It has sold very well indeed, Mr Talbot. I cannot conceal from you that without the continued popularity of that work I should be in Queer Street. It has at the very least allowed me to take a passage to, to wherever we are going, the name escapes me. And imagine, sir, Lord Nelson died down below in some stinking part of the bilges, I believe, with nothing to see him by but a ship's lantern. Who in the devil is going to make a picture of that?"

"Rembrandt perhaps."

"Ah. Rembrandt. Yes, well. At least Mr Talbot you must admire the dexterity of my management of smoke."

"Take me with you, sir."

"Smoke is the very devil. Did you not see it when Summers fired my gun? With broadsides a naval battle is nothing but a London Particular. So your true crafts-man must tuck it away to where it does not obtrude—obtrude—"

"Like a clown."

"Obtrude—"

"And interrupt some necessary business of the action."

"Obtrude—Captain, you don't drink."

The captain made another gesture with his glass, then looked round at the other three of his guests in angry frustration. But Brocklebank, his elbows now on either side of the marrow bone intended for Summers, droned on.

"I have always maintained that smoke properly han-dled can be of ma-material assistance. You are ap-proached by some captain who has had the good for-tune to fall in with the enemy and get off again. He comes to me as they did, after my lithograph. He has, for example, in company with another frigate and a small sloop—encountered the French and a battle has ensued—I beg your pardon! As the epitaph says, 'Wherever you be let your wind go free for holding mine was the death of me.' Now I ask you to imagine what would happen—and indeed my good friend, Fu-seli, you know, the Shield of Achilles, and—well. Imag-ine!"

I drank impatiently and turned to the captain.

"I think, sir, that Mr Brocklebank—"

It was of no avail and the man drooled again without noticing.

"Imagine—who pays me? If they *all* pay there can be no smoke at all! Yet they must all be seen to be hotly engaged, the devil take it! They come to blows, you know!"

"Mr Brocklebank," said the captain fretfully, "Mr Brocklebank—"

"Give me one single captain who has been successful and got his K! *Then* there will be no argument!"

"No", said Oldmeadow, cawing into his collar, "no indeed!"

Mr Brocklebank eyed him truculently.

"You doubt my word, sir? Do you, because if you do, sir—"

"I, sir? Good God no, sir!"

"He will say, 'Brocklebank,' he will say. 'I don't give a tuppenny damn for me own part, but me mother, me wife and me fifteen gals require a picture of me ship at the height of the action!' You follow? Now after I have been furnished with a copy of the gazette and had the battle described to me in minutest detail he goes off in the happy delusion that he knows what a naval battle looks like!"

The captain raised his glass. This time he emptied it at a gulp. He addressed Brocklebank in a voice which would have scared Mr Taylor from one end of the ship to the other if not farther.

"I for my part, sir, should be of his opinion!"

Mr Brocklebank, to indicate the degree of his own

cleverness, tried to lay a finger cunningly on the side of his nose but missed it.

"You are wrong, sir. Were I to rely on verisimilitude —but no. Do you suppose that my client, who has paid a deposit—for you see he may be off and lose his head in a moment—"

Summers stood up.

"I am called for, sir."

The captain, with perhaps the only glimmer of wit I have found in him, laughed aloud.

"You are fortunate, Mr Summers!"

Brocklebank noticed nothing. Indeed, I believe if we had all left him he would have continued his monologue.

"Now do you suppose the accompanying frigate is to be portrayed with an equal degree of animation? She has paid nothing! That is where smoke comes in. By the time I have done my layout she will have just fired and the smoke will have risen up round her; and as for the sloop, which will have been in the hands of some obscure lieutenant, it will be lucky to appear at all. My client's ship on the other hand will be belching more fire than smoke and will be being attacked by all the enemy at once."

"I could almost wish," said I, "that the French would afford us an opportunity for invoking the good offices of your brush."

"There's no hope of that," said the captain glumly, "no hope at all."

Perhaps his tone affected Mr Brocklebank, who went through one of those extraordinarily swift transitions which are common enough among the inebriated from cheerfulness to melancholy.

"But that is never the end of it. Your client will return and the first thing he will say is that *Corinna* or *Erato* never carried her foremast stepped as far forrard as that and what is that block doing on the main brace? Why, my most successful client—apart from the late Lord Nelson if I may so describe him—as a client I mean—was even foolish enough to object to some trifling injuries I had inflicted on the accompanying frigate. He swore she had never lost her topmast, her fore topmast I think he said, for she was scarcely in cannon shot. Then he said I had shown no damage in the region of the quarterdeck of his ship, which was not accurate. He forced me to beat two gunports into one there and carry away a great deal of the rail. Then he said, 'Could you not dash me in there, Brocklebank? I distinctly remember standin' just by the broken rail, encouragin' the crew and indicatin' the enemy by wavin' me sword towards them.' What could I do? The client is always right, it is the artist's first axiom. 'The figure will be very small, Sir Sammel,' said I. 'That is of no consequence,' said he. 'You may exaggerate me a little.' I bowed to him. 'If I do that, Sir Sammel,' said I, 'it will reduce your frigate to a sloop by contrast.' He took a turn or two up and down my studio for all the world like our captain here on the quarterdeck. 'Well', said he at last, 'you must dash me in small, then. They will know me by me cocked hat and me epaulettes. It's of no consequence to me, Mr Brocklebank, but me good lady and me gals insist on it.'"

"Sir Sammel," said the captain. "You did say 'Sir Sammel'?"

"I did. Do we move on to brandy?"

"Sir Sammel. I know him. Knew him."

"Tell us all, Captain," said I, hoping to stem the flow. "A shipmate?"

"I was the lieutenant commanding the sloop," said the captain moodily, "but I have not seen the picture."

"Captain! I positively must have a description of this," said I. "We landsmen are avid, you know, for that sort of thing!"

"Good God, the shloop! I have met the sh—the other sh—the lieutenant. Captain, you must be portrayed. We will waft away the sh—the smoke and show you in the thick of it!"

"Why so he was," said I. "Can we believe him anywhere else? You were in the thick of it, were you not?"

Captain Anderson positively snarled.

"The thick of the battle? In a sloop? Against frigates? But Captain—Sir Sammel I suppose I must say—must have thought me a young fool for he called me that, bawling through his speaking trumpet, 'Get to hell out of this, you young fool, or I'll have you broke!'"

I raised my glass to the captain.

"I drink to you, sir. But no blind eye? No deaf ear?"

"Garçon, where is the brandy? I must limn you, Captain, at a much reduced fee. Your future career—"

Captain Anderson was crouched at the table's head as if to spring. Both fists were clenched on it and his glass had fallen and smashed. If he had snarled before, this time he positively roared.

"Career? Don't you understand, you damned fool?

The war is nigh over and done with and we are for the beach, every man jack of us!"

There was a prolonged silence in which even Brocklebank seemed to find that something unusual had happened to him. His head sank, then jerked up and he looked round vacantly. Then his eyes focused. One by one, we turned.

Summers stood in the doorway.

"Sir. I have been with Mr Colley, sir. It is my belief the man is dead."

Slowly, each of us rose, coming, I suppose, from a moment of furious inhospitality to another realization. I looked at the captain's face. The red suffusion of his anger had sunk away. He was inscrutable. I saw in his face neither concern, relief, sorrow nor triumph. He might have been made of the same material as the figurehead.

He was the first to speak.

"Gentlemen. This sorry affair must end our, our meeting."

"Of course, sir."

"Hawkins. Have this gentleman escorted to his cabin. Mr Talbot. Mr Oldmeadow. Be good enough to view the body with Mr Summers to confirm his opinion. I myself will do so. I fear the man's intemperance has destroyed him."

"Intemperance, sir? A single, unlucky indulgence?"

"What do you mean, Mr Talbot?"

"You will enter it so in the log?"

Visibly, the captain controlled himself.

"That is something for me to consider in my own time, Mr Talbot."

I bowed and said nothing. Oldmeadow and I withdrew and Brocklebank was half-carried and halfdragged behind us. The captain followed the little group that surrounded the monstrous soak. It seemed that every passenger in the ship, or at least the after part of it, was congregated in the lobby and staring silently at the door of Colley's cabin. Many of the crew who were not on duty, and most of the emigrants, were gathered at the white line drawn across the deck and were staring at us in equal silence. I suppose there must have been some noise from the wind and the passage of the ship through the water but I, at least, was not conscious of it. The other passengers made way for us. Wheeler was standing on guard at the door of the cabin, his white puffs of hair, his bald pate and *lighted* face—I can find no other description for his expression of understanding all the ways and woes of the world—gave him an air of positive saintliness. When he saw the captain he bowed with the unction of an undertaker or indeed as if the mantle of poor, obsequious Colley had fallen on him. Though the work should have gone to Phillips, it was Wheeler who opened the door, then stood to one side. The captain went in. He stayed for no more than a moment, came out, motioned me to enter, then strode to the ladder and up to his own quarters. I went into the cabin with no great willingness, I can assure you! The poor man still clutched the ringbolt—still lay with his face pressed against the bolster, but the blanket had been turned back and revealed his cheek and neck. I put three hesitant fingers on his cheek and whipped them back as if they had been burned. I did not choose, indeed I did not need, to lean down and listen for the man's breathing. I came out to Colley's silent congregation and nodded to Mr Oldmeadow who went in, licking pale lips. He too came out quickly.

Summers turned to me.

"Well, Mr Talbot?"

"No living thing could be as cold."

Mr Oldmeadow turned up his eyes and slid gently down the bulkhead until he was sitting on the deck. Wheeler, with an expression of holy understanding, thrust the gallant officer's head between his knees. But now, of all inappropriate beings, who should appear but Silenus? Brocklebank, perhaps a little recovered or perhaps in some extraordinary trance of drunkenness, reeled out of his cabin and shook off the two women who were trying to restrain him. The other ladies shrieked and then were silent, caught between the two sorts of occasion. The man wore nothing but a shirt. He thrust, weaving and staggering, into Colley's cabin and shoved Summers aside with a force that made the first lieutenant reel.

"I know you all," he shouted, "all, all! I am an artist! The man is not dead but shleepeth! He is in a low fever and may be recovered by drink—"

I grabbed the man and pulled him away. Summers was there, too. We were mixed with Wheeler and stumbling round Oldmeadow—but really, death is death and if *that* is not to be treated with some seriousness—somehow we got him out into the lobby, where the ladies and gentlemen were silent again. There are some situations for which no reaction is suitable—perhaps the only one would have been for them all to retire. Somehow we got him back to the door of his hutch, he meanwhile mouthing about *spirits* and *low fever*. His women waited, silent, appalled. I was muttering in my turn.

"Come now, my good fellow, back to your bunk!"

"A low fever—"

"What the devil is a low fever? Now go in—go *in*, I say! Mrs Brocklebank—Miss Brocklebank, I appeal to you—for heaven's sake—"

They did help and got the door shut on him. I turned away, just as Captain Anderson came down the ladder and into the lobby again.

"Well gentlemen?"

I answered both for Oldmeadow and myself.

"To the best of my belief, Captain Anderson, Mr Colley is dead."

He fixed me with his little eyes.

"I heard mention of 'a low fever,' did I not?"

Summers came out, closing the door of Colley's cabin behind him. It was an act of curious decency. He stood, looking from the captain to me and back again. I spoke unwillingly—but what else could I say?

"It was a remark made by Mr Brocklebank who is, I fear, not wholly himself."

I swear the captain's cheeks creased and the twin sparks came back. He looked round the crowd of witnesses.

"Nevertheless, Mr Brocklebank has had some medical experience!"

Before I could expostulate he had spoken again and with the tyrannical accents of his service.

"Mr Summers. See that the customary arrangements are made."

"Aye, aye, sir."

The captain turned and retired briskly. Summers continued in much the same accents as his captain.

"Mr Willis!"

"Sir!"

"Bring aft the sailmaker and his mate and three or four able-bodied men. You may take what men of the off-duty watch are under punishment."

"Aye, aye, sir."

Here was none of the pretended melancholy our professional undertakers have as their stock-in-trade! Mr Willis departed *forrard* at a run. The first lieutenant then addressed the assembled passengers in his customary mild accents.

"Ladies and gentlemen, you will not wish to witness what follows. May I request that the lobby be cleared? The air of the afterdeck is to be recommended."

Slowly the lobby cleared until Summers and I were left together with the servants. The door of Brocklebank's hutch opened and the man stood there grotesquely naked. He spoke with ludicrous solemnity.

"Gentlemen. A low fever is the opposite of a high fever. I bid you good day."

He was tugged backwards and reeled. The door was shut upon him. Summers then turned to me.

"You, Mr Talbot?"

"I have the captain's request still to comply with, have I not?"

"I fancy it has ended with the poor man's death."

"We talked of *noblesse oblige* and fair play. I found myself translating the words by a single one."

"Which is?"

"Justice."

Summers appeared to consider. "You have decided who is to appear at the bar?"

"Have not you?"

"I? The powers of a captain—besides, sir, *I* have no patron."

"Do not be so certain, Mr Summers."

He looked at me for a moment in bewilderment. Then he caught his breath. "I—?"

But men of the crew were trotting aft towards us. Summers glanced at them, then back at me.

"May I recommend the afterdeck?"

"A glass of brandy is more appropriate."

I went into the passenger saloon and found Oldmeadow slumped there in a seat under the great stern window, an empty glass in his hand. He was breathing deeply and perspiring profusely. But colour was back in his cheeks. He muttered to me.

"Damned silly thing to do. Don't know what came over me."

"Is this how you behave on a stricken field, Oldmeadow? No, forgive me! I am not myself either. The dead, you see, lying in that attitude as I had so recently seen him—why even then he might have been—but now, stiff and hard as—where the devil is that steward? Steward! Brandy here and some more for Mr Oldmeadow!"

"I know what you mean, Talbot. The truth is I have

never seen a stricken field nor heard a shot fired in anger except once when my adversary missed me by a yard. How silent the ship has become!"

I glanced through the saloon door. The party of men was crowding into Colley's cabin. I shut the door and turned back to Oldmeadow.

"All will be done soon. Oldmeadow—are our feelings unnatural?"

"I wear the King's uniform yet I have never before seen a dead body except the occasional tarred object in chains. This has quite overcome me—touching it I mean. I am Cornish, you see."

"With such a name?"

"We are not all Tre, Pol and Pen. Lord, how her timbers grind. Is there a change in her motion?"

"It cannot be."

"Talbot, do you suppose—"

"What, sir?"

"Nothing."

We sat for a while and I attended more to the spreading warmth of the brandy through my veins than anything else. Presently Summers came in. Behind him I glimpsed a party of men bearing a covered object away along the deck. Summers himself had not yet recovered from a slight degree of pallor.

"Brandy for you, Summers?"

He shook his head. Oldmeadow got to his feet.

"The afterdeck and a breath of air for me, I think. Damned silly of me it was. Just damned silly."

Presently Summers and I were alone.

"Mr Talbot," he said, in a low tone, "you mentioned justice."

"Well, sir?"

"You have a journal."

"And—?"

"Just that."

He nodded meaningly at me, got up, and left. I stayed where I was, thinking to myself how little he understood me after all. He did not know that I had already used that same journal—nor that I planned this plain account to lie before one in whose judgement and integrity—

My lord, you was pleased to advise me to practise the art of flattery. But how can I continue to *try it on* a personage who will infallibly detect the endeavour? Let me be disobedient to you if only in this, and flatter you no more!

Well then, I have accused the captain of an abuse of power; and I have let stand on the page Summers's own suggestion that I myself was to some extent responsible for it. I do not know what more the name of justice can demand of me. The night is far advanced—and it is only *now* as I write these words that I remember the *Colley Manuscript* in which there may be even plainer evidence of your godson's culpability and our captain's cruelty! I will glance through what the poor devil wrote and then get me to bed.

· · ·

I have done so oh God, and could almost wish I had not. Poor, poor Colley, poor Robert James Colley! Billy Rogers, Summers firing the gun, Deverel and Cumbershum, Anderson, minatory, cruel Anderson!

If there is justice in the world—but you may see by the state of my writing how the thing has worked on me—and I—I!

There is light filtering through my louvre. It is far advanced towards morning then. What am I to do? I cannot give Colley's letter, this unbegun, unfinished letter, cannot give his letter to the captain, though *that* for sure, legalistical as it might sound, is what I ought to do. But what then? It would go overboard, be suppressed, Colley would have died of a *low fever* and that would be all. My part would disappear with it. Do I refine too much? For Anderson is captain and will have chapter and verse, justifications for everything he has done. Nor can I take Summers into my confidence. His precious *career* is at stake. He would be bound to say that though I was perhaps right to appropriate the letter I have no business to suppress it.

Well. I do not suppress it. I take the only way towards justice—natural justice I mean, rather than that of the captain or the law courts—and lay the evidence in your lordship's hands. He says he is "For the beach." If you believe as I do that he went beyond discipline into tyranny then a word from you in the right quarter will keep him there.

And I? I am writ down plainer in this record than I intended, to be sure! What I thought was behaviour consonant with my position—

Very well, then. I, too.

Why Edmund, Edmund! This is methodistical folly! Did you not believe you were a man of less sensibility than intelligence? Did you not feel, no, *believe*, that your blithely accepted system of morality for men in general owed less to feeling than to the operations of the intellect? Here is more of what you will wish to tear and not exhibit! But I have read and written all night and may be forgiven for a little lightheadedness. Nothing is real and I am already in a half-dream. I will get glue and fix the letter in here. It shall become another part of the *Talbot Manuscript*.

His sister must never know. It is another reason for not showing the letter. He died of a low fever—why, that poor girl there forrard will die of one like enough before we are done. Did I say glue? There must be some about. A hoof of Bessie. Wheeler will know, omniscient, ubiquitous Wheeler. And I must keep all locked away. This journal has become deadly as a loaded gun.

The first page, or it may be two pages, are gone. I saw them, or it, in his hand when he walked, in a trance of drunkenness, walked, head up and with a smile as if already in heaven—

Then at some time after he had fallen into a drunken slumber, he woke—slowly perhaps. There was, it may be, a blank time when he knew not who or what he was—then the time of remembering the Reverend Robert James Colley.

No. I do not care to imagine it. I visited him that first time—Did my words bring to his mind all that he had lost? Self-esteem? His fellows' respect? *My* friendship? *My* patronage? Then, *then* in that agony he grabbed the letter, crumpled it, thrust it away as he would have thrust his memory away had it been possible—away, deep down beneath the bunk, unable to bear the thought of it—

My imagination is false. For sure he willed himself to death, but not for that, not for any of that, not for a casual, a single—

Had he committed murder—or being what he was—!

It is a madness, absurdity. What women are there at *that* end of the ship for him?

And I? I might have saved him had I thought less of my own consequence and less of the danger of being bored!

Oh those judicious opinions, those interesting observations, those sparks of wit with which I once proposed to entertain your lordship! Here instead is a plain description of Anderson's *commissions* and my own—omissions.

Your lordship may now read:

COLLEY'S LETTER

so I have drawn a veil over what have been the most trying and unedifying of my experiences. My prolonged nausea has rendered those first hours and days a little less distinct in my memory, nor would I attempt to describe to you in any detail the foul air, lurching brutalities, the wantonness, the casual blasphemies to which a passenger in such a ship is exposed even if he is a clergyman! But now I am sufficiently recovered from my nausea to be able to hold a pen, I cannot refrain from harking back for a moment to my first appearance on the vessel. Having escaped the clutches of a horde of *nameless creatures* on the foreshore and having been conveyed out to our noble vessel in a most expensive manner; having then been lifted to the deck in a kind of sling—somewhat like but more elaborate than the swing hung from the beech beyond the styes—I found myself facing a young officer who carried a spyglass under his arm.

Instead of addressing me as one gentleman ought to address another he turned to one of his fellows and made the following observation.

"Oh G--, a parson! That will send old Rumble-guts flying into the foretop!"

This was but a sample of what I was to suffer. I will not detail the rest, for it is now many days, my dear sister, since we bade farewell to the shores of Old Albion. Though I am strong enough to sit at the little flap which serves me as *priedieu*, desk, table and lectern I am still not secure enough to venture further. My first duty must be, of course (after those of my calling) to make myself known to our gallant captain, who lives and has his being some two storeys, or decks as I must now call them, above us. I hope he will agree to have this letter put on a ship proceeding in a contrary direction so you may have the earliest news of me. As I write this, Phillips (my *servant!*) has been in my small cabin with a little broth and advised me against a premature visit to Captain Anderson. He says I should get up my strength a little, take some food in the passenger saloon as a change from having it here— what I could *retain* of it!—and exercise myself in the lobby or further out in that large space of deck which he calls the *waist* and which lies about the tallest of our masts.

Though unable to eat I *have* been out, and oh, my dear sister, how remiss I have been to repine at my lot! It is an earthly, nay, an oceanic paradise! The sunlight is warm and like a natural benediction. The sea is brilliant as the tails of Juno's birds (I mean the peacock) that parade the terraces of Manston Place! (Do not omit to show any little attention that may be possible in that quarter, I must remind you.) Enjoyment of such a scene is as good a medicine as a man could wish for when enhanced by that portion of the scriptures appointed for the day. There was a sail appeared briefly on the horizon and I offered up a brief prayer for our safety subject always to HIS Will. However, I took my temper from the behaviour of our officers and men, though of course in the love and care of OUR SAVIOUR I have a far securer *anchor* than any appertaining to the vessel! Dare I confess to you that as the strange sail sank below the horizon—she had never appeared wholly above it—I caught myself day-dreaming that she had attacked us and that I performed some deed of daring not, indeed, fitted for an ordained minister of the Church but even as when a boy, I dreamed sometimes of winning fame and fortune at the side of England's Hero! The sin was venial and quickly acknowledged and repented. Our heroes surrounded me on all sides and it is to them that I ought to minister!

Well, then, I could almost wish a battle for *their* sakes! They go about their tasks, their bronzed and manly forms unclothed to the waist, their abundant locks gathered in a queue, their nether garments closely fitted but flared about the ankles like the nostrils of a stallion. They disport themselves casually a hundred feet up in the air. Do not, I beg you, believe the tales spread by vicious and un-Christian men, of their brutal treatment! I have neither heard nor seen a flogging. Nothing more drastic has occurred than a judicious correction applied to the proper portion of a *young gentleman* who would have suffered as much and borne it as stoically at school.

I must give you some idea of the shape of the little society in which we must live together for I know not how many months. We, the gentry as it were, have our castle in the backward or after part of the vessel. At the other end of the waist, under a wall pierced by two entrances and furnished with stairs or, as they still call them, *ladders*, are the quarters of our Jolly Tars and the other inferior sort of passenger—the emigrants, and so forth. Above that again is the deck of the fo'castle and the quite astonishing world of the bowsprit! You will have been accustomed, as I was, to thinking of a bowsprit (remember Mr Wembury's ship-in-a-bottle!) as a stick projecting from the front end of a ship. Nay then, I must now inform you that a bowsprit is a whole mast, only laid more nearly to the horizontal than the others. It has *yards* and *mastcapping, sidestays* and even *halyards!* More than that, as the other masts may be likened to huge trees among the limbs and branches of which our fellows climb, so the bowsprit is a kind of road, steep in truth but one on which they run or walk. It is more than three feet in diameter. The masts, those other "sticks", are of such a thickness! Not the greatest beech from Saker's Wood has enough mass to supply such monsters. When I remember that some action of the enemy, or, even more appalling, some act of Nature may break or twist them off as you might twist the leaves off a carrot, I fall into a kind of terror. Indeed it was not a terror for my own safety! It was, it is, a terror at the majesty of this huge engine of war, then by a curious extension of the feeling, a kind of awe at the nature of the beings whose joy and duty it is to control such an invention in the service of their GOD and their King. Does not Sophocles (a Greek Tragedian) have some such thought in the chorus to his Philoctetes? But I digress.

The air is warm and sometimes hot, the sun lays such a lively hand on us! We must beware of him lest he strike us down! I am conscious even as I sit here at my *desk* of a warmness about my cheeks that has been occasioned by his rays! The sky this morning was of a dense blue, yet no brighter nor denser than the white-flecked blue of the broad ocean. I could almost rejoice in that powerful circling which the point of the bow-

sprit, *our* bowsprit, ceaselessly described above the
sharp line of the horizon!

Next day.
I am indeed stronger and more able to eat. Phillips
says that soon all will be well with me. Yet the weather
is somewhat changed. Where yesterday there was a
blueness and brightness, there is today little or no wind
and the sea is covered with a white haze. The bowsprit
—which in earlier days had brought on attack after
attack of nausea if I was so rash as to fix my attention
on it—stands still. Indeed, the aspect of our little world
has changed at least three times since our Dear Country sank—nay, appeared to sink—into the waves!
Where, I ask myself, are the woods and fertile fields,
the flowers, the grey stone church in which you and I
have worshipped all our lives, that churchyard in which
our dear parents—nay, the earthly remains of our dear
parents, who have surely received their reward in
heaven—where, I ask, are all the familiar scenes that
were for both of us the substance of our lives? The human mind is inadequate to such a situation. I tell myself there is some material reality which joins the place
where I am to the place where I was, even as a road
joins Upper and Nether Compton. The intellect as-
sents but the *heart* can find no certainty in it. In re-
proof I tell myself that OUR LORD is here as much as
there; or rather that here and there may be the same
place in HIS EYES!

I have been on deck again. The white mist seemed
denser, yet hot. Our people are dimly to be seen. The
ship is utterly stopped, her sails hanging down. My

footsteps sounded unnaturally loud and I did not care to hear them. I saw no passengers about the deck. There is no creak from all our wood and when I ventured to look over the side I saw not a ripple, not a bubble in the water.

Well! I am myself again—but only just!

I had not been out in the hot vapour for more than a few minutes when a thunderbolt of blinding white dropped out of the mist on our right hand and struck into the sea. The clap came with the sight and left my ears ringing. Before I had time to turn and run, more claps came one on the other and rain fell—I had almost said in rivers! But truly it seemed they were the waters over the earth! Huge drops leapt back a yard off the deck. Between where I had stood by the rail and the lobby was but a few yards, yet I was drenched before I got under cover. I disrobed as far as decency permits, then sat at this letter but not a little shaken. For the last quarter of an hour—would that I had a timepiece! —the awful bolts have dropped and the rain cascaded.

Now the storm is grumbling away into the distance. The sun is lighting what it can reach of our lobby. A light breeze has set us groaning, washing and bubbling on our way. I say the sun has appeared; but only to set.

What has remained with me apart from a lively memory of my apprehensions is not only a sense of HIS AWFULNESS and a sense of the majesty of HIS creation. It is a sense of the splendour of our vessel rather than her triviality and minuteness! It is as if I think of her as a separate world, a universe in little in which we must pass our lives and receive our reward or punishment. I trust the thought is not impious! It is a strange thought and a strong one!

It is with me still for, the breeze dying away, I ventured forth again. It is night now. I cannot tell you how high against the stars her great masts seem, how huge yet airy her sails, nor how far down from her deck the night-glittering surface of the waters. I remained motionless by the rail for I know not how long. While I was yet there, the last disturbance left by the breeze passed away so that the glitter, that image of the starry heavens, gave place to a flatness and blackness, a nothing! All was mystery. It terrified me and I turned away to find myself staring into the half-seen face of Mr Smiles, the sailing master. Phillips tells me that Mr Smiles, under the captain, is responsible for the navigation of our vessel.

"Mr Smiles—tell me how deep these waters are!"

He is a strange man, as I know already. He is given to long thought, constant observation. He is aptly named, too, for he has a kind of smiling remoteness which sets him apart from his fellow men.

"Who can say, Mr Colley?"

I laughed uneasily. He came closer and peered into my face. He is smaller even than I, and you know I am by no means a tall man.

"These waters may be more than a mile deep—two miles—who can say? We might sound at such a depth but commonly we do not. There is not the necessity."

"More than a mile!"

I was almost overcome with faintness. Here we are, suspended between the land below the waters and the sky like a nut on a branch or a leaf on a pond! I cannot convey to you, my dear sister, my sense of horror, or shall I say, my sense of our being living souls in this place where surely, I thought, no man ought to be!

I wrote that last night by the light of a most expensive candle. You know how frugal I must be. Yet I am forced in on myself and must be indulged in a light if nothing else. It is in circumstances such as these present that a man (even if he make the fullest use of the consolations of religion that are available to his individual nature), that a man, I say, requires human companionship. Yet the ladies and gentlemen at this end of the ship do not respond with any cheerful alacrity to my greetings. I had thought at first that they were, as the saying is, "shy of a parson". I pressed Phillips again and again as to the meaning of this. Perhaps I should not have done so! He need not be privy to social divisions that are no concern of his. But he did mutter it was thought among the common people that a parson in a ship was like a woman in a fishing boat—a kind of natural bringer of bad luck. This low and reprehensible superstition cannot apply to our ladies and gentlemen. It is no kind of explanation. It seemed to me yesterday that I might have a clue as to their indefinable *indifference* to me. We have with us the celebrated, or let me say, the *notorious* free thinker, Mr Prettiman, that friend of Republicans and Jacobins! He is regarded by most, I think, with dislike. He is short and stocky. He has a bald head surrounded by a wild halo—dear me, how unfortunate my choice of words has been—a wild fringe of brown hair that grows from beneath his ears and round the back of his neck.

He is a man of violent and eccentric movements that spring, we must suppose, from some well of his indignations. Our young ladies avoid him and the only one who will give him countenance is a Miss Granham, a lady of sufficient years and, I am sure, firmness of principle to afford her security even in the heat of his opinions. There is also a young lady, a Miss Brocklebank, of outstanding beauty, of whom—I say no more or you will think me arch. I believe she, at least, does not look on your brother unkindly! But she is much occupied with the indisposition of her mother, who suffers even more than I from *mal de mer*.

I have left to the last a description of a young gentleman whom I trust and pray will become my friend as the voyage advances. He is a member of the aristocracy, with all the consideration and nobility of bearing that such birth implies. I have made so bold as to salute him on a number of occasions and he has responded graciously. His example may do much among the other passengers.

This morning I have been out on deck again. A breeze had sprung up during the night and helped us on our way but now it has fallen calm again. Our sails hang down and there is a vaporous dimness everywhere, even at noon. Once more and with that same terrifying instantaneity came flashes of lightning in the mist that were awful in their fury! I fled to my cabin with such a sense of our peril from these warring elements, such a return of my sense of our suspension over this liquid profundity, that I could scarce get my hands together in prayer. However, little by little I came to myself and to peace though all outside was turmoil. I reminded myself, as I should have done before, that one good soul, one good deed, good thought, and more, one touch of Heaven's Grace was greater than all these boundless miles of rolling vapour and wetness, this intimidating vastness, this louring majesty! Indeed, I thought, though with some hesitation, that perhaps bad men in their ignorant deaths may find here the awfulness in which they must dwell by reason of their depravity. You see, my dear sister, that the strangeness of our surroundings, the weakness consequent on my prolonged nausea and a natural diffidence that has led me too readily to *shrink into my shell* has produced in me something not unlike a temporary disordering of the intellects! I found myself thinking of a seabird crying as one of those lost souls to whom I have alluded! I thanked GOD humbly that I had been allowed to detect this fantasy in myself before it became a belief.

I have roused myself from my lethargy. I have seen at least one possible reason for the indifference with which I feel myself treated. I have not made myself known to our captain and this may well have been thought a slight upon him! I am determined to undo this misapprehension as soon as possible. I shall approach him and express my sincere regret for the lack of Sabbath observance that my indisposition has occasioned in the ship, for she carries no chaplain. I must and will eradicate from my mind the ungenerous suspicion that on reaching or *joining* the ship I received less courtesy from the officers than is due to my cloth. Our Stout-hearted Defenders cannot, I am sure, be of such a sort. I will walk a little on deck now in preparation before readying myself to visit the captain. You remember my old diffidence at approaching the face of Authority and will feel for me!

I have been into the waist again and spoken once more with our sailing master. He was standing on the left-hand side of the vessel and staring with his particular intentness at the horizon; or rather, where the horizon ought to have been.

"Good morning, Mr Smiles! I should be happier if this vapour were to clear away!"

He smiled at me with that same mysterious remoteness.

"Very well, sir. I will see what can be done."

I laughed at the quip. His good humour restored me completely to myself. So that I might *exorcise* those curious feelings of the strangeness of the world I went to the side of the vessel and leaned against the railings (the bulwarks as they are called) and looked down where the timbers of our enormous vessel bulge out past her closed gunports. Her slight progress made a tiny ripple in that sea which I made myself inspect coldly, as it were. My sense of its depth—but how am I to say this? I have seen many a millpond or corner of a river seem as deep! Nor was there a spot or speck in it where our ship divided it, a closing furrow in the poet Homer's "Unfurrowed ocean." Yet I found myself facing a new puzzle—and one that would not have presented itself to the poet! (You must know that Homer is commonly supposed to have been blind.) How then can water added to water produce an opacity? What impediment to the vision can colourless-

ness and transparency spread before us? Do we not see
clear through glass or diamond or crystal? Do we not
see the sun and moon and those fainter luminaries (I
mean the stars) through unmeasured heights of pen-
dant atmosphere? Yet here, what was glittering and
black at night, grey under the racing clouds of awful
tempest, now began little by little to turn blue and
green under the sun that at last broke through the
vapour!

Why should I, a cleric, a man of GOD, one acquainted with the robust if mistaken intellects of this
and the preceding century and able to see them for
what they are—why, I say, should the material nature
of the globe so interest, so trouble and excite me? *They
that go down to the sea in ships!* I cannot think of our
Dear Country without finding myself looking not over
the horizon (in my imagination, of course) but trying
to calculate that segment of water and earth and *terrible deep rock* that I must suppose myself to stare
through in order to look in your direction and that of
our—let me say *our*—village! I must ask Mr Smiles,
who will be well enough acquainted with the angles
and appropriate mathematics of the case, as to the
precise number of degrees it is necessary to look beneath the horizon! How immeasurably strange it will
be at the Antipodes to stare (near enough I think) at
the buckles of my shoes and suppose you—forgive me,
I am off in a fantasy again! Do but think that there the
very stars will be unfamiliar and the moon stood on
her head!

Enough of fantasy! I will go now and make myself
known to our captain! Perhaps I may have some oppor-

tunity of entertaining him with the idle fancies I have alluded to above.

I have approached Captain Anderson and will narrate the plain facts to you if I can. My fingers are almost nerveless and will scarcely allow me to hold the pen. You may deduce that from the quality of this handwriting.

Well then, I attended to my clothes with more than usual care, came out of my cabin and ascended the flights of stairs to that highest deck where the captain commonly stations himself. At the front end of this deck and rather below it are the wheel and compass. Captain Anderson and the first lieutenant, Mr Summers, were staring together at the compass. I saw the moment was unpropitious and waited for a while. At last the two gentlemen finished their conversation. The captain turned away and walked to the very back end of the vessel and I followed him, thinking this my opportunity. But no sooner had he reached the rail at the back than he turned round again. As I was following closely I had to leap sideways in what must have appeared a manner hardly consonant with the dignity of my sacred office. Scarcely had I recovered my balance when he *growled* at me as if I had been at fault rather than he. I uttered a word or two of introduction which he dismissed with a grunt. He then made a remark which he did not trouble to modify with any show of civility.

"Passengers come to the quarterdeck by invitation.

I am not accustomed to these interruptions in my walk, sir. Go forrard if you please and keep to looard."

"Looard, captain?"

I found myself drawn forcibly sideways. A young gentleman was pulling me to the wheel whence he led me—I complying—to the opposite side of the ship to where Captain Anderson was. He positively hissed in my ear. That side of the deck, whichever it may be, from which the wind blows is reserved to the captain. I had therefore made a mistake but could not see how I was at fault but by an ignorance natural in a gentleman who had never been at sea before. Yet I am deeply suspicious that the surliness of the captain towards me is not to be explained so readily. Is it perhaps sectarianism? If so, as a humble servant of the Church of England—the Catholic Church of England —which spreads its arms so wide in the charitable embrace of sinners, I cannot but deplore such divisive stubbornness! Or if it is not sectarianism but a social contempt, the situation is as serious—nay, *almost* as serious! I am a clergyman, bound for an honourable if humble situation at the Antipodes. The captain has no more business to look big on me—and indeed less business—than the canons of the Close or those clergy I have met *twice* at my Lord Bishop's table! I have determined therefore to emerge more frequently from my obscurity and exhibit my cloth to this gentleman and the passengers in general so that even if they do not respect *me* they may respect *it!* I may surely hope for some support from the young gentleman, Mr Edmund Talbot, from Miss Brocklebank and Miss Granham— It is evident I must return to the captain, offer him my sincere apologies for my inadvertent trespass, then raise the question of Sabbath Observance. I would beg to offer Communion to the ladies and gentlemen—and of course to the common people who should desire it. There is, I fear, only too plainly room for much improvement in the conduct of affairs aboard the vessel. There is (for example) a daily ceremony of which I had heard and would now wish to prevent—for you know how paternally severe my Lord Bishop has been in his condemnation of drunkenness among the lower orders! Yet here it is only too true! The people are indeed given strong drink regularly! A further reason for instituting worship must be the opportunities it will afford for animadverting on the subject! I shall return to the captain and proceed by a process of mollification. I must indeed be all things to all men.

I have attempted to be so and have failed abjectly, humiliatingly. It was, as I wrote before, in my mind to ascend to the captain's deck, apologize for my previous trespass, beg his permission to use it and then raise the question of regular worship. I can scarcely bring myself to recount the truly awful scene that followed on my well-meant attempt to bring myself to the familiar notice of the officers and gentlemen. As soon as I had written the foregoing paragraph I went up to the lower part of the quarterdeck where one of the lieutenants stood by the two men at the wheel. I lifted my hat to him and made an amiable comment.

"We are now in finer weather, sir."

The lieutenant ignored me. But this was not the

worst of it. There came a kind of growling roar from the back rail of the ship.

"Mr Colley! Mr Colley! Come here, sir!"

This was not the kind of invitation I had looked for. I liked neither the tone nor the words. But they were nothing to what followed as I approached the captain.

"Mr Colley! Do you wish to subvert all my officers?"

"Subvert, sir?"

"It was my word, sir!"

"There is some mistake—"

"It is yours then, sir. Are you aware of the powers of a captain in his own ship?"

"They are rightly extensive. But as an ordained minister—"

"You are a passenger, sir, neither more nor less. What is more, you are not behaving as decent as the rest—"

"Sir!"

"You are a nuisance, sir. You was put aboard this ship without a note to me. There is more courtesy shown me about a bale or a keg, sir. Then I did you the credit to suppose you could read—"

"Read, Captain Anderson? Of course I can read!"

"But despite my plainly written orders, no sooner had you recovered from your sickness than you have twice approached and exasperated my officers—"

"I know nothing of this, have read nothing—"

"They are my Standing Orders, sir, a paper prominently displayed near your quarters and those of the other passengers."

"My attention was not drawn—"

"Stuff and nonsense, sir. You have a servant and the orders are there."

"My attention—"

"Your ignorance is no excuse. If you wish to have the same freedom as the other passengers enjoy in the after part of the vessel—or do you wish not to live among ladies and gentlemen, sir? Go—examine the paper!"

"It is my right—"

"Read it, sir. And when you have read it, get it by heart."

"How, sir! Will you treat me like a schoolboy?"

"I will treat you like a schoolboy if I choose, sir, or I will put you in irons if I choose or have you flogged at the gratings if I choose or have you hanged at the yard-arm if I choose—"

"Sir! Sir!"

"Do you doubt my authority?"

I saw it all now. Like my poor young friend Josh— you remember Josh—Captain Anderson was mad. Josh was always well enough in his wits except when frogs were in question. *Then* his mania was clear for all to hear, and later, alas, for all to see. Now here was Captain Anderson, well enough for the most part, but by some unfortunate chance fixing on me in his mania for an object to be humiliated—as indeed I was. I could do nothing but humour him for there was, mad or no, that in his enraged demeanour which convinced me he was capable of carrying out at least some of his threats. I answered him as lightly as possible but in a voice, I fear, sadly tremulous.

"I will indulge you in this, Captain Anderson."

"You will carry out my orders."

I turned away and withdrew silently. Directly I was out of his presence I found my body bathed in perspiration yet strangely cold, though my face, by some contrast, was as strangely hot. I discovered in myself a deep unwillingness to meet any eye, any face. As for my own eyes—I was weeping! I wish I could say they were tears of manly wrath but the truth is they were tears of shame. On shore a man is punished at the last by the Crown. At sea the man is punished by the captain who is visibly present as the Crown is not. At sea a person's manhood suffers. It is a kind of contest—is that not strange? So that men—but I wander in my narrative. Suffice it to say that I found, nay, groped my way back to the neighbourhood of my cabin. When my eyes had cleared and I had come to myself a little I searched for the captain's written Orders. They were indeed displayed on a wall near the cabins! Now I did remember too that during the convulsions of my sickness Phillips had talked to me about *Orders* and even *the captain's Orders*; but only those who have suffered as I can understand how slight an impression the words had made on my fainting spirits. But here they were. It was unfortunate, to say the least. I had, by the most severe standards, been remiss. The Orders were displayed in a case. The glass was somewhat blurred on the inside by a condensation of atmospheric water. But I was able to read the writing, the material part of which I copy here.

Passengers are in no case to speak to officers who are executing some duty about the ship. In no

case are they to address the officer of the watch
during his hours of duty unless expressly enjoined
to do so by him.

I saw now what a hideous situation I was in. The officer of the watch, I reasoned, must have been the first
lieutenant, who had been with the captain, and at my
second attempt the lieutenant who had stood by the
men at the wheel. My fault was quite inadvertent but
none the less real. Even though the manner of Captain
Anderson to me had not been and perhaps never would
be that of one gentleman to another, yet some form of
apology was due to him and through him to those
other officers whom I might have hindered in the exe-
cution of their duty. Then too, forbearance must be in
the very nature of my calling. I therefore easily and
quickly committed the essential words to memory and
returned at once to the raised decks which are included
in the seaman's term "Quarterdeck". The wind was
increased somewhat. Captain Anderson paced up and
down the side, Lieutenant Summers talked to another
lieutenant by the wheel, where two of the ship's people
guided our huge vessel creaming over the billows. Mr
Summers pointed to some rope or other in the vast
complication of the rigging. A young gentleman who
stood behind the lieutenants touched his hat and
skipped nimbly down the stairs by which I had ascended. I approached the captain's back and waited
for him to turn.

Captain Anderson walked through me!

I could almost wish that he had in truth done so—
yet the hyperbole is not inapt. He must have been very

deep in thought. He struck me on the shoulder with his swinging arm and then his chest struck me in the face so that I went reeling and ended by measuring my length on the white-scrubbed planking of the deck!

I got my breath back with difficulty. My head was resounding from a concussive encounter with the wood. Indeed, for a moment it appeared that not one but two captains were staring down at me. It was some time before I realized that I was being addressed.

"Get up, sir! Get up at once! Is there no end to your impertinent folly?"

I was scrabbling on the deck for my hat and wig. I had little enough breath for a rejoinder.

"Captain Anderson—you asked me—"

"I asked nothing of you, sir. I gave you an order."

"My apology—"

"I did not ask for an apology. We are not on land but at sea. Your apology is a matter of indifference to me—"

"Nevertheless—"

There was, I thought, and indeed was frighted by the thought, a kind of stare in his eyes, a suffusion of blood in all his countenance that made me believe he might well assault me physically. One of his fists was raised and I own that I crouched away a few steps without replying. But then he struck the fist into the other palm.

"Am I to be outfaced again and again on my own deck by every ignorant landsman who cares to walk there? Am I? Tell me, sir!"

"My apology—was intended—"

"I am more concerned with your person, sir, which is

more apparent to me than your mind and which has formed the habit of being in the wrong place at the wrong time—repeat your lesson, sir!"

My face felt swollen. It must have been as deeply suffused as his. I perspired more and more freely. My head still rang. The lieutenants were studiously and carefully examining the horizon. The two seamen at the wheel might have been cast in bronze. I believe I gave a shuddering sob. The words I had learned so recently and easily went clean out of my head. I could see but dimly through my tears. The captain grumbled, perhaps a thought—indeed I hope so—a thought less fiercely.

"Come, sir. Repeat your lesson!"

"A period for recollection. A period—"

"Very well. Come back when you can do it. Do you understand?"

I must have made some reply, for he concluded the interview with his hectoring roar.

"Well, sir—what are you waiting for?"

I did not so much go to my cabin as flee to it. As I approached the second flight of stairs I saw Mr Talbot and the two young gentlemen he had with him—three more witnesses to my humiliation!—hurry out of sight into the lobby. I fell down the stairs, the ladders as I suppose I must call them, hurried into my cabin and flung myself down by my bunk. I was shaking all over, my teeth were chattering. I could hardly breathe. Indeed I believe, nay, I confess that I should have fallen into a fit, a syncope, a seizure or the like—something at all events that would have ended my life, or reason at least, had I not heard young Mr Talbot outside the

cabin speak in a firm voice to one of the young gentlemen. He said something like—Come, young midshipman, one *gentleman* does not take pleasure in the persecution of another! At that my tears burst forth freely
but with what I may call a healing freedom! God bless
Mr Talbot! There is one *true* gentleman in this ship
and I pray that before we reach our destination I may
call him *Friend* and tell him how much his true consideration has meant to me! Indeed, I now knelt,
rather than crouched by my bunk and gave thanks for
his consideration and understanding—for his noble
charity! I prayed for us both. Only then was I able to
sit at this table and consider my situation with something like a rational coolness.

However I turned the thing over and over, I saw
one thing clearly enough. As soon as I saw it I came
near to falling into a panic all over again. There was—
there *is* no doubt—I am the object of a particular animosity on the part of the captain! It was with a thrill
of something approaching terror that I re-created in my
imagination that moment when he had, as I expressed
it, "walked through me". For I saw now that it was not
an accident. His arm, when it struck me, moved not
after the common manner in walking but continued
its swing with an unnatural momentum—augmented
immediately after by the blow from his chest that ensured my fall. I knew, or my person knew, by some
extraordinary faculty, that Captain Anderson had
deliberately struck me down! He is an enemy to religion—it can only be that! Oh what a spotted soul!

My tears had cleansed my mind. They had exhausted but not defeated me. I thought first of my

cloth. He had tried to dishonour that; but I told myself, *that* only I could do. Nor could he dishonour me
as a common fellow-being since I had committed no
fault, no sin but the venial one of omitting to read his
Orders! For that, my sickness was more to blame than
I! It is true I had been foolish and was perhaps an
object of scorn and amusement to the officers and the
other gentlemen with the exception of Mr Talbot. But
then—and I said this in all humility—so would my
Master have been! At that I began to understand that
the situation, harsh and unjust as it might seem, was
a lesson to me. He puts down the mighty and exalteth
the humble and meek. Humble I was of necessity before all the brutal powers which are inherent in absolute command. Meek, therefore, it behoved me to be.
My dear sister—

Yet this is strange. Already what I have written
would be too painful for your—for her—eyes. It must
be amended, altered, softened; and yet—

If not to my sister then to whom? To THEE? Can
it be that like THY saints of old (particularly Saint
Augustine) I am addressing THEE, OH MOST MERCIFUL
SAVIOUR?

I have prayed long. That thought had flung me to
my knees—was at once a pain and a consolation to me.
Yet I was able to put it away at last as too high for me!
To have—oh, indeed, not touched the hem of those
garments—but to have glanced for a moment towards
THOSE FEET—restored me to a clearer view of myself and of my situation. I sat, then, and reflected.

I concluded at last that it would be proper to do

either of two things. Item: never to return to the quarterdeck, but for the remainder of our passage hold myself aloof from it with dignity; the other: to go to the quarterdeck, repeat Captain Anderson's Orders to him and to as many gentlemen as might be present, add some such cool remark as "And now, Captain Anderson, I will trouble you no further," then withdraw, absolutely declining to use that part of the vessel in any circumstances whatever—unless perhaps Captain Anderson himself should condescend (which I did not believe) to offer me an apology. I spent some time emending and refining my farewell speech to him. But at last I was driven to the consideration that he might not afford me the opportunity of uttering it. He is a master of the brutal and quelling rejoinder. Better then to pursue the first course and give him no further cause or opportunity to insult me.

I must own to a great feeling of relief at reaching this decision. With the aid of PROVIDENCE I might contrive to avoid him until the end of our voyage. However, my first duty, as a Christian, was to forgive him, monster as he was. I was able to do this but not without recourse to much prayer and some contemplation of the awful fate that awaited him when he should find himself at last before the THRONE. There, I knew him for my brother, was his keeper, and prayed for us both.

That done, to trifle for a moment with profane literature, like some Robinson Crusoe, I set to and considered what part of the vessel remained to me as my—as I expressed it—my *kingdom*! It comprised my cabin, the corridor or lobby outside it, the passenger saloon, where I might take such sustenance as I was bold enough to in the presence of the other ladies and gentlemen who had been all witnesses of my humiliation. There were too the necessary offices on this side of the vessel and the deck, or *waist* as Phillips calls it, as far as the white line at the main mast which separates us from the common people, be they either seamen or emigrants. That deck was to be for my airing in fine weather. There I might meet the better disposed of the gentlemen—and *ladies* too! There—for I knew he used it—I should further and deepen my friendship with Mr Talbot. Of course, in wet and windy weather I must be content with the lobby and my cabin. I saw that even if I were to be confined to these areas I might still pass the months ahead without too much discomfort and avoid what is most to be feared, a melancholy leading on to madness. All would be well.

This was a decision and a discovery that gave me more earthly pleasure, I believe, than anything I have experienced since parting from those scenes so dear to me. Immediately I went out and paced round my island—my *kingdom!*—in the meantime reflecting on all those who would have welcomed such an expansion of their territory as the attainment of liberty—I mean those who in the course of history have found themselves imprisoned for a just cause. Though I have, so to speak, abdicated from that part of the vessel which ought to be the prerogative of my cloth and consequent station in our society, the waist is in some ways to be preferred to the quarterdeck! Indeed I have seen Mr Talbot not merely walk to the white line, but cross

211

RITES OF PASSAGE

it and go among the common people in a generous and democratic freedom!

Since writing those last words I have furthered my acquaintance with Mr Talbot! It was he of all people who did in fact search me out! He is a true friend to religion! He came to my cabin and begged me in the most friendly and open manner to favour the ship's people in the evening with a short address! I did so in the passenger saloon. I cannot pretend that many of the *gentry*, as I may call them, paid much attention to what they heard and only one of the officers was present. I therefore addressed myself particularly to those hearts I thought readily open to the message I have to give—to a young lady of great piety and beauty and to Mr Talbot himself, whose devotion does credit not only to him in person but through him to his whole order. Would that the gentry and Nobility of England were all imbued with a like spirit!

It must be the influence of Captain Anderson; or perhaps they ignore me from a refinement of manners, a delicacy of feeling—but though I salute our ladies and gentlemen from the waist when I see them up there on the quarterdeck, they seldom acknowledge the salutation! Yet now, truth to tell, and for the past three days there has been nothing to salute—no waist to walk on since it is awash with sea water. I find myself not sick as I was before—I am become a proper sailor! Mr Talbot, however, is sick indeed. I asked Phillips what was the matter and the man replied with an evident

sarcasm—*belike it was summat he ate!* I did dare to
cross the lobby softly and knock, but there was no
reply. Daring still further I lifted the latch and entered. The young man lay asleep, a week's beard on his
lips and chin and cheeks—I scarce dare put down here
the impression his slumbering countenance made on
me—it was as the face of ONE who suffered for us all—
and as I bent over him in some irresistible compulsion
I do not deceive myself but there was the sweet aroma
of holiness itself upon his breath! I did not think myself worthy of his lips but pressed my own reverently
on the one hand that lay outside the coverlet. Such is
the power of goodness that I withdrew as from an
altar!

The weather has cleared again. Once more I take my
walks in the waist and the ladies and gentlemen theirs
on the quarterdeck. Yet I find myself a good sailor and
was about in the open before other people!

The air in my cabin is hot and humid. Indeed, we
are approaching the hottest region of the world. Here I
sit at my writing-flap in shirt and unmentionables and
indite this letter, if letter it be, which is in some sort my
only friend. I must confess to a shyness still before the
ladies since the captain gave me my great *set-down*.
Mr Talbot, I hear, improves and has been visible for
some days, but with a diffidence before my cloth and
indeed it may be with some desire to spare me embarrassment, he holds aloof.

Since writing that, I have walked again in the waist.
It is now a mild and sheltered place. Walking there I
have come to the opinion of our brave sailors which

landsmen have ever held of them! I have observed these common people closely. These are the good fellows whose duty it is to steer our ship, to haul on the ropes and do strange things with our sails in positions which must surely be perilous, so high they go! Their service is a continual round and necessary, I must suppose, to the progress of the vessel. They are for ever cleaning and scraping and painting. They create marvellous structures from the very substance of rope itself! I had not known what can be done with rope! I had seen here and there on land ingenuities of woodcarving in imitation of rope; here I saw rope carved into the imitation of wood! Some of the people do indeed carve in wood or in the shells of coconuts or in bone or perhaps ivory. Some are making the models of ships such as we see displayed in the windows of shops or inns or alehouses near seaports. They seem to be people of infinite ingenuity.

All this I watch with complacency from far off in the shelter of the wooden wall with its stairways that lead up to where the *privileged* passengers live. Up there is silence, or the low murmur of conversation or the harsh sound of a shouted order. But forward, beyond the white line, the people work and sing and keep time to the fiddle when they play—for like children, they play, dancing innocently to the sound of the fiddle. It is as if the childhood of the world were upon them. All this has thrown me into some perplexity. The ship is crowded at the front end. There is a small group of soldiers in uniform, there are a few emigrants, the women seeming common as the men. But when I ignore all but the ship's people, I find *them* objects of astonishment to me. They cannot, for the most part, read or write. They know nothing of what our officers know. But these fine, manly fellows have a complete— what shall I call it? "Civilization" it is not, for they have no city. Society it might be, save that in some ways they are *joined* to the superior officers, and there are classes of men between the one and the other— warrant officers they are called!—and there appear to be grades of authority among the sailors themselves. What are they then, these beings at once so free and so dependent? They are *seamen*, and I begin to understand the word. You may observe them when they are released from duty to stand with arms linked or placed about each other's shoulders. They sleep sometimes on the scrubbed planking of the deck, one it may be, with his head pillowed on another's breast! The innocent pleasures of friendship—in which I, alas, have as *yet* so little experience—the joy of kindly association or even that bond between two persons which, Holy Writ directs us, passes the love of women, must be the cement that holds their company together. It has indeed seemed to me from what I have jestingly represented as "my kingdom" that the life of the front end of the vessel is sometimes to be preferred to the vicious system of control which obtains *aft of the mizzen* or even *aft of the main!* (The precision of these two phrases I owe to my servant Phillips.) Alas that my calling and the degree in society consequent on it should set me so firmly where I no longer desire to be!

We have had a spell of bad weather—not very bad, but sufficient to keep most of our ladies in their cabins. Mr Talbot keeps his. My servant assures me that the young man is not seasick, yet I have heard strange sounds emanating from behind his locked door. I had the temerity to offer my services and was both disconcerted and concerned to wring from the poor young gentleman the admission that he was wrestling with his soul in prayer! Far, far be it from me to blame him —no, no, I would not do so! But the sounds were those of _enthusiasm!_ I much fear that the young man for all his rank has fallen victim to one of the extremer systems against which our Church has set her face! I must and will help him! But that can only be when he is himself again and moves among us with his customed ease. These attacks of a too passionate devotion are to be feared more than the fevers to which the inhabitants of these climes are subject. He is a layman; and it shall be my pleasant duty to bring him back to that decent moderation in religion which is, if I may coin a phrase, the genius of the Church of England!

He has reappeared; and avoids me, perhaps in an embarrassment at having been detected at his too protracted devotions; I will let him be for the moment and pray for him while we move day by day, I hope, towards a mutual understanding. I saluted him from far off this morning as he walked on the quarterdeck but he affected to take no notice. Noble young man! He who has been so ready to help others will not deign, on his own behalf, to ask for help!

This morning in the waist I have been spectator once again of that ceremony which moves me with a mixture of grief and admiration. A barrel is set on the deck. The seamen stand in line and each is given successively a mug of liquid from the barrel which he drains off after exclaiming, "The King! GOD bless him!" I would His Majesty could have seen it. I know of course that the liquid is the devil's brew and I do not swerve one jot or tittle from my previous opinion that strong drink should be prohibited from use by the lower orders. For sure, ale is enough and too much —but let them have it!

Yet here, *here* on the bounding main, under the hot sun and with a whole company of bronzed young fellows bared to the waist—their hands and feet hard with honest and dangerous toil—their stern yet open faces weathered by the storms of every ocean, their luxuriant curls fluttering from their foreheads in the breeze— *here*, if there was no overthrowing of my opinion, there was at least a modification and mitigation of it. Watching one young fellow in particular, a narrow-waisted, slim-hipped yet broad-shouldered *Child of Neptune*, I felt that some of what was malignant in the potion was cancelled by where and who was concerned with it. For it was as if these beings, these young men, or some of them at least and one of them in particular, were of the giant breed. I called to mind the legend of Talos, the man of bronze whose artificial frame was filled with liquid fire. It seemed to me that such an evidently fiery liquid as the one (it is *rum*) which a mistaken benevolence and paternalism provides for the sea-service was the proper *ichor* (this was the blood of the Grecian Gods, supposedly) for beings of such semi-divinity, of such truly heroic proportions! Here and there among them the marks of the discipline were evident and they bore these parallel scars with indifference and even pride! Some, I verily be-

lieve, saw them as marks of distinction! Some, and that
not a few, bore on their frames the scars of unquestioned honour—scars of the cutlass, pistol, grape or
splinter. None were maimed; or if they were, it was in
such a minor degree, a finger, eye or ear perhaps, that
the blemish hung on them like a medal. There was
one whom I called in my mind my own particular hero!
He had nought but four or five white scratches on the
left side of his open and amiable countenance as if
like Hercules he had struggled with a wild beast!
(Hercules, you know, was fabled to have wrestled
with the Nemaean Lion.) His feet were bare and his
nether limbs—*my* young hero I refer to, rather than
the legendary one! His nether garments clung to his
lower limbs as if moulded there. I was much taken
with the manly grace with which he tossed off his mug
of liquor and returned the empty vessel to the top of
the barrel. I had an odd fancy. I remembered to have
read somewhere in the history of the union that when
Mary, Queen of Scots, first came into her kingdom she
was entertained at a feast. It was recorded that her
throat was so slender and her skin so white that as she
swallowed wine the ruby richness of the liquid was
visible through it to the onlookers! This scene had always exercised a powerful influence over my infant
spirits! It was only now that I remembered with what
childish pleasure I had supposed my future spouse
would exhibit some such particular comeliness of person—in addition of course to the more necessary
beauties of mind and spirit. But now, with Mr Talbot
shy of me, I found myself, in my *kingdom* of lobby,
cabin and waist, unexpectedly dethroned and a new

monarch elevated there! For this young man of bronze
with his flaming ichor—and as he drank the liquor
down it seemed to me that I heard a furnace roar and
with my inward eye saw the fire burst forth—it seemed
to me with my *outer* eye that he could be no other than
the king! I abdicated freely and yearned to kneel before him. My whole heart went out in a passionate
longing to bring this young man to OUR SAVIOUR,
first and surely richest fruit of the harvest I am sent
forth to garner! After he retired from the barrel, my
eye followed him without my volition. But he went
where I, alas, could not go. He ran out along that
fourth mast laid more nearly horizontal, the bowsprit I
mean, with its complication of ropes and tackles and
chains and booms and sails. I was reminded of the old
oak in which you and I were wont to climb. But he
(the king) ran out there or up there and stood at the
tip of the very thinnest spar and looked down into the
sea. His whole body moved easily to counter our slight
motion. Only his shoulder leaned against a rope, so
that he lounged as he might against a tree! Then he
turned, ran back a few paces and *lay down* on the surface of the thicker part of the bowsprit as securely as I
might in my bed! Surely there is nothing so splendidly
free as a young fellow in the branches of one of His
Majesty's *travelling trees*, as I may call them! Or for-
ests, even! There lay the king, then, crowned with
curls—but I grow fanciful.

We are in the doldrums. Mr Talbot still avoids me.
He has been wandering round the ship and descending
into her very bowels as if searching for some private

place where, perhaps, he may continue his devotions without hindrance. I fear sadly that my approach was untimely and did more damage than good. I pray for him. What can I do more?

We are motionless. The sea is polished. There is no sky but only a hot whiteness that descends like a curtain on every side, dropping, as it were, even below the horizon and so diminishing the circle of the ocean that is visible to us. The circle itself is of a light and luminescent blue. Now and then some sea creature will shatter the surface and the silence by leaping through it. Yet even when nothing leaps there is a constant shuddering, random twitches and vibrations of the surface, as if the water were not only the home and haunt of all sea creatures but the skin of a living thing, a creature vaster than Leviathan. The heat and dampness combined would be quite inconceivable to one who had never left that pleasant valley which was our home. Our own motionlessness—and this I believe you will not find mentioned in the accounts of sea voyages—has increased the effluvias that rise from the waters immediately round us. Yesterday morning there was a slight breeze but we were soon still again. All our people are silent, so that the striking of the ship's bell is a loud and startling sound. Today the effluvias became intolerable from the necessary soiling of the water round us. The boats were hoisted out from the *boom* and the ship towed a little way from the odious place; but now if we do not get any wind it will all be to do again. In my cabin I sit or lie in shirt and breeches and even so find the air hardly to be borne. Our ladies and gentlemen keep their cabin in a like case, lying abed I think, in hope that the weather and the place may pass. Only Mr Talbot roams as if he can find no peace—poor young man! May GOD be with him and keep him! I have approached him once but he bowed slightly and distantly. The time is not yet.

How next to impossible is the exercise of virtue! It requires a constant watchfulness, constant guard—oh my dear sister, how much must you and I and every Christian soul rely at every moment on the operation of Grace! There has been an altercation! It was not, as you might expect, among the poor people in the front of the ship but here among the gentlemen, nay, among the very officers themselves!

It was thus. I was sitting at my writing-flap and re-cutting a quill when I heard a scuffle outside in the lobby, then voices, soft at first but raised later.

"You dog, Deverel! I saw you come from the cabin!"

"What are you about then, Cumbershum, for your part, you rogue!"

"Give it to me, sir! By G—— I will have it!"

"And unopened at either end— You sly dog, Cumbershum, I'll read it, I swear I will!"

The scuffle became noisy. I was in shirt and breeches, my shoes under the bunk, my stockings hung over it, my wig on a convenient nail. The language became so much more blasphemous and filthy that I could not let the occasion pass. Not thinking of my appearance I got up quickly and rushed out of the cabin, to find the two officers struggling violently for possession of a missive. I cried out.

"Gentlemen! Gentlemen!"

I seized the nearest to me by the shoulder. They stopped the fight and turned to me.

"Who the devil is this, Cumbershum?"

"It's the parson, I think. Be off, sir, about your own business!"

"I am about my business, my friends, and exhort you in a spirit of Christian Charity to cease this unseemly behaviour, this unseemly language, and make up your quarrel!"

Lieutenant Deverel stood looking down at me with his mouth open.

"Well by thunder!"

The gentleman addressed as Cumbershum—another lieutenant—stuck his forefinger so violently towards my face that had I not recoiled, it would have entered my eye.

"Who in the name of all that's wonderful gave you permission to preach in this ship?"

"Yes, Cumbershum, you have a point."

"Leave this to me, Deverel. Now, parson, if that's what you are, show us your authority."

"Authority?"

"D — n it man, I mean your commission!"

"Commission!"

"Licence they call it, Cumbershum, old fellow, licence to preach. Right parson—show us your licence!"

I was taken aback, nay, confounded. The truth is, and I record it here for you to pass to any young clergyman about to embark on such a voyage, I had deposited the licence from my Lord Bishop with other private papers—not, as I supposed, needed on the voyage—in my trunk, which had been lowered somewhere into the bowels of the vessel. I attempted to explain this briefly to the officers but Mr Deverel interrupted me.

"Be off with you, sir, or I shall take you before the captain!"

I must confess that this threat sent me hurrying back into my cabin with some considerable trepidation. For a moment or two I wondered whether I had not after all succeeded in abating their mutual wrath, for I heard them both laughing loudly as they walked away. But I concluded that such heedless—I will not call them more—such heedless spirits were far more likely to be laughing at the *sartorial* mistake I had made and the result of the interview with which they had threatened me. It was clear that I had been at fault in allowing myself a public appearance less *explicit* than that sanctioned by custom and required by decorum. I began hurriedly to dress, not forgetting my bands, though my throat in the heat felt them as an unfortunate constriction. I regretted that my gown and hood were packed or, should I say, *stowed* away with my other impedimenta. At length, then, clothed in at least some of the visible marks of the dignity and authority of my calling, I issued forth from my cabin. But of course the two lieutenants were nowhere to be seen.

But already, in this equatorial part of the globe, after

being fully dressed for no more than a moment or two
I was bathed in perspiration. I walked out into the
waist but felt no relief from the heat. I returned to the
lobby and my cabin determined to be more comfortable yet not knowing what to do. I could be, without
the sartorial adornment of my calling, mistaken for an
emigrant! I was debarred from intercourse with the
ladies and gentlemen and had been given no opportunity other than that first one of addressing the common people. Yet to endure the heat and moisture in a
garb appropriate to the English countryside seemed
impossible. On an impulse derived, I fear, less from
Christian practice than from my reading of the classi-
cal authors, I opened the Sacred Book and before I
was well aware of what I was doing I had employed
the moment in a kind of *Sortes Virgilianae*, or con-
sultation of the oracle, a process I had always thought
to be questionable even when employed by the holiest
servants of the Lord. The words my eyes fell on were
II Chronicles viii. 7–8. "The Hittites, and the Amo-
rites, and the Perizzites, and the Hivites, and the Jebu-
sites which were not of Israel"—words which in the
next moment I had applied to Captain Anderson and
Lieutenants Deverel and Cumbershum, then flung
myself on my knees and implored forgiveness!

I record this trivial offence merely to show the oddi-
ties of behaviour, the perplexities of the understanding, in a word, the *strangeness* of this life in this strange
part of the world among strange people and in this
strange construction of English oak which both trans-
ports and imprisons me! (I am aware, of course, of the

amusing "paranomasia" in the word "transport" and hope the perusal of it will afford you some entertainment!)

To resume. After a period at my devotions I considered what I had better do in order to avoid any future mistake as to my *sanctified* identity. I divested myself once more of all but shirt and breeches, and thus divested, I employed the small mirror which I have for use when shaving to examine my appearance. This was a process of some difficulty. Do you remember the knothole in the barn through which in our childish way we were wont to keep watch for Jonathan or our poor, sainted mother, or his lordship's bailiff, Mr Jolly? Do you remember, moreover, how, when we were tired of waiting, we would see by moving our heads how much of the exterior world we could spy through the knot? Then we would pretend to be seized of all we saw, from Seven Acre right up to the top of the hill? In such a manner did I contort myself before the mirror and the mirror before me! But here I am—if indeed this letter should ever be sent—instructing a member of the Fair Sex in the employment of a mirror and the art of, dare I call it, "Self-admiration"? In my own case, of course, I use the word in its original sense of surprise and wonder rather than self-satisfaction! There was much to wonder at in what I saw but little to approve. I had not fully understood before how harshly the sun can deal with the male countenance that is exposed to its more nearly vertical rays.

My hair, as you know, is of a light but indeterminate hue. I now saw that your cropping of it on the day before our parting—due surely to our mutual distress—

had been sadly uneven. This unevenness seems to have been accentuated rather than diminished by the passage of time so that my head presented an appearance not unlike a patch of ill-reaped stubble. Since I had not been able to shave during my first *nausea* (the word indeed derives from the Greek word for a ship!) and had feared to do so in the later period when the ship was in violent motion—and at last have been dilatory, fearing the pain I should inflict on my sunscorched skin, the lower part of my face was covered with bristles. They were not long, since my beard is of slow growth—but of varying hue. Between these two *crop-yielding areas*, as I may call them, of scalp and beard, king Sol had exerted his full sway. What is sometimes called a widow's peak of rosy skin delineated the exact extent to which my wig had covered my forehead. Below that line the forehead was plum-coloured and in one place burst with the heat. Below that again, my nose and cheeks appeared red as on fire! I saw at once that I had deceived myself entirely if I supposed that appearing in shirt and breeches and in this *guise* I should exert the authority inhering in my profession. Nay—are these not of all people those who judge a man by his uniform? My "uniform," as I must in all humility call it, must be sober black with the pure whiteness of bleached linen and bleached hair, the adornments of the Spiritual Man. To the officers and people of this ship, a clergyman without his bands and wig would be of no more account than a beggar.

True, it was the sudden sound of an altercation and the desire to do good that had drawn me forth from my seclusion, but I was to blame. I drew in my breath with something like fear as I envisaged the appearance I must have presented to them—with a bare head, unshaven, sunblotched, unclothed! It was with confusion and shame that I remembered the words addressed to me individually at my ordination—words I must ever hold sacred because of the occasion and the saintly divine who spake them—"Avoid scrupulosity, Colley, and always present a decent appearance." Was *this* that I now saw in the mirror of my imagination the figure of a labourer in that country where "the fields are white to harvest"? Among those with whom I now dwell, a respectable appearance is not merely a *desideratum* but a *sine qua non.* (I mean, my dear, not merely desirable but necessary.) I determined at once to take more care. When I walked in what I had thought of as my kingdom, I would not only be a man of GOD—I would be *seen* to be a man of GOD!

Things are a little better. Lieutenant Summers came and begged the favour of a word with me. I answered him through the door, begging him not to enter as I was not yet prepared in clothes or visage for an interview. He assented, but in a low voice as if afraid that others would hear. He asked my pardon for the fact that there had been no more services in the passenger saloon. He had repeatedly *sounded* the passengers and had met with indifference. I asked him if he had asked Mr Talbot and he replied after a pause that Mr Talbot had been much occupied with his own affairs. But he, Mr Summers, thought that there might be a chance of what he called a *small gathering* on the next Sabbath. I found myself declaring through the door with a passion quite unlike my usual even temper—

"This is a Godless vessel!"

Mr Summers made no reply so I made a further remark.

"It is the influence of a certain person!"

At this I heard Mr Summers change his position outside the door as if he had suddenly looked round him. Then he whispered to me.

"Do not, I beg you, Mr Colley, entertain such thoughts! A small gathering, sir—a hymn or two, a reading and a benediction—"

I took the opportunity to point out that a morning service in the waist would be far more appropriate; but Lieutenant Summers replied with what I believe to be a degree of embarrassment that *it could not be.* He then withdrew. However, it is a small victory for religion. Nay—who knows when that heart of awful flint may be brought to yield as yield at last it must?

I have discovered the name of my Young Hero. He is one Billy Rogers, a sad scamp, I fear, whose boyish heart has not yet been touched with Grace. I shall try to make an opportunity of speaking with him.

I have passed the last hour in *shaving!* It was indeed painful and I cannot say that the result justifies the labour. However, it is done.

I heard an unwonted noise and went into the lobby. As I did so, I felt the deck tilt under me—though very slightly—but alas! The few days of almost total calm have unfitted me for the motion and I have lost the "sea legs" I thought I had acquired! I was forced to retire precipitately to my cabin and bunk. There I was better placed and could feel that we have some wind, favourable, light and easy. We are moving on our way again; and though I did not at once care to trust to my legs I felt that elevation of the spirits which must come to any traveller when after some let or hindrance he discovers himself to be on the move towards his destination.

A day's rest lies in that line I have drawn above these words! I have been out and about, though keeping as much as possible away from the passengers and the people. I must re-introduce myself to them, as it were, by degrees until they see not a bare-headed clown but a man of God. The people work about the ship, some hauling on this rope, others *casting off* or slackening that one with a more cheerful readiness than is their wont. The sound of our progress through the water is much more clearly audible! Even I, landsman that I am and must remain, am sensible of a kind of lightness in the vessel as if she too were not inanimate but a partaker in the general gaiety! The people earlier were everywhere to be seen climbing among her limbs and branches. I mean, of course, that vast paraphernalia which allows all the winds of heaven to advance us towards the desired haven. We steer south, ever south, with the continent of Africa on our left hand but hugely distant. Our people have added even more area to the sails by attaching small *yards* (poles, you would call them) from which is suspended lighter material beyond the outer edge of our usual *suit!* (You will detect the degree to which by a careful attention to the conversations going on round me I have become imbued with the language of navigation!) This new area of sail increases our speed, and, indeed, I have just heard one young gentleman cry to another—I omit an unfortunate expletive—"How the old lady lifts up her p-tt-c-ts and makes a run for it!" Perhaps these additional areas are to be called "p-tt-c-ts" in nautical parlance; for you cannot imagine with what impropriety the people and even the officers name the various pieces of equipment about the vessel! This continues even in the presence of a clergyman and the ladies, as if the seamen concerned were wholly unconscious of what they have said.

Once again a day has passed between two paragraphs! The wind has dropped and my trifling indisposition with it. I have dressed, nay, even shaved once more and moved for a while into the waist. I should endeavour, I think, to define for you the position in which I find myself vis-à-vis the other gentlemen, not to say ladies. Since the captain inflicted a public humiliation on me I have been only too aware that of all the passengers I am in the most peculiar position. I do not know how to describe it, for my opinion of how I am regarded alters from day to day and from hour to hour! Were it not for my servant Phillips and the first lieutenant Mr Summers, I believe I should speak to no one; for poor Mr Talbot has been either indisposed or restlessly moving towards what I can only suppose to be a crisis of faith, in which it would be my duty and profound pleasure to help him, but he avoids me. He will not inflict his troubles on any one! Now as for the rest of the passengers and officers, I do sometimes suspect that, influenced by the attitude of Captain Anderson, they disregard me and my sacred office with a frivolous indifference. Then in the next moment I suppose it to be a kind of delicacy of feeling not always to be found among our countrymen that prevents them forcing any attention on me. Perhaps—and I only say perhaps—there is an inclination among them to let me be and make belief that no one has noticed anything! The ladies, of course, I cannot expect to approach me and I should think the less of any one who did so. But this (since I have still limited my movements to the area that I called, jestingly, my *kingdom*) has by now resulted in a degree of isolation which I have suffered in more than I should have supposed. Yet all this must change! I am determined! If either indifference or delicacy prevents them from addressing me, then I must be bold and address *them!*

I have been again into the waist. The ladies and gentlemen, or those who were not in their cabins, were parading on the quarterdeck where I must not go. I did bow to them from far off to show how much I desire some familiar intercourse but the distance was too great and they did not notice me. It must have been the poor light and the distance. It could have been nothing else. The ship is motionless, her sails hanging vertically down and creased like aged cheeks. As I turned from surveying the strange parade on the quarterdeck—for here, in this field of water everything is strange—and faced the forward part of the ship I saw something strange and new. The people are fastening what I at first took to be an awning before the fo'castle—*before*, I mean, from where I stood below the stairs leading up to the quarterdeck—and at first I thought this must be a shelter to keep off the sun. But the sun is dropping low and, as we have eaten our animals, the pens had been broken up, so the shelter would protect nothing. Then again, the material of which the "awning" is composed seems unnecessarily heavy for such a purpose. It is stretched across the deck at the height of the bulwarks from which it is suspended, or stretched, rather, by ropes. The seamen call the material "tarpaulin" if I am not mistaken; so the phrase "Honest Tar" here finds its original.

After I had written those words I resumed my wig and coat (they shall never see me other than properly dressed again) and went back to the waist. Of all the strangenesses of this place at the world's end surely the change in our ship at this moment is the strangest! There is silence, broken only by bursts of laughter. The people, with every indication of enjoyment, are lowering buckets over the side on ropes that run through pulleys or *blocks*, as we call them here. They heave up sea water—which must, I fear, be most impure since we have been stationary for some hours—and spill it into the tarpaulin, which is now bellied down by the weight. There seems no way in which this can help our progress; the more so as certain of the people (my Young Hero among them, I am afraid) have, so to say, relieved nature into what is none other than a container rather than awning. This, in a ship, where by the propinquity of the ocean, such arrangements are made as might well be thought preferable to those our fallen state makes necessary on land! I was disgusted by the sight and was returning to my cabin when I was involved in a strange occurrence! Phillips came towards me hastily and was about to speak when a voice spoke or rather shouted at him from a dim part of the lobby.

"Silence, Phillips, you dog!"

The man looked from me into the shadows from which none other than Mr Cumbershum emerged and stared him down. Phillips retired and Cumbershum stood looking at me. I did not and do not like the man. He is another Anderson I think, or will be should he ever attain to captaincy! I went hastily into my cabin. I took off my coat, wig and bands and composed myself to prayer. Hardly had I begun when there came a timid knocking at the door. I opened it to find Phillips there again. He began to whisper.

"Mr Colley, sir, I beg you—"

"Phillips, you dog! Get below or I'll have you at the grating!"

I stared round in astonishment. It was Cumbershum again and Deverel with him. Yet at first I only recognized them by Cumbershum's voice and Deverel's air of unquestioned elegance, for they too were without hat or coat. They saw me, who had promised myself never to be seen so, and they burst out laughing. Indeed, their laughter had something maniacal about it. I saw they were both to some degree in drink. They concealed from me objects which they held in their hands and they bowed to me as I entered my cabin with a ceremony I could not think sincere. Deverel is a gentleman! He cannot, sure, intend to harm me!

The ship is extraordinarily quiet. A few minutes ago I heard the rustling steps of the remainder of our passengers go through the lobby, mount the stairs and pass over my head. There is no doubt about it. The people at this end of the ship are gathered on the quarterdeck. Only *I* am excluded from them!

I have been out again, stole out into the strange light for all my resolutions about dress. The lobby was silent. Only a confused murmur came from Mr Talbot's cabin. I had a great mind to go to him and beg his protection; but knew that he was at private prayer. I stole out of the lobby into the waist. What I saw as I stood, petrified as it were, will be stamped on my mind till my dying day. *Our* end of the ship—the two raised portions at the back—was crowded with passengers and officers, all silent and all staring forward over my head. Well might they stare! There never was such a sight. No pen, no pencil, not that of the greatest artist in history could give any idea of it. Our huge ship was motionless and her sails still hung down. On her right hand the red sun was setting and on her left the full moon was rising, the one directly across from the other. The two vast luminaries seemed to stare at each other and each to modify the other's light. On land this spectacle could never be so evident because of the interposition of hills or trees or houses, but here we see down from our motionless vessel on all sides to the very edge of the world. Here plainly to be seen were the very scales of GOD.

The scales tilted, the double light faded and we were wrought of ivory and ebony by the moon. The people moved about forward and hung lanterns by the dozen from the rigging, so that I saw now that they had erected something like a bishop's *cathedra* beyond the ungainly paunch of tarpaulin. I began to understand. I began to tremble. I was alone! Yes, in that vast ship with her numberless souls I was alone in a place where on a sudden I feared the Justice of GOD unmitigated by HIS Mercy! On a sudden I dreaded both GOD and man! I stumbled back to my cabin and have endeavoured to pray.

NEXT DAY

I can scarcely hold this pen. I *must* and *will* recover my composure. What a man does defiles him, not what is done by others— My shame, though it burn, has been inflicted on me.

I had completed my devotions, but sadly out of a state of recollection. I had divested myself of my garments, all except my shirt, when there came a thunderous knocking at the cabin door. I was already, not to refine upon it, fearful. The thunderous blows on the door completed my confusion. Though I had speculated on the horrid ceremonies of which I might be the victim, I thought then of shipwreck, fire, collision or the violence of the enemy. I cried out, I believe.

"What is it? What is it?"

To this a voice answered, loud as the knocking.

"Open this door!"

I answered in great haste, nay, panic.

"No, no, I am unclothed—but what is it?"

There was a very brief pause, then the voice answered me dreadfully.

"Robert James Colley, you are come into judgement!"

These words, so unexpected and terrible, threw me into utter confusion. Even though I knew that the voice was a human voice I felt a positive contraction of the heart and know how violently I must have clutched my hands together in that region, for there is a contusion over my ribs and I have bled. I cried out in answer to the awful summons.

"No, no, I am not in any way ready, I mean I am unclothed—"

To this the same unearthly voice and in even more terrible accents uttered the following reply.

"Robert James Colley, you are called to appear before the throne."

These words—and yet *part* of my mind knew them for the foolery they were—nevertheless completely inhibited my breathing. I made for the door to shoot the bolt but as I did so the door burst open. Two huge figures with heads of nightmare, great eyes and mouths, black mouths full of a mess of fangs drove down at me. A cloth was thrust over my head. I was seized and hurried away by irresistible force, my feet not able to find the deck except every now and then. I am, I know, not a man of quick thought or instant apprehension. For a few moments I believe I was rendered totally insensible, only to be brought to myself again by the sound of yelling and jeering and positively demonic laughter. *Some* touch of presence of mind, however, as I was borne along all too securely muffled, made me cry out "Help! Help!" and briefly supplicate MY SAVIOUR.

The cloth was wrenched off and I could see clearly —all too clearly—in the light of the lanterns. The foredeck was full of the people and the edge of it lined with figures of nightmare akin to those who had hurried me away. He who sat on the throne was bearded and crowned with flame and bore a huge fork with three prongs in his right hand. Twisting my neck as the cloth came off I could see the after end of the ship, *my rightful place*, was thronged with *spectators!* But there were too few lanterns about the quarterdeck for me to see clearly, nor had I more than a moment to look for a friend, for I was absolutely at the disposal of my captors. Now I had more time to understand my situation and the cruelty of the "jest", some of my fear was swallowed up in shame at appearing before the ladies and gentlemen, not to refine upon it, half-naked. I, who had thought never to appear but in the ornaments of the Spiritual Man! I attempted to make a smiling appeal for some covering as if I consented to and took part in the jest but all went too fast. I was made to kneel before the "throne" with much wrenching and buffeting, which took away any breath I had contrived to retain. Before I could make myself heard, a question was put to me of such grossness that I will not remember it, much less write it down. Yet as I opened my mouth to protest, it was at once filled with such nauseous stuff I gag and am like to vomit remembering it. For some time, I cannot tell how long, this operation was repeated; and when I would not open my mouth the stuff was smeared over my face. The questions, one after another, were of such a nature that I cannot write any of them down. Nor could they have been contrived by any but the most depraved of souls. Yet each was greeted with a storm of cheering and that terrible British sound which has ever daunted the foe; and then it came to me, was forced in upon my soul the awful truth—*I was the foe!*

It could not be so, of course. They were, it may be, hot with the devil's brew—they were led astray—it

could not be so! But in the confusion and—to me—
horror of the situation the thought that froze the very
blood in my veins was only this—*I was the foe!*

To such an excess may the common people be led
by the example of those who should guide them to
better things! At last the leader of their revels deigned
to address me.

"You are a low, filthy fellow and must be sham-
poo'd."

Here was more pain and nausea and hindrance to
my breathing, so that I was in desperate fear all the
time that I should die there and then, victim of their
cruel sport. Just when I thought my end was come I
was projected backwards with extreme violence into
the paunch of filthy water. Now here was more of
what was strange and terrible to me. I had not harmed
them. They had had their sport, their will with me.
Yet now as I struggled each time to get out of the wal-
lowing, slippery paunch, I heard what the poor victims
of the French Terror must have heard in their last moments and oh!—it is crueller than death, it must be—
it must be so, nothing, *nothing* that men can do to
each other can be compared with that snarling, lustful,
storming appetite—

By now I had abandoned hope of life and was endeavouring blindly to fit myself for my end—as it were
betwixt the saddle and the ground—when I was aware
of repeated shouts from the quarterdeck and then the
sound of a tremendous explosion. There was compara-
tive silence in which a voice shouted a command. The
hands that had been thrusting me down and in now
lifted me up and out. I fell upon the deck and lay

there. There was a pause in which I began to crawl away in a trail of filth. But there came another shouted order. Hands lifted me up and bore me to my cabin. Someone shut the door. Later—I do not know how much later—the door opened again and some Christian soul placed a bucket of hot water by me. It may have been Phillips but I do not know. I will not describe the contrivances by which I succeeded in getting myself comparatively clean. Far off I could hear that the devils—no, no, I will not call them that—the *people* of the forward part of the ship had resumed their sport with other victims. But the sounds of merriment were jovial rather than bestial. It was a bitter draught to swallow! I do not suppose that in any other ship they have ever had a "parson" to play with. No, no, I will *not* be bitter, I will forgive. They are my brothers even if they feel not so—even if *I* feel not so! As for the gentlemen—no, I will not be bitter; and it is true that one among them, Mr Summers perhaps, or Mr Talbot it may be, did intervene and effect an interruption to their brutal sport even if late in it!

I fell into an exhausted sleep, only to experience most fearful nightmares of judgement and hell. They waked me, praise be to GOD! For had they continued, my reason would have been overthrown.

I have prayed since then and prayed long. After prayer and in a state of proper recollection I have thought.

I believe I have come some way to being myself again. I see without any disguise *what happened*. There is much health in that phrase *what happened*. To clear away the, as it were, undergrowth of my own feelings, my terror, my disgust, my indignation, clears a path by which I have come to exercise a proper judgement. I am a victim at several removes of the displeasure that Captain Anderson has evinced towards me since our first meeting. Such a *farce* as was enacted yesterday could not take place without his approval or at least his tacit consent. Deverel and Cumbershum were his agents. I see that my shame—except in the article of outraged modesty—is quite unreal and does my understanding little credit. Whatever I had *said* —and I have begged my SAVIOUR'S forgiveness for it—what I *felt* more nearly was the opinion of the ladies and gentlemen in regard to me. I was indeed more sinned against than sinning but must put my own house in order, and learn all over again—but there is no end to that lesson!—to forgive! What, I remind myself, have the servants of the LORD been promised in this world? If it must be so, let persecution be my lot henceforward. I am not alone.

I have prayed again and with much fervour and risen from my knees at last, I am persuaded, a humbler and a better man. I have been brought to see that the insult to *me* was as nothing and no more than an invitation to turn the other cheek!

Yet there remains the insult offered not to me, but through me to ONE whose NAME is often in their mouths though seldom, I fear, in their thoughts! The true insult is to my cloth and through it to the Great Army of which I am the last and littlest soldier. MY MASTER HIMSELF has been insulted and though HE may—as I am persuaded HE will—forgive it, I have a duty to deliver a rebuke rather than suffer *that* in silence!

Not for ourselves, O LORD, but for THEE!

I slept again more peacefully after writing those words and woke to find the ship running easily before a moderate wind. The air, I thought, was a little cooler. With a start of fear which I had some difficulty in controlling I remembered the events of the previous evening. But then the *interior* events of my fervent prayer returned to me with great force and I got down from my bunk or I may say, leapt down from it, with joy as I felt my own renewed certainties of the Great Truths of the Christian Religion! My devotions were, you must believe, far, far more prolonged than usual!

After I rose from my knees I took my morning draught, then set myself once more to shave carefully. My hair would have benefited from your ministrations! (But you shall never read this! The situation becomes increasingly paradoxical—I may at some time *censor* what I have written!) I dressed with equal care, bands, wig, hat. I directed the servant to show me where my trunk was *stowed* and after some argument was able to descend to it in the gloomy interior parts of the ship. I took out my Hood and Square and extracted his lordship's licence which I put in the tail-pocket of my coat. Now I had—not *my* but MY MASTER's quarrel just, I was able to view a meeting with anyone in the ship as an encounter no more to be feared than—well, as you know, I once spoke with a highwayman! I climbed, therefore, to the upper portion of the quarterdeck with a firm step and beyond it to the raised platform at its back or after end, where Captain Anderson was commonly to be seen. I stood and looked about me. The wind was on the starboard quarter and brisk. Captain Anderson walked up and down. Mr Talbot with one or two other gentlemen stood by the rail and he touched the brim of his beaver and moved forward. I was gratified at this evidence of his wish to befriend me, but for the moment I merely bowed and passed on. I went across the deck and stood directly in Captain Anderson's path, taking off my hat as I did so. He did not *walk through me*, as I expressed it, on this occasion. He stopped and stared, opened his mouth, then shut it again.

The following exchange then took place.

"Captain Anderson, I desire to speak with you."

He paused for a moment or two. Then—

"Well, sir. You may do so."

I proceeded in calm and measured accents.

"Captain Anderson. Your people have done my office wrong. You yourself have done it wrong."

The hectic appeared in his cheek and passed away. He lifted his chin at me, then sank it again. He spoke, or rather muttered, in reply.

"I know it, Mr Colley."

"You confess as much, sir?"

He muttered again.

"It was never meant—the affair got out of hand. You have been ill-used, sir."

I answered him serenely.

"Captain Anderson, after this confession of your fault I forgive you freely. But there were, I believe, and I am content to suppose they were acting not so much under your orders as by force of your example, there were other officers involved and not merely the commoner sort of people. *Theirs* was perhaps the most outrageous insult to my cloth! I believe I know them, sir, disguised as they were. Not for my sake, but for their own, they must admit the fault."

Captain Anderson took a rapid turn up and down the deck. He came back and stood with his hands clasped behind him. He stared down at me, I was astonished to see, not merely with the highest colouring but with rage! Is it not strange? He had confessed his fault yet mention of his officers threw him back into a state which is, I fear, only too customary with him. He spoke angrily.

"You will have it all, then."

"I defend MY MASTER's Honour as you would defend the King's."

For a while neither of us said anything. The bell was struck and the members of one watch changed places with another. Mr Summers, together with Mr Willis, took over from Mr Smiles and young Mr Taylor. The change was, as usual, ceremonious. Then Captain Anderson looked back at me.

"I will speak to the officers concerned. Are you now satisfied?"

"Let them come to me, sir, and they shall receive my forgiveness as freely as I have given it to you. But there is another thing—"

Here I must tell you that the captain uttered an imprecation of a positively blasphemous nature. However, I employed the wisdom of the serpent as well as the meekness of the dove and affected at *this* time to take no notice! It was not the moment to rebuke a naval officer for the use of an imprecation. That, I already told myself, should come later!

I proceeded.

"There are also the poor, ignorant people in the front end of the ship. I must visit them and bring them to repentance."

"Are you mad?"

"Indeed no, sir."

"Have you no care for what further mockery may be inflicted on you?"

"You have your uniform, Captain Anderson, and I have mine. I shall approach them in that garb, those *ornaments* of the Spiritual Man!"

"Uniform!"

"You do not understand, sir? I shall go to them in those garments which my long studies and ordination enjoin on me. I do not wear them here, sir. You know me for what I am."

"I do indeed, sir."

"I thank you, sir. Have I your permission then, to go forward and address them?"

Captain Anderson walked across the planking and expectorated into the sea. He answered me without turning.

"Do as you please."

I bowed to his back, then turned away myself. As I came to the first stair Lieutenant Summers laid a hand on my sleeve.

"Mr Colley!"

"Well, my friend?"

"Mr Colley, I beg you to consider what you are

about!" Here his voice sank to a whisper. "Had I not discharged Mr Prettiman's weapon over the side and so startled them all, there is no knowing how far the affair might have gone. I beg you, sir—let me assemble them under the eyes of their officers! Some of them are violent men—one of the emigrants—"

"Come, Mr Summers. I shall appear to them in the raiment in which I might conduct a service. They will recognize that raiment, sir, and respect it."

"At least wait until after they have been given their rum. Believe me, sir, I know whereof I speak! It will render them more amiable, calmer—more receptive, sir, to what you have to say to them— I beg you, sir! Otherwise, contempt, indifference—and who knows what else—?"

"And the lesson would go unheeded, you think, the opportunity lost?"

"Indeed, sir!"

I considered for a moment.

"Very well, Mr Summers. I will wait until later in the morning. I have some writing in the meantime which I wish to do."

I bowed to him and went on. Now Mr Talbot stepped forward again. He asked in the most agreeable manner to be admitted to a familiar degree of friendship with me. He is indeed a young man who does credit to his station! If privilege were always in the hands of such as he—indeed, it is not out of the question that at some future date—but I run on!

I had scarcely settled myself to this writing in my cabin when there came a knock at the door. It was the lieutenants, Mr Deverel and Mr Cumbershum, my two *devils* of the previous night! I looked my severest on them, for indeed they deserved a little chastisement before getting forgiveness. Mr Cumbershum said little but Mr Deverel much. He owned freely that they had been mistook and that he had been a little in drink, like his companion. He had not thought I would take the business so much to heart but the people were accustomed to such sport when crossing the equator, only he regretted that they had misinterpreted the captain's general permission. In fine, he requested me to treat the whole thing as a jest that had got out of hand. Had I then worn such apparel as I was now suited in, no one would have attempted—in fact the d-v-l was in it if they had meant any harm and now hoped I would forget the whole business.

I paused for a while as if cogitating, though I knew already what I would do. It was no moment at which to admit my own sense of unworthiness at having appeared before our people in a garb that was less than fitting. Indeed, these were the sort of men who needed a *uniform*—both one to wear, and one to look up to!

I spoke at last.

"I forgive you freely, gentlemen, as I am enjoined to do by MY MASTER. Go, and sin no more."

On that, I shut the cabin door. Outside it, I heard one of them, Mr Deverel, I think, give a low, but prolonged whistle. Then as their steps receded I heard Mr Cumbershum speak for the first time since the interview began.

"I wonder who the d-v-l his Master is? D'you think he's *in* with the d-mned Chaplain to the Fleet?"

Then they had departed. I own I felt at peace for

the first time for many, many days. All was now to be well. I saw that little by little I might set about my work, not merely among the common people but later, among the officers and gentry who would not be, could not be now so insensible to the WORD as had appeared! Why—even the captain himself had shown some small signs—and the power of Grace is infinite. Before assuming my canonicals I went out into the waist and stood there, free at last—why, no doubt now the captain would revoke his first harsh prohibition to me of the quarterdeck! I gazed down into the water, the blue, the green, the purple, the snowy, sliding foam! I saw with a new feeling of security the long, green weed that wavers under the water from our wooden sides. There was, it seemed too, a peculiar richness in the columns of our rounded sails. Now is the time; and after due preparation I shall go forward and rebuke these unruly but truly lovable children of OUR MAKER! It seemed to me then—it still seems so— that I was and am consumed by a great love of all things, the sea, the ship, the sky, the gentlemen and the people and of course OUR REDEEMER above all! Here at last is the happiest outcome of all my distress and difficulty! ALL THINGS PRAISE HIM!

As your lordship knows, Colley wrote no more. After death—nothing. There must be nothing! The only consolation I have myself over the whole business is that I can ensure that his poor sister will never know the truth of it. Drunken Brocklebank may roar in his cabin, "Who killed cock Colley?" but *she* shall never know what weakness killed him, nor whose hands—mine among them—struck him down.

When I was roused by Wheeler from a too brief and uneasy sleep, I found that the first part of the morning was to be passed in an enquiry. I was to sit, with Summers and the captain. Upon my objecting that the body should—in these hot latitudes—be buried first of all, Wheeler said nothing. It is plain that the captain means to cloak his and our persecutions of the man under a garment of proper, official proceedings! We sat, then, behind the table in the captain's cabin and the witnesses were paraded. The servant who had attended Colley told us no more than we knew. Young Mr Taylor, hardly subdued by the man's death but in a proper awe of the captain, repeated that he had seen Mr Colley agree to taste of the rum in a spirit of something or other, he could not recollect quite what—On my suggesting that the word might be "reconciliation" he accepted it. What was Mr Taylor doing there, forrard? (This from Mr Summers.) Mr Tommy Taylor was inspecting the stowage of the cables with a view to having the cable to the bower anchor rousted out and walked end-for-end. This splendid jargon satisfied the naval gentlemen, who nodded together as if they had been spoken to in plain English. But what was Mr Taylor doing, in that case, out of the cable locker? Mr Taylor had finished his inspection and was coming up to report and had stayed for a while, never having seen a parson in that state before. And then? (This from the captain.) Mr Taylor had "proceeded aft, sir, to inform Mr Summers" but had been "*given a bottle* by Mr Cumbershum before I could do so."

The captain nodded and Mr Taylor retired with what looked like relief. I turned to Summers.

"A bottle, Summers? What the devil did they want with a bottle?"

The captain growled.

"A bottle is a rebuke, sir. Let us get on."

The next witness was one East, a respectable emigrant, husband to the poor girl whose emaciated face had so struck me. He could read and write. Yes, he had seen Mr Colley and knew the reverend gentleman by sight. He had not seen him during the "badger bag," as the sailors called it, but he had heard tell. Perhaps we had been told how poorly his wife was and he was in near enough constant attendance on her, himself and Mrs Roustabout taking turns, though near her own time. He had only glimpsed Mr Colley among the seamen, did not think he had said much before taking a cup with them. The applause and laughter we had heard? That was after the few words the gentleman had spoken when he was being social with the sailors. The growls and anger? He knew nothing about that. He only knew the sailors took the gentleman away with them, down where the young gentleman had been among the ropes. He had had to look after his wife, knew nothing more. He hoped we gentlemen would think it no disrespect but that was all anyone knew except the sailors who had the reverend gentleman in charge.

He was allowed to withdraw. I gave it as my opinion that the only man who might enlighten us would be the fellow who had brought or carried him back to us in his drunken stupor. I said that he might know how much Colley drank and who had given it to him or forced it on him. Captain Anderson agreed and said that he had ordered the man to attend. He then addressed us in not much above a whisper:

"My *informant* advises me this is the witness we should press."

It was my turn.

"I believe," I said, and braced myself—"we are doing what you gentlemen would call 'making heavy weather of it'! The man was made drunk. There are some men, as we now know to our cost, whose timidity is such that they are wounded almost to death by another's anger and whose conscience is so tender they will die of what, let us say, Mr Brocklebank would accept as a peccadillo, if that! Come, gentlemen! Could we not confess that his intemperance killed him but that our general indifference to his welfare was likely enough the cause of it!"

This was bold, was it not? I was telling our tyrant that he and I together— But he was regarding me with astonishment.

"Indifference, sir?"

"Intemperance, sir," said Summers, quickly, "let us leave it at that."

"One moment, Summers. Mr Talbot. I pass over your odd phrase, 'our general indifference'. But do you not understand? Do you think that a single bout of drinking—"

"But you yourself said, sir—let us include all under a *low fever!*"

"That *was* yesterday! Sir, I tell you. It is likely enough that the man, helplessly drunk, suffered a criminal assault by one, or God knows how many men, and the absolute humiliation of it killed him!"

"Good God!"

This was a kind of convulsion of the understanding. I do not know that I thought anything at all for minutes together. I, as it were, *came to*, to hear the captain talking.

"No, Mr Summers. I will have no concealment. Nor will I tolerate frivolous accusations which touch me myself in my conduct of the ship and in my attitude to the passengers in her."

Summers was red in the face. "I have made a submission, sir. I beg your pardon if you find it beyond the line of my duty."

"Very well, Mr Summers. Let us get on."

"But captain," said I, "no man will admit to *that!*"

"You are young, Mr Talbot. You cannot guess what channels of information there are in a ship such as this, even though her present commission has been of such a short duration."

"Channels? Your informant?"

"I would prefer us to get on," said the captain heavily. "Let the man come in."

Summers himself went out and fetched Rogers. It

was the man who had brought Colley back to us. I have seldom seen a more splendid young fellow. He was naked to the waist and of a build that one day might be over-corpulent. But now he could stand as a model to Michelangelo! His huge chest and columnar neck were of a deep brown hue, as was his broadly handsome face save where it was scarred by some parallel scratches of a lighter tone. Captain Anderson turned to me.

"Summers tells me you have claimed some skill in cross-examination."

"Did he? Did I?"

Your lordship will observe that I was by no means at my best in all this sorry episode. Captain Anderson positively beamed at me.

"Your witness, sir."

This I had not bargained for. However, there was no help for it.

"Now, my good man. Your name, if you please!"

"Billy Rogers, my lord. Foretop man."

I accepted the honorific. May it be an omen!

"We want information from you, Rogers. We want to know in precise detail what happened when the gentleman came among you the other day."

"What gentleman, my lord?"

"The parson. The reverend Mr Colley, who is now dead."

Rogers stood in the full light of the great window. I thought to myself that I had never seen a face of such wide-eyed candour.

"He took a drop too much, my lord, was overcome, like."

RITES OF PASSAGE

It was time to *go about*, as we nautical fellows say.

"How came you by those scars on your face?"

"A wench, my lord."

"She must have been a wild cat, then."

"Nigh on, my lord."

"You will have your way, whether or no?"

"My lord?"

"You would overcome her disinclination for her own good?"

"I don't know about all that, my lord. All I know is she had what was left of my pay in her other hand and would have been through the door like a pistol shot if I had not took a firm hold of her."

Captain Anderson beamed sideways at me.

"With your permission, my lord—"

Devil take it, the man was laughing at me!

"Now, Rogers. Never mind the women. What about the men?"

"Sir?"

Mr Colley suffered an outrage there in the fo'-castle. Who did it?"

The man's face was without any expression at all. The captain pressed him.

"Come, Rogers. Would it surprise you to know that you yourself are suspected of this particular kind of beastliness?"

The man's whole stance had altered. He was a little crouched now, one foot drawn a few inches behind the other. He had clenched his fists. He looked from one to the other of us quickly, as if trying to see in each face what degree of peril confronted him. I saw that he took us for *enemies*!

"I know nothing, Captain sir, nothing at all!"

"It may not have anything to do with you, my man. But you will know who it was."

"Who was who, sir?"

"Why, the one or many among you who inflicted a criminal assault on the gentleman so that he died of it!"

"I know nothing—nothing at all!"

I had got my wits back.

"Come, Rogers. You were the one man we saw with him. In default of any other evidence your name must head the list of suspects. What did you sailors do?"

I have never seen a face of more well-simulated astonishment.

"What did *we* do, my lord?"

"Doubtless you have witnesses to testify to your innocence. If you are innocent then help us to bring the criminals to book."

He said nothing, but still stood at bay. I took up the questioning again.

"I mean, my good man, you can either tell us who did it, or at the very least you can furnish us with a list of the people you suspect or know to be suspected of this particular form of, of interest, of assault."

Captain Anderson jerked up his chin.

"Buggery, Rogers, that's what he means. Buggery."

He looked down, shuffled some papers before him and dipped his pen in the ink. The silence prolonged itself into our expectancy. The captain himself broke it at last with a sound of angry impatience.

"Come along, man! We cannot sit here all day!"

There was another pause. Rogers turned his body

rather than his head to us, one after the other. Then he looked straight at the captain.

"Aye aye, sir."

It was only then that there was a change in the man's face. He thrust his upper lip down, then as if in an experimental manner tried the texture of his lower lip judiciously with his white teeth.

"Shall I begin with the officers, sir?"

It was of the utmost importance that I should not move. The slightest flicker of my eye towards either Summers or the captain, the slightest contraction of a muscle would have seemed a fatal accusation. I had absolute faith in them both as far as this accusation of *beastliness* was concerned. As for the two officers themselves, doubtless they also had a mutual faith, yet they too did not dare risk any movement. We were waxworks. Rogers was waxworks too.

It had to be the captain who made the first move and he knew it. He laid his pen down beside the papers and spoke gravely.

"Very well, Rogers. That will be all. You may return to your duties."

The colour came and went in the man's face. He let out his breath in a prolonged gasp. He knuckled his forehead, began to smile, turned and went away out of the cabin. I cannot say how long the three of us sat without word or movement. For my part, it was something as simple and ordinary as the fear of doing or saying the wrong thing; yet the "wrong thing" would be, so to speak, raised to a higher power, to such a power as to be fearful and desperate. I felt in the long moments of our silence as if I could not allow myself to think at all, otherwise my face might redden and the perspiration begin to creep down my cheeks. I made by a most conscious effort my mind as nearly blank as might be and waited on the event. For surely of the three of us it was least my part to speak. Rogers had caught us in a mantrap. Can your lordship understand how already touches of suspicion came to life in my mind whether I would or no and flitted from the name of this gentleman to that?

Captain Anderson rescued us from our catalepsy. He did not move but spoke as if to himself.

"Witnesses, enquiries, accusations, lies, more lies, courts-martial—the man has it in his power to ruin us all if he be brazen enough, as I doubt not he is, for it would be a hanging matter. Such accusations cannot be disproved. Whatever the upshot, something would stick."

He turned to Summers.

"And there, Mr Summers, ends our investigation. Have we other informants?"

"I believe no, sir. Touch pitch—"

"Just so. Mr Talbot?"

"I am all at sea, sir! But it is true enough. The man was at bay and brought out his last weapon; false witness, amounting to blackmail."

"In fact," said Summers, smiling at last, "Mr Talbot is the only one of us to have profited. He had at least a temporary elevation to the peerage!"

"I have returned to earth, sir—though since I was addressed as 'my lord' by Captain Anderson, who can conduct marriages and funerals—"

"Ah yes. Funerals. You will drink, gentlemen? Call Hawkins in, Summers, will you? I must thank you, Mr Talbot, for your assistance."

"Of little use I fear, sir."

The captain was himself again. He beamed.

"A low fever then. Sherry?"

"Thank you, sir. But is everything concluded? We still do not know what happened. You mentioned informants—"

"This is a good sherry," said the captain brusquely. "I believe, Mr Summers, you are averse to drinking at this time of the day and you will wish to oversee the various arrangements for the unfortunate man's committal to the deep. Your health, Mr Talbot. You will be willing to sign, or rather counter-sign, a report?"

I thought for a while.

"I have no official standing in this ship."

"Oh, come, Mr Talbot!"

I thought again.

"I will make a statement and sign that."

Captain Anderson looked sideways up at me from under his thick brows and nodded without saying anything. I drained my glass.

"You mentioned informants, Captain Anderson—"

But he was frowning at me.

"Did I, sir? I think not!"

"You asked Mr Summers—"

"Who replied there were none," said Captain Anderson loudly. "None at all, Mr Talbot, not a man jack among them! Do you understand, sir? No one has come sneaking to me—no one! You can go, Hawkins!"

I set down my glass and Hawkins took it away. The captain watched him leave the stateroom, then turned to me again.

"Servants have ears, Mr Talbot!"

"Why certainly, sir! I am very sure my fellow Wheeler has."

The captain smiled grimly.

"Wheeler! Oh yes indeed! *That* man must have ears and eyes all over him—"

"Well then, until the sad ceremony of this afternoon I shall return to my journal."

"Ah, the journal. Do not forget to include in it, Mr Talbot, that whatever may be said of the passengers, as far as the people and my officers are concerned this is a *happy* ship!"

At three o'clock we were all assembled in the waist. There was a guard, composed of Oldmeadow's soldiers, with flintlocks, or whatever their ungainly weapons are called. Oldmeadow himself was in full dress and unblooded sword, as were the ship's officers. Even our young gentlemen wore their dirks and expressions of piety. We passengers were dressed as sombrely as possible. The seamen were drawn up by watches, and were as presentable as their varied garments permit. Portly Mr Brocklebank was erect but yellow and drawn from potations that would have reduced Mr Colley to a ghost. As I inspected the man I thought that Brocklebank would have gone through the whole of Colley's ordeal and fall with no more than a bellyache and a sore head. Such are the varied fabrics of the human tapestry that surrounds me! Our ladies, who must surely have had such an occasion in their minds when they fitted themselves for the voyage, were in mourning—even Brocklebank's two doxies, who supported him on either side. Mr Prettiman was present at this *superstitious ritual* by the side of Miss Granham, who had led him there. What is all his militant Atheism and Republicanism when pitted against this daughter of a canon of Exeter Cathedral? I made a note as I saw him fretting and barely contained at her side, that *she* was the one of the two with whom I must speak and to whom I must convey the kind of delicate admonition I had intended for our notorious Freethinker!

You will observe that I have recovered somewhat from the effect of reading Colley's letter. A man cannot be forever brooding on what is past nor on the tenuous connection between his own unwitting conduct and someone else's deliberately criminal behaviour! Indeed, I have to own that this ceremonious naval occasion was one of great interest to me! One seldom attends a funeral in such, dare I call them, exotic surroundings! Not only was the ceremony strange, but all the time—or some of it at least—our actors conducted their dialogue in Tarpaulin language. You know how I delight in that! You will already have noted some particularly impenetrable specimens as, for instance, mention of a *badger bag*—does not Servius (I believe it was he) declare there are half a dozen cruxes in the *Aeneid* which will never be solved, either by emendation or inspiration or any method attempted by scholarship? Well then, I shall entertain you with a few more *naval cruxes*.

The ship's bell was struck, muffled. A party of sailors appeared, bearing the body on a plank and under the union flag. It was placed with its feet towards the starboard, or honourable side, by which admirals and bodies and suchlike rarities make their exits. It was a longer body than I had expected but have since been told that two of our few remaining cannon balls were attached to the feet. Captain Anderson, glittering with bullion, stood by it. I have also been told since, that he and all the other officers were much exercised as to the precise nature of the ceremonies to be observed when, as young Mr Taylor expressed it, "piping a sky pilot over the side".

Almost all our sails were *clewed up* and we were what the *Marine Dictionary* calls, technically speaking —and when does it not?—*hove to*, which ought to mean we were stationary in the water. Yet the spirit of farce (speaking perfectly exquisite Tarpaulin) attended Colley to his end. No sooner was the plank laid on the deck than I heard Mr Summers mutter to Mr Deverel:

"Depend upon it, Deverel, without you aft the driver a handspan she will make a sternboard."

Hardly had he said this when there came a heavy and rhythmical thudding from the ship's hull under water as if *Davey Jones* was serving notice or perhaps getting hungry. Deverel shouted orders of the *warrar-roohoowassst!* variety, the seamen leapt, while Captain Anderson, a prayerbook clutched like a grenade, turned on Lieutenant Summers.

"Mr *Summers!* Will you have the sternpost out of her?"

Summers said nothing but the thudding ceased. Captain Anderson's tone sank to a grumble.

"The pintles are loose as a pensioner's teeth."

Summers nodded in reply.

"I know it, sir. But until she's rehung—"

"The sooner we're off the wind the better. God curse that drunken superintendant!"

He stared moodily down at the union flag, then up at the sails which, as if willing to debate with him, boomed back. They could have done no better than the preceding dialogue. Was it not superb?

At last the captain glanced round him and positively started, as if seeing us for the first time. I wish I could say that he *started like a guilty thing upon a fearful summons* but he did not. He started like a man in the smallest degree remiss who has absentmindedly forgotten that he has a body to get rid of. He opened the book and grunted a sour invitation to us to pray—and so on. Certainly he was anxious enough to get the thing over, for I have never heard a service read so fast. The ladies scarce had time to get out their handkerchiefs (tribute of a tear) and we gentlemen stared for a moment as usual into our beavers, but then, reminded that this unusual ceremony was too good to miss, all looked up again. I hoped that Oldmeadow's men would fire a volley but he has since told me that owing to some difference of opinion between the Admiralty and the War Office, they have neither flints nor powder. However, they presented arms in approximate unison and the officers flourished their swords. I wonder—was all this proper for a parson? I do not know, neither do they. A fife shrilled out and someone rattled on a muffled drum, a kind of overture, or post-lude should I call it, or would *envoi* be a better word?

You will observe, my lord, that *Richard is himself again*—or shall we say that I have recovered from a period of fruitless and *perhaps* unwarranted regret?

And yet—at the last (when Captain Anderson's grumbling voice invited us to contemplate that time when there shall be no more sea) six men shrilled out a call on the bosun's pipe. Now, your lordship may never have heard these pipes so I must inform you that they have just as much music in them as the yowling of cats on heat! And yet and yet and *yet!* Their very harsh and shrill unmusicality, their burst of high sound leading to a long descent that died away through an uneasy and prolonged fluttering into silence, seemed to voice something beyond words, religion, philosophy. It was the simple voice of Life mourning Death.

I had scarcely time to feel a touch of complacency at the directness of my own emotions when the plank was lifted and tilted. The mortal remains of the Reverend Robert James Colley shot from under the union flag and entered the water with a single loud phut! as if he had been the most experienced of divers and had made a habit of rehearsing his own funeral, so expertly was it done. Of course the cannon balls assisted. This subsidiary use of their mass was after all in keeping with their general nature. So the remains of Colley dropping *deeper than did ever plummet sound* were to be thought of as now finding the solid base of all. (At these necessarily ritualistic moments of life, if you cannot use the prayer book, have recourse to Shakespeare! Nothing else will do.)

Now you might think that there was then a moment or two of silent tribute before the mourners left the churchyard. Not a bit of it! Captain Anderson shut his book, the pipes shrilled again, this time with a kind of temporal urgency. Captain Anderson nodded to Lieutenant Cumbershum, who touched his hat and *roared*:

"*Leeeoonnawwll!*"

Our obedient vessel started to turn as she moved forward and lumbered clumsily towards her original course. The ceremonially ordered ranks broke up, the people climbed everywhere into the rigging to spread our full suit of sails and add the stun's'ls to them again. Captain Anderson marched off, grenade, I mean prayerbook in hand, back to his cabin, I suppose to make an entry in his journal. A young gentleman scrawled on the traverse board and all things were as they had been. I returned to my cabin to consider what statement I should write out and sign. It must be such as will cause his sister least pain. It shall be a *low fever*, as the captain wishes. I must conceal from him that I have already laid a trail of gunpowder to where your lordship may ignite it. God, what a world of conflict, of birth, death, procreation, betrothals, marriages for all I know, there is to be found in this extraordinary ship!

(&)

There! I think the ampersand gives a touch of eccentricity, does it not? None of your dates, or letters of the alphabet, or presumed *day of the voyage!* I might have headed this section "addenda" but that would have been dull—far too, too dull! For we have come to an end, there is nothing more to be said. I mean—there is, of course, there is the daily record, but my journal, I found on looking back through it, had insensibly turned to the record of a drama—Colley's drama. Now the poor man's drama is done and he stands there, how many miles down, on his cannon balls, alone, as Mr Coleridge says, all, all alone. It seems a different sort of *bathos* (your lordship, as Colley might say, will note the amusing "paranomasia") to return to the small change of day to day with no drama in it, but there are yet some pages left between the rich bindings of your lordship's gift to me, and I *have* tried to stretch the burial out, in the hope that what might be called *The Fall and Lamentable End of Robert James Colley together with a Brief Account of his Thalassian Obsequies* would extend right to the last page. All was of no avail. His was a real life and a real death and no more to be fitted into a given book than a misshapen foot into a given boot. Of course my journal will continue beyond this volume—but in a book obtained for me by Phillips from the purser and not to be locked. Which reminds me how trivial the explanation of men's fear and silence concerning the purser proved to be. Phillips told me, for he is more open than

Wheeler. All the officers, including the captain, owe the purser money! Phillips calls him *the pusser*.

Which reminds me again—I employed Phillips because no matter how I shouted, I could not rouse Wheeler. He is being sought now.

He *was* being sought. Summers has just told me. The man has disappeared. He has fallen overboard. Wheeler! He has gone like a dream, with his puffs of white hair, and his shining baldness, his *sanctified* smile, his complete knowledge of everything that goes on in a ship, his paregoric, and his willingness to obtain for a gentleman anything in the wide, wide world, provided the gentleman pays for it! Wheeler, as the captain put it, *all over ears and eyes!* I shall miss the man, for I cannot hope for as great a share in the services of Phillips. Already I have had to pull off my own boots, though Summers, who was present in my cabin at the time, was good enough to help. Two deaths in only a few days!

"At least", said I to Summers with meaning, "no one can accuse me of having a hand in *this* death, can they?"

He was too breathless to reply. He sat back on his heels, then stood up and watched me pull on my embroidered slippers.

"Life is a formless business, Summers. Literature is much amiss in forcing a form on it!"

"Not so, sir, for there are both death and birth aboard. Pat Roundabout—"

"Roundabout? I thought it was 'Roustabout'!"

"You may use either indifferently. But she is delivered of a daughter to be named after the ship."

"Poor, poor child! But that was the mooing I heard then, like Bessie when she broke her leg?"

"It was, sir. I go now to see how they do."

So he left me, these blank pages still unfilled. News, then, news! What news? There *is* more to be recorded but germane to the captain, not Colley. It should have been fitted in much earlier—at Act Four or even Three. Now it must come limping after the drama, like the satyr play after the tragic trilogy. It is not a *dénouement* so much as a pale illumination. Captain Anderson's detestation of the clergy! You remember. Well now, perhaps, you and I *do* know all.

Hist, as they say—let me bolt my hutch door!

Well then—Deverel told me. He has begun to drink heavily—heavily that is in comparison with what he did before, since he has always been intemperate. It seems that Captain Anderson—fearful not only of my journal but also of the other passengers who *now* with the exception of steely Miss Granham believe "Poor Colley" was mistreated—Anderson, I say, rebuked the two men, Cumbershum and Deverel, savagely for their part in the affair. This meant little to Cumbershum, who is made of wood. But Deverel, by the laws of the service, is denied the satisfaction of a gentleman. He broods and drinks. Then last night, deep in drink, he came to my hutch and in the dark hours and a muttered, slurred voice gave me what he called necessary observations on the captain's history for my journal. Yet he was not so drunk as to be unaware of danger. Picture us then, by the light of my candle, seated side by side on the bunk, Deverel whispering viciously into my ear

as my head was inclined to his lips. There was, it
appears, and there is, a noble family—not I believe
more than distantly known to your lordship—and their
land marches with the Deverels'. They, Summers
would say, have used the privilege of their position and
neglected its responsibilities. The father of the present
young lord had in keeping a lady of great sweetness of
disposition, much beauty, little understanding and, as
it proved, some fertility. The use of privilege is sometimes expensive. Lord L—— (this is perfect Richardson, is it not?) found himself in need of a fortune,
and that instantly. The fortune was found but her family in a positively Wesleyan access of righteousness in-
sisted on the dismissal of the sweet lady, against whom
nothing could be urged save lack of a few words spoke
over her by a parson. Catastrophe threatened. The
dangers of her position struck some sparks from the
sweet lady, the fortune hung in the balance! At this
moment, as Deverel whispered in my ear, Providence
intervened and the incumbent of one of the three livings that lay in the family's gift was killed in the
hunting field! The heir's tutor, a dull sort of fellow, accepted of the living and the sweet lady and what Deverel called her curst cargo together. The lord got his
fortune, the lady a husband and the Reverend Anderson a living, a wife and an heir *gratis*. In due course
the boy was sent to sea, where the casual interest of his
real father was sufficient to elevate him in the service.
But now the old lord is dead and the young one has no
cause to love his bastard half-brother!

All this by an unsteady candle light, querulous re-

RITES OF PASSAGE

marks in his sleep from Mr Prettiman, with snores and farts from Mr Brocklebank in the other direction. Oh that cry from the deck above us—

"Eight bells and all's well!"

Deverel, at this witching hour, put his arm about me with drunken familiarity and revealed why he had spoken so. This history was the *jest* he had meant to tell me. At Sydney Cove, or the Cape of Good Hope, should we put in there, Deverel intends—or the drink in him intends—to resign his commission, call the captain out and shoot him dead! "For", said he in a louder voice and with his shaking right hand lifted, "I can knock a crow off a steeple with one barker!" Hugging and patting me and calling me his *good Edmund* he informed me I was to act for him when the time came; and if, *if* by some luck of the devil, he himself was taken off, why the information was to be put fully in my famous journal—

I had much ado to get him taken to his cabin without rousing the whole ship. But here is news indeed! So *that* is why a certain captain so detests a parson! It would surely be more reasonable in him to detest a lord! Yet there is no doubt about it. Anderson has been wronged by a lord—or by a parson—or by life— Good God! I do not care to find excuses for Anderson!

Nor do I care as much for Deverel as I did. It was a misjudgement on my part to esteem him. He, perhaps, illustrates the last decline of a noble family as Mr Summers might illustrate the original of one! My wits are all to seek. I found myself thinking that had I been so much the victim of a lord's gallantry I would have become a *Jacobin!* I? Edmund Talbot?

It was then that I remembered my own half-formed intention to bring Zenobia and Robert James Colley together to rid myself of a possible embarrassment. It was so like Deverel's *jest* I came near to detesting myself. When I realized how he and I had talked, and how he must have thought me like-minded with the "Noble family" my face grew hot with shame. Where will all this end?

However, one birth does not equal two deaths. There is a general dullness among us, for say what you will, a burial at sea, however frivolously I treat it, cannot be called a laughing matter. Nor will Wheeler's disappearance lighten the air among the passengers.

Two days have passed since I diffidently forbore to ask Summers to help me on with my slippers! The officers have not been idle. Summers—as if this were a Company ship rather than a man of war—has determined we shall not have too much time left hanging on our hands. We have determined that the after end of the ship shall present the forrard end with a *play!* A *committee* has been formed *with the captain's sanction!* This has thrown me will-he, nill-he, into the company of Miss Granham! It has been an edifying experience. I found that this woman, this handsome, cultivated maiden lady, holds views which would freeze the blood of the average citizen in his veins! She does *literally* make no distinction between the uniform worn by our officers, the woad with which our unpolished ancestors were said to paint themselves and the tattooing rife in the South Seas and perhaps on the mainland of Australia! Worse—from the point of view of society—she, daughter of a canon, makes no distinction between the Indian's Medicine Man, the Siberian Shaman, and a Popish priest in his vestments! When I expostulated that she bid fair to include our own clergy she would only admit them to be less offensive because they made themselves less readily distinguishable from other gentlemen. I was so staggered by this conversation I could make no reply to her and only discovered the reason for the awful candour with which she spoke when (before dinner in the passenger saloon) it was announced that she and Mr Prettiman are *officially* engaged! In the unexpected security of her *fiançailles* the lady feels free to say anything! But with what an eye she has seen us! I blush to remember the many things I have said in her presence which must have seemed like the childishness of the schoolroom.

However, the announcement has cheered everyone up. You may imagine the public felicitations and the private comments! I myself sincerely hope that Captain Anderson, gloomiest of Hymens, will marry them aboard so that we may have a complete collection of all the ceremonies that accompany the forked creature from the cradle to the grave. The pair seem attached— they have fallen in love *after their fashion!* Deverel introduced the only solemn note. He declared it was a great shame the man Colley had died, otherwise the knot might be tied there and then by a parson. At this, there was a general silence. Miss Granham, who had furnished your humble servant with her views on priests in general might, I felt, have said nothing. But instead, she came out with a quite astonishing statement.

"He was a truly degraded man."

"Come, ma'am," said I, "*de mortuis* and all that! A single unlucky indulgence— The man was harmless enough!"

"Harmless," cried Prettiman with a kind of bounce, "a priest harmless?"

"I was not referring to drink," said Miss Granham in her steeliest voice, "but to vice in another form."

"Come, ma'am—I cannot believe—as a lady you cannot—"

"*You*, sir," cried Mr Prettiman, "*you* to doubt a lady's word?"

"No, no! Of course not! Nothing—"

"Let it be, dear Mr Prettiman, I beg of you."

"No, ma'am, I cannot let it go. Mr Talbot has seen fit to doubt your word and I will have an apology—"

"Why," said I laughing, "you have it, ma'am, unreservedly! I never intended—"

"We learnt of his vicious habits accidentally," said Mr Prettiman. "A priest! It was two sailors who were descending one of the rope ladders from the mast to the side of the vessel. Miss Granham and I—it was dark—we had retired to the shelter of that confusion of ropes at the foot of the ladder—"

"Chain, ratlines—Summers, enlighten us!"

"It is no matter, sir. You will remember, Miss Granham, we were discussing the inevitability of the process by which true liberty must lead to true equality and thence to—but that is no matter, neither. The sailors were unaware of our presence so that without meaning to, we heard all!"

"Smoking is bad enough, Mr Talbot, but at least gentlemen go no further!"

"My dear Miss Granham!"

"It is as savage a custom, sir, as any known among coloured peoples!"

Oldmeadow addressed her in tones of complete incredulity. "By Jove, ma'am—you cannot mean the fellow chewed tobacco!"

There was a roar of laughter from passengers and officers alike. Summers, who is not given to idle laughter, joined in.

"It is true," said he, when there was less noise. "On one of my earlier visits I saw a large bunch of leaf tobacco hung from the deckhead. It was spoilt by mildew and I threw it overboard."

"But Summers," said I. "I saw no tobacco! And that kind of man—"

"I assure you, sir. It was before you visited him."

"Nevertheless, I find it almost impossible to believe!"

"You shall have the facts," said Prettiman with his usual choler. "Long study, a natural aptitude and a necessary habit of defence have made me expert in the recollection of casual speech, sir. You shall have the words the sailors spoke *as* they were spoken!"

Summers lifted both hands in expostulation.

"No, no—spare us, I beg you! It is of little moment after all!"

"Little moment, sir, when a lady's word—it cannot be allowed to pass, sir. One of these sailors said to the other as they descended side by side—'Billy Rogers was laughing like a bilge pump when he come away from the captain's cabin. He went into the heads and I sat by him. Billy said he'd knowed most things in his time but he had never thought to get a chew off a parson!'"

The triumphant but fierce look on Mr Prettiman's face, his flying hair and the instant decline of his educated voice into a precise imitation of a ruffian sort threw our audience into whoops. This disconcerted the philosopher even more and he stared round him wildly. Was anything ever more absurd? I believe it was this diverting circumstance which marked a change in our general feelings. Without the source of it being evident there strengthened among us the determination to get on with our play! Perhaps it was Mr Prettiman's genius for comedy—oh, unquestionably we must have him for our comic! But what might have been high words between the social philosopher and your humble servant passed off into the much pleasanter business of discussing *what* we should act and *who* should produce and *who* should do this and that!

Afterwards I went out to take my usual constitutional in the waist; and lo! there by the break of the fo'castle was "Miss Zenobia" in earnest conversation with Billy Rogers! Plainly, he is her *Sailor Hero* who can "*Wate no longer*". With what kindred spirit did he concoct his misspelt but elaborate billet-doux? Well, if he attempts to come aft and visit her in her hutch I will see him flogged for it.

Mr Prettiman and Miss Granham walked in the waist too but on the opposite side of the deck, talking with animation. Miss Granham said (I heard her and believe she intended me to hear) that *as he knew* they should aim first at supporting those parts of the administration that might be supposed still uncorrupted. Mr Prettiman trotted beside her—she is taller than he —nodding with vehemence at the austere yet penetrating power of her intellect. They will influence each other—for I believe they are as sincerely attached as such extraordinary characters can be. But oh yes, Miss Granham, I shall not keep an eye on him—I shall keep an eye on you! I watched them pass on over the white line that separates the social orders and stand right up in the bows, talking to East and that poor, pale girl, his wife. Then they returned and came straight to where I stood in the shade of an awning we have stretched from the starboard shrouds. To my astonishment, Miss Granham explained that they had been *consulting with Mr East!* He is, it seems, a craftsman and has to do with the setting of type! I do not doubt that they have in view his future employment. However, I did not allow them to see what an interest I took in the matter and turned the conversation back to the question of what play we should show the people. Mr Prettiman proved to be as indifferent to that as to so much of the common life he is allegedly concerned with in his philosophy! He dismissed Shakespeare as a writer who made too little comment on the evils of society! I asked, reasonably enough, what society consisted in other than human beings only to find that the man did not understand me—or rather, that there was a screen between his unquestionably powerful intellect and the perceptions of common sense. He began to orate but was deflected skilfully by Miss Granham, who declared that the play *Faust* by the German author Goethe would have been suitable—

"But," said she, "the genius of one language cannot be translated into another."

"I beg your pardon, ma'am?"

"I mean," said she, patiently, as to one of her *young gentlemen*, "you cannot translate a work of genius entirely from one language to another!"

"Come now, ma'am," said I, laughing, "here at least I may claim to speak with authority! My godfather has translated Racine entire into English verse; and in the opinion of connoisseurs it equals and at some points surpasses the original!"

The pair stopped, turned and stared at me as one. Mr Prettiman spoke with his usual febrile energy.

"Then I would have you know, sir, that it must be unique!"

I bowed to him.

"Sir," said I, "it is!"

With that and a bow to Miss Granham I took myself off. I *scored*, did I not? But really—they are a provokingly opinionated pair! Yet if they are provoking and comic to *me* I doubt not that they are intimidating to others! While I was writing this I heard them pass my hutch on the way to the passenger saloon and listened as Miss Granham *cut up* some unfortunate character.

"Let us hope he learns in time, then!"

"Despite the disadvantage of his birth and upbringing, ma'am, he is not without wit."

"I grant you," said she, "he always tries to give a

comic turn to the conversation and indeed one cannot help finding his laughter at his own jests infectious. But as for his opinions in general—Gothic is the only word to be applied to them!"

With that they passed out of earshot. They cannot mean Deverel, surely—for though he has some pretension to wit, his birth and upbringing are of the highest order, however little he may have profited from them. Summers is the more likely candidate.

I do not know how to write this. The chain would seem too thin, the links individually too weak—yet something within me insists they *are* links and all joined, so that I now understand what happened to pitiable, clownish Colley! It was night, I was heated and restless, yet my mind as in a fever—a *low* fever indeed!—went back over the whole affair and would not let me be. It seemed as if certain sentences, phrases, situations were brought successively before me—and these, as it were, glowed with a significance that was by turns farcical, gross and tragic.

Summers must have guessed. There *was* no leaf-tobacco! He was trying to protect the memory of the dead man!

Rogers in the enquiry with a face of well-simulated astonishment—"What did *we* do, my lord?" Was that astonishment well-simulated? Suppose the splendid animal was telling the naked, the physical truth! Then Colley in his letter—*what a man does defiles him, not what is done by others*—Colley in his letter, infatuated with the "king of my island" and longing to kneel before him—Colley in the cable locker, drunk for the

RITES OF PASSAGE

first time in his life and not understanding his condition and in a state of mad exuberance—Rogers owning in the heads that he had knowed most things in his life but had never thought *to get a chew off a parson!* Oh, doubtless the man consented, jeeringly, and encouraged the ridiculous, schoolboy trick—even so, not Rogers but Colley committed the *fellatio* that the poor fool was to die of when he remembered it.

Poor, poor Colley! Forced back towards his own kind, made an equatorial fool of—deserted, abandoned by me who could have saved him—overcome by kindness and a gill or two of the intoxicant—

I cannot feel even a pharisaical complacency in being the only gentleman not to witness his ducking. Far better had I seen it so as to protest at that childish savagery! Then my offer of friendship might have been sincere rather than—

I shall write a letter to Miss Colley. It will be lies from beginning to end. I shall describe my growing friendship with her brother. I shall describe my admiration for him. I shall recount all the days of his *low fever* and my grief at his death.

A letter that contains everything but a shred of truth! How is that for a start to a career in the service of my King and Country?

I believe I may contrive to increase the small store of money that will be returned to her.

It is the last page of your journal, my lord, last page of the "ampersand"! I have just now turned over the pages, ruefully enough. Wit? Acute observations? Entertainment? Why—it has become, perhaps, some kind of sea-story but a sea-story with never a tempest, no shipwreck, no sinking, no rescue at sea, no sight nor sound of an enemy, no thundering broadsides, heroism, prizes, gallant defences and heroic attacks! Only one gun fired and that a blunderbuss!

What a thing he stumbled over in himself! Racine declares—but let me quote your own words to you.

Lo! where toils Virtue up th'Olympian ſteep—
With like ſmall ſteps doth Vice t'wards Hades creep!

True indeed, and how should it be not? It is the smallness of those steps that enables the Brocklebanks of this world to survive, to attain a deboshed and saturated finality which disgusts everyone but themselves! Yet not so Colley. He was the exception. Just as his iron-shod heels shot him rattling down the steps of the ladders from the quarterdeck and afterdeck to the waist; even so a gill or two of the *fiery ichor* brought him from the heights of complacent austerity to what his sobering mind must have felt as the lowest hell of self-degradation. In the not too ample volume of man's knowledge of Man, let this sentence be inserted. Men can die of shame.

The book is filled all but a finger's breadth. I shall lock it, wrap it and sew it unhandily in sailcloth and thrust it away in the locked drawer. With lack of sleep and too much understanding I grow a little crazy, I think, like all men at sea who live too close to each other and too close thereby to all that is monstrous under the sun and moon.

WE HOPE YOU ENJOYED THIS BOOK

IF YOU'D LIKE A FREE LIST
OF OTHER BOOKS AVAILABLE FROM
PLAYBOY PAPERBACKS,
JUST SEND YOUR REQUEST TO:

PLAYBOY PAPERBACKS
BOOK MAILING SERVICE
P.O. BOX 690
ROCKVILLE CENTRE, NEW YORK 11571

From Playboy Paperbacks, novels guaranteed to entertain, delight and captivate you

_____	16988 AT THE SHORES Thomas Rogers	$2.95
_____	16944 BLUE LADIES Bettz Burr	$2.95
_____	16691 BUT NOT TO KEEP Roger Kahn	$2.75
_____	21000 THE CONFESSION OF A CHILD OF THE CENTURY Thomas Rogers	$3.50
_____	16921 FAME AND FORTUNE Joanne Kaye	$2.25
_____	16724 GOOD RIDDANCE Barbara Abercrombie	$2.50
_____	16906 LOVE AND BETRAYAL Joanne Kaye	$2.25
_____	16681 MEMENTO Michael M. Mooney	$2.75
_____	16929 MORGAN'S PASSING Anne Tyler	$3.50
_____	16897 THE PLAYHOUSE Elaine Ford	$2.25
_____	16537 RAG TRADE Lewis Orde	$2.75
_____	16872 A RAGE IN PARADISE Gary Brandner	$2.95
_____	16895 RAGS AND RICHES Joanne Kaye	$2.25
_____	16981 THE RAJ Donald H. Robinson	$3.50
_____	16567 REQUIEM FOR A DREAM Hubert Selby	$2.25
_____	16846 ROUGH STRIFE Lynn Sharon Schwartz	$2.75
_____	16982 SATIN AND STARS Joanne Kaye	$2.50
_____	16830 STEPPING Nancy Thayer	$2.95
_____	16787 THAT VANDERBILT WOMAN Philip van Rensselaer	$2.75
_____	16934 TIME OF DESECRATION Alberto Moravia	$3.50
_____	16945 TWO WOMEN Alberto Moravia	$3.50

282-4

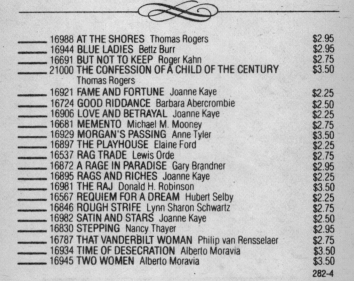

PLAYBOY PAPERBACKS
Book Mailing Service
P.O. Box 690 Rockville Centre, New York 11571

NAME_____

ADDRESS_____

CITY_____STATE_____ZIP_____

Please enclose 50¢ for postage and handling if one book is ordered;
25¢ for each additional book. $1.50 maximum postage and handling
charge. No cash, CODs or stamps. Send check or money order.

Total amount enclosed: $_____

NOVELS BY
SHIRLEY HAZZARD

WINNER OF THE 1981
NATIONAL BOOK CRITICS CIRCLE AWARD

_____	16859 THE TRANSIT OF VENUS	$3.50
_____	16874 THE EVENING OF THE HOLIDAY	$2.25
_____	16901 THE BAY OF NOON	$2.50
_____	16928 PEOPLE IN GLASS HOUSES	$2.50
_____	16913 CLIFFS OF FALL	$2.50

1081-10

❖ **PLAYBOY PAPERBACKS**
Book Mailing Service
P.O. Box 690 Rockville Centre, New York 11571

NAME_____

ADDRESS_____

CITY_____STATE_____ZIP_____

Please enclose 50¢ for postage and handling if one book is ordered;
25¢ for each additional book. $1.50 maximum postage and handling
charge. No cash, CODs or stamps. Send check or money order.

Total amount enclosed: $_____

GREAT BOOKS OF ADVENTURE AND SUSPENSE

GREAT BOOKS OF ADVENTURE AND SUSPENSE

_____ 16852 ON THE EIGHTH DAY Lawrence Okun, M.D. $2.25

_____ 16831 THE SCORPION SIGNAL Adam Hall $2.95

_____ 16800 THE SECRET OF MI6 Lou Smith $2.50

_____ 21048 SHADOW OF THE KNIFE Kenneth R. McKay $2.95

_____ 16860 SHOW ME A HERO Patrick Alexander $2.95

_____ 16857 TIME OF RECKONING Walter Wager $2.75

_____ 16810 20,000 ALARMS $2.50
              Lt. Richard Hamilton with Charles Barnard

_____ 16848 THE WAVE Christopher Hyde $2.95

_____ 16779 WHEN LOVE WAS NOT ENOUGH Clifford Mason $2.50

282-3

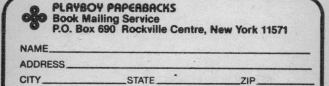

PLAYBOY PAPERBACKS
Book Mailing Service
P.O. Box 690 Rockville Centre, New York 11571

NAME_____

ADDRESS_____

CITY_____STATE_____ZIP_____

Please enclose 50¢ for postage and handling if one book is ordered;
25¢ for each additional book. $1.50 maximum postage and handling
charge. No cash, CODs or stamps. Send check or money order.

Total amount enclosed: $_____

FOUR SWASHBUCKLING TALES OF THE HIGH SEAS

BY C. Northcote Parkinson

___16728	*DEAD RECKONING*	$2.25
___16636	*DEVIL TO PAY*	$2.25
___16685	*THE FIRESHIP*	$2.25
___16713	*TOUCH AND GO*	$2.25

PLAYBOY PAPERBACKS
Book Mailing Service
P.O. Box 690 Rockville Centre, New York 11571

NAME_____

ADDRESS_____

CITY_____STATE_____ZIP_____

Please enclose 50¢ for postage and handling if one book is ordered; 25¢ for each additional book. $1.50 maximum postage and handling charge. No cash, CODs or stamps. Send check or money order.

Total amount enclosed: $_____

WAR BOOKS FROM PLAYBOY PAPERBACKS

_____ 21158	THE BATTLE FOR MOSCOW Col. Albert Seaton	$2.75
_____ 16629	THE BATTLE OF LEYTE GULF Edwin P. Hoyt	$2.50
_____ 16634	BLOODY AACHEN Charles Whiting	$2.25
_____ 16879	BLOODY BUNA Lida Mayo	$2.50
_____ 16609	THE DEVIL'S VIRTUOSOS David Downing	$2.25
_____ 16597	DUNKIRK Robert Jackson	$2.25
_____ 16716	POINT OF NO RETURN Wilbur H. Morrison	$2.50
_____ 21089	THE SECRET OF STALINGRAD Walter Kerr	$2.50
_____ 16655	U-BOATS OFFSHORE Edwin P. Hoyt	$2.25
_____ 21122	WAKE ISLAND Duane Schultz	$2.50

282-5

PLAYBOY PAPERBACKS
Book Mailing Service
P.O. Box 690 Rockville Centre, New York 11571

NAME_____

ADDRESS _____

CITY_____STATE_____ZIP_____

Please enclose 50¢ for postage and handling if one book is ordered;
25¢ for each additional book. $1.50 maximum postage and handling
charge. No cash, CODs or stamps. Send check or money order.

Total amount enclosed: $_____

A MARVELOUS SELECTION
OF TOP-NOTCH MYSTERY THRILLERS
FOR YOUR READING PLEASURE

Charles Alverson

_____ 16530	GOODEY'S LAST STAND	$1.95
_____ 16603	NOT SLEEPING, JUST DEAD	$1.95

Margot Arnold

_____ 16639	THE CAPE COD CAPER	$1.95
_____ 16534	EXIT ACTORS, DYING	$1.75
_____ 16684	ZADOK'S TREASURE	$1.95

Michael Collins

_____ 16593	ACT OF FEAR	$1.75
_____ 16812	THE BLOOD-RED DREAM	$2.25
_____ 16991	BLUE DEATH	$2.25
_____ 16672	THE BRASS RAINBOW	$1.95
_____ 16773	NIGHT OF THE TOADS	$2.25
_____ 16822	THE NIGHTRUNNERS	$2.25
_____ 16915	SHADOW OF A TIGER	$2.25
_____ 16930	THE SILENT SCREAM	$2.25
_____ 16855	THE SLASHER	$2.25
_____ 16903	WALK A BLACK WIND	$2.25

Phillips Lore

_____ 16694	THE LOOKING GLASS MURDERS	$1.95
_____ 16652	MURDER BEHIND CLOSED DOORS	$1.95
_____ 16587	WHO KILLED THE PIE MAN?	$1.75

1081-23

 PLAYBOY PAPERBACKS
Book Mailing Service
P.O. Box 690 Rockville Centre, New York 11571

NAME_____

ADDRESS_____

CITY_____STATE_____ZIP_____

Please enclose 50¢ for postage and handling if one book is ordered;
25¢ for each additional book. $1.50 maximum postage and handling
charge. No cash, CODs or stamps. Send check or money order.

Total amount enclosed: $_____